D0776742

The
Reluctant Bride

The
Reluctant Bride

Barbara Cartland

THORNDIKE
CHIVERS

This Large Print edition is published by Thorndike Press®, Waterville, Maine USA and by BBC Audiobooks, Ltd, Bath, England.

Published in 2005 in the U.S. by arrangement with Cartland Promotions.

Published in 2005 in the U.K. by arrangement with Cartland Promotions.

U.S. Hardcover 0-7862-7679-7 (Candlelight)
U.K. Hardcover 1-4056-3433-2 (Chivers Large Print)

The text of this Large Print edition is unabridged.
Other aspects of the book may vary from the original edition.

Set in 16 pt. Plantin by Al Chase.

Printed in the United States on permanent paper.

British Library Cataloguing-in-Publication Data available

Library of Congress Cataloging-in-Publication Data

Cartland, Barbara, 1902–
    The reluctant bride / by Barbara Cartland.
        p. cm. — (Thorndike Press large print Candlelight)
    ISBN 0-7862-7679-7 (lg. print : hc : alk. paper)
    1. Large type books.   I. Title.   II. Thorndike Press large
print Candlelight series.
PR6005.A765R45 2005
823′.912—dc22   2005014670

The
Reluctant Bride

1

There was a sudden crash followed by a slow rumble overhead, and Lady Lambourn, who had been dozing, started up in her chair.

"Good gracious! Whatever can that be?" she asked apprehensively.

Her daughter rose from the window-seat where she had been sewing, crossed the room and laid her hand on her mother's shoulder.

"I am afraid, Mama, it is the ceiling in the tapestry bedchamber," she answered. "After the last rains the water seeped in and discoloured the plaster. Old Wheaton warned us it might fall, but nothing was done to repair it."

"That is the third ceiling!" Lady Lambourn exclaimed. "The house seems to be collapsing about our very ears."

"Repairs cost money, Mama," Camilla said quietly, "like everything else."

Lady Lambourn looked up at her daughter and there were tears in her tired eyes.

"Camilla, what will become of us?" she asked. "Heaven knows we have nothing left to sell, and I said before he went that your father's journey to London would be fruitless."

"I was afraid too," Camilla answered, "but dear Papa is always optimistic. He was quite certain that he would encounter someone who would help us."

"Sir Horace has been optimistic all his life," his wife said with a deep sigh. "He never gives up hope, even when the odds seem most against him. But things now are desperate, and when Gervase returns from the sea he will find us in a debtors' prison!"

"No, no, Mama, that will never happen!" Camilla said consolingly.

"I dream about it every night," Lady Lambourn insisted pathetically. "If only I was not so weak and so helpless, I could perhaps appeal to someone who used to know us in the old days. So many people came to our house when your Papa was an Ambassador. I had more friends than any woman in the world, but now where are they?"

"Where indeed?" Camilla echoed with a note of bitterness in her voice. "But we were not the only ones to lose money when the country banks closed last year. It was a terrible time for thousands like ourselves. In fact Papa says the date 1816 will be engraved on more tombstones than any other date for centuries."

"We are at least alive," Lady Lambourn murmured, "but sometimes I wonder for how long."

"You must not be depressed, Mama," Camilla begged, kneeling down beside her mother and putting her arms round her. "Perhaps Gervase will come back rich — and then you can go to Bath and get well. I know the hot springs would make all the difference to your legs."

"I would much rather we had the money for you to visit London and have a gay time such as you should be enjoying at your age," Lady Lambourn retorted. "It is wrong that you should be cooped up here, Camilla."

"Do not worry about me, Mama," her daughter interrupted quickly. "You know that when I was in London at the beginning of last year I did not enjoy myself, even though Aunt Georgina was as kind to me as anyone could possibly be. All I want is to live here in peace with you and Papa, and to know that we are able to have a decent meal on the table and a roof over our heads."

"That hardly seems likely at the moment," Lady Lambourn said miserably. "I feel so ashamed that the servants have not received their wages for over six months. I can hardly look at Agnes when she brings in my tea, struggling with the silver which used to be looked after by a butler and three footmen."

"Agnes does not mind," Camilla declared with a smile. "She has been with us all her life, and you know as well as I do, Mama, that she is part of the family. Why, she said to me only last night, 'When we get rich again, Miss Camilla, we will be able to laugh about all this.' Our troubles are Agnes's troubles, and our joys, when they come, will be hers as well."

"When they come!" Lady Lambourn ejaculated. "What can be keeping your father? Let us pray that he has not borrowed gold from some kind friend and thought to increase it at the tables."

"Father is not a gambler," Camilla assured her mother. "You know that any money he saved when he was in the Diplomatic Service was invested, it was just unfortunate that he put a great deal of it into French francs."

"We lost nearly everything we possessed because of that monster Napoleon," Lady Lambourn cried. "Then came the shock of the banks closing last year, when we all expected victory to make us much richer. It is cruel, Camilla! I feel so helpless."

"So do I," Camilla said, rising from her feet and bending forward to kiss her mother on the cheek. "But there is nothing we can do now but pray. Remember, Mama, you have always believed that prayer can help us when all else fails."

"I have always believed that in the past," Lady Lambourn admitted, "but now, my love, I am afraid."

Camilla gave a little sigh and turned again to the window. The April sunshine coming through the lattice panes was warm on her little pointed face, and Lady Lambourn, looking across the room, caught her breath at the fragility of her child as she saw her silhouetted against the light.

"Camilla is too thin," she thought, and yet it was not surprising as their food supply had diminished week by week, day by day. They owed money to the butcher in the village, and there were no gamekeepers now to bring in the rabbits and pigeons which had been their main diet during the hard winter. Everyone had gone except Agnes and old Wheaton, who had been with them over fifty years and was half blind and so rheumaticky that he could only crawl about his work.

Lady Lambourn shut her eyes for a

moment and remembered the distinguished guests who had thronged their house in London when she and Sir Horace had returned from Europe just before the war. As an Ambassador he had been *persona grata* with all the diplomats at the Court of St. James's, and they had flocked to greet him, eager for news from Europe and proffering an almost extravagant welcome to the popular Sir Horace and his lovely wife.

They had brought presents for Camilla, expensive trifles, but she had often found them far less interesting than her old toys which she had treasured since she was very small. She had been beautiful even then, a fairy-like child with golden hair and deep blue eyes, which would study seriously everyone who spoke to her.

"She will be the Toast of the Town," the diplomats told Lady Lambourn. "In a few years' time your house will be besieged by ardent beaux."

Lady Lambourn had accepted that they spoke the truth, and Camilla's childlike loveliness had developed over the years into a breathtaking beauty. But now there was no money to spend on fashionable gowns and there was no house in London, only a crumbling Elizabethan manor and an estate which lay rotting, its fields full of weeds and nettles because there were no labourers to work on them.

"Oh, Camilla, I had such plans for you!" Lady Lambourn exclaimed, and the cry seemed to come from her very heart.

Camilla was not listening to her mother and she held up her hand as if to ask for silence.

"I think, Mama — I am almost certain — it is the sound of wheels," she cried, and turning she ran from the room. Lady Lambourn heard her footsteps cross the hall and the sound of the latch being raised at the front door.

Unable to move in her wheel-chair, she could only clasp her hands together and pray, almost fiercely.

"Please, God, let my dear one have brought some hope for the future."

There was a sound of voices, and then the drawing-room door, which Camilla had left ajar, was flung open and Sir Horace stood there.

Notwithstanding his years, he was an extremely handsome man, with iron-grey hair brushed back from a square forehead. An exquisitely tied cravat, still spotless and uncrumpled despite his journey, and his many-tiered riding-coat, which he had not yet discarded, made him seem almost unnaturally tall and at the same time elegant.

There was something triumphant in the way he paused at the doorway, and he did not need to speak because his wife saw the expression on his face.

"Horace!" and her voice deepened, "Horace, my love!"

As her husband walked across the room and bent to kiss her, she raised her trembling hands towards him. Her fingers, some of them misshapen, still had some resemblance of beauty, and her care of them showed in the polished nails and the crisp, exquisite lace which veiled her wrists.

"Have you been successful?"

Lady Lambourn could hardly speak the words for the beating of her heart.

"More than successful!" Sir Horace declared, and his voice seemed to ring out round the room.

"Oh, Papa, tell us!"

Camilla was at his side, her eyes upturned to his, her fair curls seeming to dance with excitement.

The depression had gone, the whole room seemed to vibrate with a new tempo from the moment of Sir Horace's arrival. There was no longer an atmosphere of anxiety and despair; now, almost as if a light illuminated every corner, there was hope and a rising faith.

"You are all right, my dear?" Lady Lambourn enquired. It was a question she never failed to ask whenever Sir Horace returned from one of his journeys.

"I am all right," Sir Horace assured her. "Everything is all right and I want above all things to tell you about it; but first, Camilla, instruct the servants to bring from my travelling carriage the presents I have bought you both."

"Presents, Papa? What sort of presents?"

"A pâté for one, a shoulder of mutton for another," Sir Horace replied. "A whole case of the best cognac — besides some of the finest Indian tea for your Mama."

"How wonderful!" Camilla exclaimed, running from the room, knowing that Agnes and Wheaton would require her assistance in bringing the packages into the house. The coachman would be too concerned with the horses to be of much help.

When she had gone Sir Horace put his wife's hands to his lips.

"Our troubles are over, my dear."

"But how? What has happened?" Lady Lambourn demanded. "And if it is a loan, will it not have to be repaid?"

"It is not a loan," Sir Horace began, and

then broke off as Camilla returned.

"Papa!" she cried. "There was a footman on the box of the travelling carriage and he tells me that you have engaged him. Is that correct?"

"Yes indeed," Sir Horace replied. "I had no time to find other servants, but doubtless many of our old employees can be re-engaged from the village. This footman was available, so I brought him with me."

"Where does the money for all this come from?" Camilla asked, and now the first excitement had gone from her voice and her eyes looked troubled.

Sir Horace took off his riding-coat and threw it on a chair.

"I am ready to tell you all about it, Camilla," he said, "but first may I have a drink? I assure you I have come here at such breakneck speed that I did not stop, even to water the horses. I was so anxious to relate to you and Mama what has occurred."

"I will get you a bottle of your new brandy," Camilla smiled.

"No!" Sir Horace said sharply. "Tell the footman to bring it. There is no need now for you to demean yourself as you have done these past months."

A little smile dimpled Camilla's cheeks.

"I have never thought it was demeaning

16

myself to wait on you, Papa," she answered softly. Sir Horace, forgetting his thirst, put out his hand to take hers and draw her close to him.

"My dearest, my most beloved daughter," he said. "The reason I am so excited about the news I bring is that it concerns you. That is what matters more than anything else to me."

"It concerns me?" Camilla looked surprised.

"Come and sit down."

Sir Horace seated himself in the winged armchair which was close to Lady Lambourn, and Camilla sat on a low stool facing him.

"Tell me, Papa," she begged, "I cannot bear the suspense any longer."

"Nor I either," Lady Lambourn interposed, "but, Horace, you have no idea what it means to me to see you smiling again. You went away miserable, grey, an old man, but you have come back to me in looks and voice as young as your son."

"That is how I feel," Sir Horace told her.

"But won't you tell us why?" Camilla prompted.

Sir Horace cleared his throat and leant back in his chair.

"You remember that I have often spoken

to you, Camilla, of Meldenstein."

"Yes indeed," Camilla said, "and the Princess — my godmama — has remembered my birthday every year since I was a child. Last year she sent me the most adorable lace cloak, most useful for wearing at the opera, but unfortunately I have no chance of attending an opera."

"That is now changed," Sir Horace said. "You will need your opera cape, my child, or indeed a far finer one."

"Why, what do you mean?" Camilla asked.

"I will start at the beginning," Sir Horace said, then paused as the door opened. The footman, over six feet tall, wearing a claret-coloured livery with brightly polished buttons, came into the room carrying a tray.

"I thought, sir, you would wish a glass of wine after your journey," he said respectfully.

"Thank you, James," Sir Horace answered, and turning to Lady Lambourn he said: "My dear, this is James. I have already informed him that for a few days we shall be short-handed in the house. After that we shall be able to fill all the posts which have been vacant for so long."

The footman set the salver with the decanter beside Sir Horace, filled the glass,

18

and bowing, first to Lady Lambourn and then to Camilla, left the room.

"Excellent fellow," Sir Horace commented as he closed the door quietly behind him. "He has been in the service of the Duke of Devonshire and is well trained."

Lady Lambourn said nothing — she merely stared in bewilderment at the door which had closed behind the footman and turned her face towards her husband.

"I will start at the beginning," Sir Horace began again. "When I reached London I was in despair. You know, dearest, although I tried to put on a brave face, I felt as though we had reached the end of everything, and there was nothing, nothing I could do to save us all from disaster. I went to my club — I thought that in White's there was certain to be one friend who had known me in the past, and to whom I might humble myself sufficiently to ask for a helping hand."

"Poor Papa, how you must have hated the thought of having to beg," Camilla murmured.

"I was thinking only of you and your mother," Sir Horace replied. "Well, I saw a few acquaintances but no one I knew well, and I was just wondering whether I dare spend the little money I had on ordering dinner when a voice behind me exclaimed, 'Sir Horace, the very man I want to see!' "

"Who was it?" Lady Lambourn enquired eagerly.

"Do you remember Ludovick von Helm?" Sir Horace asked his wife.

Lady Lambourn wrinkled her brow.

"Ludovick von Helm," she repeated, "I seem to recall the name. Yes, of course, he was at Meldenstein, a rather ambitious young courtier. I remember him now."

"His ambitions have been realised," Sir Horace said, "he is now the Prime Minister."

"Indeed," Lady Lambourn remarked. "Is anything left of Meldenstein? I thought Napoleon had overrun all those principalities."

"Von Helm tells me that very little harm was done to Meldenstein compared with the other states," Six Horace replied. "They made no effort to resist Napoleon, and therefore nothing was damaged. They were forced to billet a large number of soldiers as they passed through the country *en route* for Russia, but, amazingly enough, financially Meldenstein is as rich as she was before the war."

"How is that possible?" Lady Lambourn asked.

"Because, my dear, as you know, the

Princess is an English woman and the State funds were invested in England. They must have had some bad moments during the war when they thought that at any moment England would be defeated by a Napoleonic invasion. Now we are the victors, and Meldenstein's money is not only intact but has multiplied during the war years."

"Well, I am glad someone could benefit by the war," Lady Lambourn commented bitterly.

"What was more, Prince Hedwig — you remember him, my dear — was not in the country. Von Helm tells me that he was travelling in the East when war broke out. Only after Waterloo could he return to his own land, which was administered during his absence by his mother."

"She is English," Lady Lambourn pointed out. "How could Napoleon tolerate an Englishwoman ruling over a state he had conquered?"

"Apparently the Princess charmed him. The stories of Napoleon's susceptibility to a pretty woman are not exaggerated. He allowed the Princess to remain, placing of course, some chattel of his own in supreme command, who was also charmed by our dear friend to grant her and the country many concessions which less-fortunate principalities did not enjoy."

"I am glad everything has turned out so well for them," Lady Lambourn said, "and Elaine was always a true friend. But tell me how this affects us."

"Well, intimately," Sir Horace said, "for von Helm had come to England with a mission, which was to find me and ask if my daughter — our daughter, my dear — would accept the hand of His Supreme Highness Prince Hedwig of Meldenstein."

There was a moment's utter silence after Sir Horace had spoken, and then in a very small voice, so low that he could hardly hear it, Camilla asked:

"You mean, Papa, that he wishes to marry me?"

"That is what he has requested," Sir Horace replied, "and I need hardly say what this offer meant, in a moment when I was in the deepest despair. Meldenstein has always been my second home, I went there when I was young as Third Secretary in the British Legation — my first diplomatic post. The Prince and his beautiful wife were kindness itself. I was sent to Rome, Paris, and then back to Meldenstein again as Minister. It was the happiest time of my life."

"But I have never seen the Prince," Camilla protested.

"Is he coming to England?" Lady Lambourn asked.

Sir Horace looked uncomfortable.

"You must understand, my dear," he replied, "that it would not be possible for His Supreme Highness to leave his country at this particular moment, having been away all through the war. There is a great deal for him to do; he has to meet his people. Their loyalty and, I am sure, their adoration of him is undiminished. At the same time, von Helm explained that it would be impossible for him to undertake another journey so soon upon his return. That is why von Helm came himself. The Prime Minister! You can understand that it is indeed an honour that a man in such a position should come in person to urge his Prince's suit."

Camilla rose to her feet and walked to the mantelpiece, and stood looking down at the unlit fire.

"Did you accept, Papa?" she asked quietly.

Again Sir Horace seemed a little uncomfortable.

"Naturally I did not jump at the suggestion without discussion," he answered. "But the Prime Minister had everything cut and dried. He had details of the marriage

23

settlement with him. Shall I tell you what they were?"

Camilla did not reply, so looking at his wife Sir Horace continued:

"His Supreme Highness is prepared to settle on his bride a hundred thousand pounds on the day of the marriage. As he realises that the preparation of her trousseau will involve heavy special expenses, the Prime Minister was empowered to hand me immediately ten thousand pounds."

"Ten thousand pounds," Lady Lambourn repeated faintly. "Oh, Horace! What an immense sum!"

"That is the sort of generosity I should expect from Meldenstein," Sir Horace said enthusiastically, but his eyes went towards his daughter standing with her back to him, her hands gripping the marble mantelpiece as if for support.

There was a moment's silence. Then Sir Horace said in a very different tone: "You are pleased, Camilla?"

"He has never seen me," Camilla said, "how can he wish to marry me?"

"Where Royalty is concerned these things are always arranged," Sir Horace replied.

"Surely the . . . two people . . . concerned . . . meet before anything is . . . decided?"

"Not always," Sir Horace said. "As you

know, the Regent had not seen Princess Caroline of Brunswick until she had crossed the Channel."

"And that has certainly been a disastrous marriage," Camilla said quickly.

"Of course, there is no comparison," Sir Horace said, realising his error. "Prince Hedwig has an English mother — your godmother — who has been a very good friend of ours for years. From all I have heard His supreme Highness is a delightful young man."

"How old is he?" Camilla asked.

There was a moment's pause.

"Thirty-eight or thirty-nine," Sir Horace said, almost as though the words were forced from him.

"Why has he not married before?" Camilla asked.

"I have already explained that," her father replied, a note of irritation in his voice. "He was in the East. You could hardly expect him to marry out there. Now he has returned, and a wedding will be exceedingly popular in Meldenstein."

"And so a bride has to be found," Camilla said in a low voice. "Anyone would do, so why choose me?"

"Camilla, I do not like your tone," Sir Horace replied sharply. "This is a great honour which has been accorded us. The same family have ruled in Meldenstein for nearly a thousand years, and the fact that it has become a tradition in the last three generations for the reigning Prince to marry an English wife has formed very close links with this country. Indeed, there is no other foreign state where I would wish you to reign save Meldenstein."

Camilla turned round. Her cheeks were very pale, her huge eyes dark and fearful, seemed almost too big for her little face.

"I do not wish to reign anywhere," she declared passionately. "I am not suited for such a life, as you well know, Papa. What knowledge have I of Courts? You and Mama are different. You have always held important diplomatic posts, and have mixed with Kings and Queens, with princes and their families. But I am different. I have lived quietly here ever since I grew up, with the exception of one short visit to London, where I felt lost and insignificant. I should not be accepted in Royal circles. I should be out of place and you would be embarrassed by my ignorance."

Sir Horace rose to his feet.

"Camilla, you must not say such things."

He walked across the room and put his arm round her.

"My dear, you are very beautiful. Wherever you go men will bow to your beauty and women will accept you as being undoubtedly the fairest of your sex. You will be happy at Meldenstein, I know it. Its Court is not subject to overpowering protocol like that of the Hapsburgs in Vienna, or the Court of Spain, where one only has to breathe to do the wrong thing. People in Meldenstein are simple and happy, from the Prince down to the lowest subject."

"But how do you know that I shall be happy," Camilla asked, "with a man I have never seen, a man who is nearly twenty years older than I am, a man who may dislike me as much as I may dislike him when he condescends to meet me?"

Sir Horace stared at his daughter. Then he dropped his arm, and his expression hardened.

"Very well," he said in a hard voice. "I see that I have made a mistake. I thought that you would be pleased at the change in our circumstances. I believed you would have felt that to be the reigning Princess in a place like Meldenstein — one of the most beautiful little countries in the world — was preferable to starving slowly to death in this tumble-down house. I was wrong."

Sir Horace walked across the room and

back again to face Camilla.

"I imagined too," he continued, "that you would be glad that your mother could go to Bath to relieve the suffering she has borne so bravely for so long, that you would have been pleased for our home to be repaired, the estate put in proper order for Gervase's return, but I was under a misapprehension."

Sir Horace paused and his tone grew sarcastic.

"You are concerned that you have not met this man who is prepared to behave so generously towards you and your family. I will write to him and say my daughter does not consider him a proper suitor for her hand because he will not throw over his Royal commitments to his country at this vital moment in its history, to come posting across the Channel and kneel at the feet of a fastidious young wench, who for all her much-vaunted attractions has not yet received a decent offer of marriage!"

Sir Horace had not raised his voice but his face was pale and his breath came sharply as if he had been running. It was obviously with a supreme effort at self-control that he added more quietly, but in an icy tone:

"Perhaps, Camilla you will oblige me by ringing the bell and requesting the footman

— whose wages I will now be unable to pay — to bring me pen and paper, so that a letter expressing your sentiments may be conveyed at once to His Serene Highness, Prince Hedwig of Meldenstein."

Sir Horace stopped speaking but it seemed as if his voice, almost like the lash of a whip, still echoed in the quietness of the room. Lady Lambourn gave a little sob and put her hands up to her face. For a moment Camilla stood irresolute and then she said in a dull voice:

"It is all right, Papa, I will do it, of course I will marry the Prince. I have no alternative, have I?"

"The choice is, of course, yours, my dear," Sir Horace said, picking up his glass of brandy and tossing it off as though he felt in need of sustenance.

"You are quite right, Papa," Camilla went on, "it is a great honour for which I should be extremely thankful. At least the house will be repaired and there will be new ceilings under which we can sleep without getting wet."

"That is a sensible girl!" Sir Horace said, the colour returning to his face. "I thought you would see reason. Indeed, we shall have to work quickly, for the Prime Minister has already returned to Meldenstein. His

Serene Highness will be arranging for proper representatives to come here next month to escort you and, of course, your Mama and me to the wedding."

"Next month!" Camilla echoed. "It is impossible for me to be ready so soon."

"The marriage is to be celebrated in June," Sir Horace replied. "It is a beautiful month in Meldenstein, and all the Royal weddings have taken place there during the second week of the month. It is the traditional time of good fortune."

"So the Prime Minister has already left with your acceptance," Camilla said. "You never thought for one moment that I might refuse, did you, Papa?"

It seemed for a moment as if Sir Horace would answer sharply. Then his diplomatic training made him say coaxingly: "My dearest child, I know only too well what you feel, but what other answer could I give? You are aware of why I went to London. Do you suppose that I was not in the very depths of despair at the position in which we found ourselves. I was penniless, Camilla, can you not understand what that means? To have no money in the bank, to have sold everything that was saleable!"

Sir Horace picked up his wife's hand.

"Look at your mother's fingers without a

ring," he commanded. "Look at the safe almost empty of silver, the spaces on the walls where the pictures hung, the furniture gone from the Salon, the stables bereft of all the best horses."

He flung out his arms dramatically, like a well-trained actor.

"Do you not think," he continued, "that I have not been ashamed of letting month after month go by and being unable to pay even Agnes and Wheaton, turning away labourers from the farm, the gardeners from the garden and the keepers from the woods? Old Groves, who has been with us forty years, retired without a pension!"

He put his hands on Camilla's shoulders and said softly:

"I have never been a millionaire, Camilla, but I have, in the past, lived like a gentleman. I am humiliated having my pockets to let, knowing that few people, apparently not even you, my dearest daughter, understand what agonies I am suffering from my impecuniosity. So when a chance came to right all the wrongs suffered inadvertently but nevertheless disastrously by those to whom we have a responsibility, I could not believe that you would make me regret it."

The gentleness and persuasion in her father's voice brought the tears to Camilla's eyes.

"I am sorry, Papa," she murmured. "Forgive me. It was just that for a moment I was frightened of what lies ahead. I would marry anyone, even if it were the Devil himself, to make you happy and Mama well. And I love my home. I want it to be repaired and in good shape for Gervase when he leaves the Navy. It was very selfish and wrong of me to speak as I did. I am sorry, Papa."

She turned her face up to her father's and now, as the tears ran down her cheeks, he saw, just as Lady Lambourn had done, how thin and fragile she looked. He caught her in his arms.

"My dearest, my little girl," he said, and his voice broke. "You know that all I want is your happiness, and believe me this will make you happy, I swear it."

"I am happy, I am, Papa," Camilla said, as if by repeating the words she could convince herself. "It was just the surprise and shock of what you had to say. Now everything is all right, and, please, before we do anything else, will you pay Agnes and Wheaton, and give them much more than they expected."

Sir Horace pulled her closer.

"I will do it this very minute," he said,

"and I will tell Agnes to cook the saddle of lamb for dinner. I vow we shall all feel less emotional when we have had some food."

He kissed Camilla's wet cheek, gave her a last close hug and went from the room. For a moment she stood looking after him and then, without speaking, she knelt down beside her mother's chair and laid her fair head against Lady Lambourn's breast.

"I am sorry, Mama, I must have upset you."

"No, darling," Lady Lambourn replied, "I know full well what you are feeling. We all want to meet the man of our dreams and fall in love with him."

She put one hand on her daughter's soft hair.

"You have not already lost your heart to someone else, have you, my dearest?"

Lady Lambourn's voice betrayed some anxiety. There was just a second's hesitation before Camilla replied:

"No . . . no . . . of course not, Mama."

2

The tapers in the chandeliers were burning low when a Gentleman, exquisitely attired, sauntered with a bored, cynical expression up the marble staircase. The noise of the crowd thronging the reception rooms was, he thought, not unlike the parrot-house at the Zoo.

He was unimpressed by the glittering jewels of the women in their transparent gauze and gold-threaded muslins, or by the diamonded decorations which adorned the chests of the men, who reminded him of a crowd of peacocks preening themselves as a prelude to mating.

Several people spoke to him, but with a brief nod the Gentleman passed on until finally he found his hostess holding court to a dozen or so of her male guests, every sentence uttered by her lilting voice bringing a guffaw of laughter or exclamations of flattery to their lips.

Lady Jersey knew every feminine trick to command the admiration of the other sex, to entice, entrance and to enthral. Petite, and not unlike a small, over-decorated bird, she had held for years the Regent's attention and his affections by the sheer persistence with which she had pursued him.

For the Regent it had been a wholly new and exciting experience to find himself not the seducer but the seduced. When finally their *affaire de cœur* ended, Lady Jersey, still looking younger than her daughters, but far older in experience and infinitely more cunning, had many other lovers eager to fall victim to her charms.

Although her place at the Regent's side had been taken by Lady Hertford, Lady Jersey was still undoubtedly the most powerful of the leaders of society and one whom it was social suicide to ignore or to offend.

It was therefore with a more pleasant expression on his face that the Gentleman who had just arrived stepped forward to bow and kiss the small hand held out to him.

"Hugo Cheverly!" Lady Jersey ejaculated, "I declare I am going to give you a scold. Have you any idea what time of the morning it is?"

"Pray forgive me," he answered, "I was delayed."

"At some gaming hell, I presume," Lady

Jersey said tartly. "Well, I am distressed that what I can offer you in the way of hospitality is not more interesting than the excitement of losing what little money you have on the green-baize tables."

"Your Ladyship is mistaken," he answered. "I have come here with all possible push from the country. If my horse had not been so inconsiderate as to cast a shoe I should have been here earlier. I am repentant, so I beg of you to be merciful to me."

He looked down into her disbelieving face, which showed little sign of her years, despite the late hours she kept and the constant strain of scheming and intriguing which would have taken its toll of any woman of less vitality. Now, with the quick change of mood which made her admirers find her so captivating, Lady Jersey tapped her guest's arm with her fan and said:

"Of course I forgive you, Hugo! What woman could resist that lazy indifference which, I swear, is a monstrously provoking challenge to any poor female?"

She smiled, and Hugo Cheverly, bored though he might have been, found himself smiling back. There was something audaciously direct about Lady Jersey which never failed to appeal to his sense of humour. As he bent and raised her hand to his lips once more, she said with quite a surprising tenderness in her tone:

"Now you have arrived, go and flutter the hearts of the simpering little doves who had been awaiting you. You will not find much competition when it comes to countenance."

"I want to talk to you sometime," he answered in a low voice. "Not here, not with all that crowd to overhear. I will call on you tomorrow. When will you be alone?"

Lady Jersey laughed.

"When am I ever alone?" she asked. "But come about tea-time and I will see what I can do."

She dismissed him with a wave of her fan, and as he moved away someone asked:

"Who is that? I do not recall having seen him here before."

"He is Captain Hugo Cheverly, and has only just arrived in London," Lady Jersey replied, "from the Army of Occupation across the Channel."

"Cheverly!" the courtier ejaculated. "Is not that the Alveston family name?"

"Hugo is a cousin of the present Duke," Lady Jersey explained, "but a poor one and with no prospects of succeeding, as Alveston has two sons and every likelihood of breeding half a dozen more."

"I never did care for the Duke," a bemedalled army officer ejaculated. "He instructed me once how to win the war. I never could abide these armchair critics!"

"You are lucky if you have to listen to them only from a chair," Lady Jersey said mischievously. "Where a woman is concerned, it is far too often from the bed."

There was a roar of laughter which reached Hugo Cheverly's ears as he moved out of one Salon into another. It seemed to him that London had not changed since he was there five years before. The same faces, the same flippant, drawling voices, the same glitter which could often be intolerably tarnished. Even the same scandal repeated and re-repeated from mouth to mouth.

He could hear as he passed sniggering whispered asides he knew only too well. "Prinny's debts", "Maria Fitzherbert's tears", "The King's madness", "Lady Hertford's greed"! It seemed almost incredible there could be anything new to say about any of them!

For a moment Hugo Cheverly hated them. What did those frivolous scatter-brains know of war or the men who fought for them? He no longer saw the expensive glitter or heard the high-pitched chatter, instead he saw and heard Montbrun's splendid horsemen at the Battle of Fuentes, trampling, bounding, shouting for the word to charge, and riding at times almost up to the British bayonets.

Outnumbered, trapped, the Light Division had seemed doomed he remembered, and yet Cotton's cavalry repeatedly charging had immobilised the French. With very few killed and more taken prisoner, Wellington's army had been the victors.

"What had it meant in London?" Hugo Cheverly questioned, recalling men blown to pieces, men parched with thirst, their faces blackened and scorched with powder and gore, men marching on with blistered feet to another battle with a song and a rough jest.

Supposing he told this blue-blooded vapourish company of the horrors he had seen — of the agonies suffered by wounded men, of the dead lying stiff or dying still faintly stirring, hillocks of soiled and blood-stained scarlet and blue amongst dismounted guns, shattered ammunition wagons and broken horse trappings? Who would listen?

It was a warm night and the hundreds of lighted tapers and the crowd of guests continually moving to and fro, made the salons almost intolerably hot. Seeing an open window Hugo Cheverly moved towards it and found himself on a small balcony overlooking the garden, which was discreetly lit with fairy-lights.

Below him he could see several well-known figures perambulating round a sparkling fountain, and beyond them in the shadows he noticed with a somewhat grim satisfaction several couples locked in passionate and indiscreet embraces. Concealed from those near the fountain by shrubs and a profusion of flowers, they had forgotten that they could be seen from the upper windows of the house.

Yawning, Hugo Cheverly decided there was no one he wanted to speak to, and he was just wondering if he could leave unobserved when a voice behind him asked quietly:

"Are you so very bored?"

He turned quickly to see a Vision almost blindingly bedecked with rubies and diamonds. She wore a tiara of them on her dark hair, a great necklace encircled her swan-like neck and cascaded over the daringly low-cut bodice of her evening gown. There were rubies and diamonds on her wrists, and he thought that they looked almost like blood against the whiteness of her skin — a skin which he knew, as he carried her ungloved hand to his lips, was as soft and smooth as a gardenia.

"I did not expect to see you here."

Her voice was low, and her Russian accent gave the words much more than their conventional meaning.

Hugo Cheverly released the hand which seemed to cling to his, and said harshly:

"I was convinced you would have left by now."

"Then you were trying to avoid me! I thought you might be. Is that why you have not returned to London for so long?"

"Anastasia, this conversation is exceeding foolish, as well you know," Hugo Cheverly said sternly. "Five years have passed since we last met. We have nothing to say to each other."

The woman facing him gave a little laugh, which lacked any sound of humour.

"That, my dear, is where you are wrong, I have a great deal to say to you. We cannot converse here. Escort me home. I was just about to leave and have already said my farewells to our hostess."

"No."

The monosyllable was sharp and almost rude, and Hugo Cheverly looked away across the garden, his clear-cut features silhouetted against the darkness of the sky.

"Hu-go, I must see you, I must. You cannot refuse! And if you do, what will you gain? We are both in London, we are bound to meet night after night. Therefore first we must talk to each other."

"No!"

The reply was still uncompromising. A small white hand crept forward to touch him on the arm.

"Please, Hu-go."

She had a way of saying his name which had an appeal all of its own, with a little pause between the first syllable and the second, a pause which he knew only too well had an irresistible attraction for him.

"It is impossible, everything is over, Anastasia! You know that. We cannot put back the clock."

"I have only asked to talk with you, surely you cannot refuse me that. Just a few minutes of your time, Hu-go."

The white hand crept down his arm and now he felt her fingers against the skin of his hand, soft, compelling, hypnotic. How well he knew the power of those small, sensitive fingers which could squeeze a man's heart until even love was dry and lifeless.

"No, Anastasia," he said angrily. Then as he looked down at her, the expression in his eyes hardened, his lips twisted wryly and he smiled.

"Why not?" he asked. "If the war has taught me nothing else, it has taught me not to be a coward in the face of the enemy. I will take you home."

She looked up at him from under her eyelashes, her red mouth smiling provocatively.

"Your gallantry overwhelms me," she murmured. The words were not sarcastic, rather an invitation, and once again he smiled, while the lines of cynicism made his handsome face look almost sardonic.

They moved slowly together through the Reception Rooms, which were not so crowded as they had been only a little while earlier. Already people were leaving and as they came down the Grand Staircase into the marble hall, the flunkeys were calling the carriages.

"Your coach, m'lady," a gilt-braided footman asked.

Hugo Cheverly answered him.

"The Countess of Wiltshire's coach," he said in a voice which was somehow unnecessarily loud and had a note of defiance in it.

As they waited he did not speak, standing aside as the Countess bowed, smiled or spoke to the other guests who had come down the stairs and were waiting in the hall

43

for a conveyance to carry them home or on to further activities.

At last the footman called Anastasia's name in stentorian tones, and they moved forward to find an extremely elegant coach drawn by a pair of silver-bridled chestnuts, a coat of arms emblazoned on the panel, two coachmen on the box and two footmen behind. One of them sprang down to open the door and let down the steps, and hold the fur rug in his arms as Anastasia stepped into the comfort of a padded vehicle which must have cost — Hugo noted grimly — many more guineas than he could earn in a year.

The rug was placed over their knees, the door was closed, and the horses moved forward, the coach travelling incredibly smoothly owing to the excellence of its springing.

"You were always desirous of comfort," Hugo Cheverly said, and she did not pretend to misunderstand him.

"I revel in it," she answered, "and you know full well that I could not live without it."

"The years roll back," Hugo remarked. "I remember this conversation taking place a dozen times under rather different circumstances."

She did not answer him, and after a moment he turned his head to look at her and saw by the light of the flares outside the houses they were passing that her dark eyes were raised to his, her lips parted. He turned away.

"This is madness," he said, "as we both well know."

"I have longed for your return, Hu-go. I hoped night after night to meet you somewhere."

"There is no point or reason in what we are doing," Hugo Cheverly said angrily.

She did not reply.

At that moment they reached a house in Berkeley Square. The horses came to a standstill, and they heard a footman scramble down from the box.

"Well, we have met each other," Hugo Cheverly said. "Good night, Anastasia."

"Hu-go, you cannot leave me like this, I have got to speak with you. Come in, there is no one at home, my husband is in the country."

"All the more reason for you to behave circumspectly," Hugo replied.

"Come in with me or I will make a scene," she threatened. "You would not wish for that in front of the servants."

The coach door was opened, she stepped

out on to the red carpet rolled across the pavement and Hugo Cheverly followed her. Just for a moment he hesitated as though he would walk away, and then with an almost imperceptible shrug of his shoulders he entered the house. He noted that, though it was so late, there were four flunkeys in attendance.

"Is there champagne in the little Salon?" Lady Wiltshire enquired.

"Yes, m'lady, and sandwiches."

"If I need anything more I will ring."

She swept ahead of him, her dress glittering in the candlelight. He followed her slowly, and when the double mahogany doors had been closed behind him, he saw he was in a room that was essentially feminine.

There were lilies everywhere — how well he remembered their pungent, haunting fragrance. The hangings were coral satin — a perfect background for the darkness of her hair and the pale alabaster of her skin. She stood shimmering against the mantelpiece, staring at him for a long moment, to take in every detail of his face and figure. Then she flung wide her arms.

"Hu-go!"

He came towards her, but he did not touch her.

"Listen, Anastasia," he said. "You made your choice, there is no going back, we cannot pick up the threads."

"Why not?" Her question was suddenly fierce, her eyes flashing, her lips pouting.

"Because you are married," he replied slowly, as if explaining something to a child. "Because you chose money rather than love. You did it deliberately, and now that I have had time to think about it I realise how sensible you were. I could not have given you those baubles which become you so well, I could not have paid the wages of even one of the obsequious servants who pander to your slightest whim. I could not give you this, or anything like it."

His gesture took in the room with its pictures, its expensive *objets d'art* on carved gilt tables, its almost over-opulent luxury from the painted ceiling to the Aubusson carpet on the floor.

"But you still love me."

The words came in a triumphant and seductive murmur from between her red lips.

Deliberately Hugo Cheverly turned away and walked towards the side-table on which a tray held cut-glass decanters and crystal glasses. He poured himself a glass of champagne from the bottle resting in a crested silver ice-cooler, and without turning round

47

tossed it off as though he was desperately in need of solace.

"You do!" Anastasia said behind him. "You do! I know it. A woman can never be mistaken."

It was then he turned round.

"I do not love you, Anastasia," he said quietly, "I loathe and despise you for what you have done to me. You bewitched me, haunted me and made me more miserable than I believed it was possible for any man to be. Thank God I am no longer in your thrall. I was afraid when I saw you tonight, afraid of what you might do to me. The scars from the agony which you made me suffer are still too recent for me to forget them, but, fortunately, what I feared I might feel for you is no longer there. You are lovely, yes lovelier than when we parted. Wealth becomes you, my dear. Your husband can provide a very expensive frame for what was always a very pretty picture. That was something I was unable to do."

"But, Hu-go, how could you have given me anything except your love?" Anastasia asked.

"And that was not enough, was it?" Hugo Cheverly retorted, with that wry smile which somehow she did not remember.

He turned and poured himself another

glass of champagne.

"Well, Anastasia," he went on, in a voice which showed he had complete control of himself, "what is there for us to talk about? The past is finished and over; the future as far as we are concerned does not exist; the present, well let me tell you again you are a very beautiful woman, and that tiara, which must have cost many thousands of golden guineas, becomes you mightily."

"Stop Hu-go, you are making me hate you," Anastasia said sharply.

She lifted up her arms and took the tiara from her head. She looked younger, at the same time even more attractive without the sparkling jewels which distracted from the slanting seduction of her eyes and the scarlet invitation of her mouth. She put the tiara casually down on a table and came towards him.

"We have so much to talk about, you and I," she said in a soft voice. "Not of the past — you are quite right there — or of the future, but now. We are together again and when we are together, whether you think you love me or not, there is, I believe, a link between us which can never be broken, something in me which responds to something in you, and that you cannot deny."

"And why should I wish to?" Hugo

Cheverly asked. "You have not changed, Anastasia. You always want what it is hard for you to get, and so for the moment, because you now have everything else you wanted — money, position, importance — you still want me. Well, it is too late. I am no longer a slave to come running at the snap of your fingers, I no longer kneel humbly at your feet desperate for the favours you would grant me if I please you or withhold if I do not. I am free, Anastasia, free, and I did not know it until tonight."

"Are you so sure?"

She did not sound annoyed at what he had said to her; not even piqued, but just curious. He realised it must have been a long time since anyone had spoken frankly to this incredibly lovely creature who was spoiled from the top of her shining head to the soles of her tiny feet.

"Suppose," Anastasia suggested, coming a little nearer, "you held me in your arms again and kissed as you used to do and with such fire, Hu-go. Oh, how strong, possessive and . . . brutal you could be at times. Do you think you could manage then to be so unconcerned? Could you still look at me with the indifference that I hear now in your voice, but I am not quite certain if I see it in your eyes."

50

Hugo Cheverly put down his glass of champagne.

"Hear me, Anastasia," he said. "I am no friend of your husband, in fact, I have but a passing acquaintance with him, so I am under no particular obligation where his honour is concerned. But I have a rooted objection — stupid of me, of course — to seducing a woman in her husband's bed. So, if you will forgive me for appearing discourteous, I will bid you good night. Otherwise we might both do things we would regret later on."

"No, Hu-go, we would not regret them," Anastasia said firmly, "and as to seducing me in my husband's bed, I no longer have a husband, save in name."

She did not move, but Hugo Cheverly felt as if she came nearer to him and took a step back.

"What the devil do you mean by that?" he demanded.

"I mean, as you well knew when I married, that my Lord Wiltshire is thirty years older than I. He is proud of me, he gives me everything that I ask for, but he is not particularly interested in me as a woman. I am just one of his possessions, and if he had the choice between me and his horses I am quite certain what his choice would be."

"It is not my business," Hugo Cheverly said sharply.

Anastasia laughed. It was low and soft, and unmistakably now a laugh of amusement.

"What has happened to you, Hu-go? You used not to be so fastidious! Your lady-loves, like Lady Jersey, would not believe that you had suddenly taken to psalm-singing if they had not heard it with their own ears. What has happened to the gallant who swept every woman off her feet, whose escapades with the fair sex were spoken of breathlessly and whispered from boudoir to boudoir? Men never change, or are you indeed but a coward still running away, despite all your brave words?"

"No, Anastasia, you shall not make a monkey of me again," Hugo Cheverly replied. "Good night and be damned to you! You made your choice five years ago. There are other women in the world, thank God!"

He turned towards the door, but as he reached it, he could not forbear to look back. Anastasia was standing at the far end of the room, and he saw with surprise that on one side of the fireplace a panel had opened to reveal a small aperture in which he could dimly discern the beginning of a flight of stairs.

"The staircase, Hu-go," Anastasia said, following his eyes, "is one leading up to my bedroom. I found it in the house when I came here. You must admit it is exceeding convenient."

"What do you mean, convenient?"

Hugo Cheverly walked back towards her. She made an expressive gesture with her hands.

"My dear Hu-go, I cannot believe that after you left me — you expected me to wear the willow indefinitely for our lost love. I have an old husband, but youth does not last for ever. I am still young, Hu-go."

"Curse you, Anastasia!" he said bitterly as he came near to her. "I knew you would never behave yourself unless you married someone strong enough to take a whip to you."

"And who would be likely to do that — save you, Hu-go?"

"What sort of men have you loved?" he asked, and now his hands went out to grip her bare shoulders. "Tell me! I have a mind to strangle you, for that is what you deserve."

His hands were on her shoulders, but now with a swift movement of her body she was close against his chest. Almost without realising it his arms went around her.

"Oh, Hu-go, Hu-go," she murmured, "I adore you when you are jealous. Punish me for what I have done! Hurt me, beat me! But hold me in your arms and kiss me, because I have missed you more than I deemed it possible to miss anyone."

He made a sound that was half anger, half pain, and then his lips were on hers, kissing her passionately, wildly, possessively, with a brutality which left her bruised and quivering as she held him closer and closer. Then gently, so that he hardly realised what she was doing, she led him through the open panel by the fireplace and up the narrow staircase.

3

Camilla stood at the window and looked out over the garden. The lilacs were in full bloom, purple mauve and white; the pink cherry blossom was blowing in the breeze; and the syringa bushes filled the air with their pungent compelling fragrance.

She sat down an the window-seat and felt she could never see enough of the home she loved so dearly. Tomorrow she would be gone, leaving behind all that was familiar, all that was an indivisible part of the eighteen years she had lived here.

"It is like having part of one's body amputated," Camilla thought to herself, and tried to suppress the pain she could feel in her heart at the thought of saying good-bye.

She had managed to turn a brave face to her father through all the weeks of preparation. There had been visits to London to spend what seemed to Camilla a fortune on gowns and redingotes, hats, gloves, shoes and reticules. Many of her dresses were so grand that she felt as though she would be afraid to wear them; but she knew they were fitting for the position she would hold as a reigning princess.

Gauzes and lamés, brocades and satins, velvets and silks, she now possessed them all, and at this moment they were being packed in the big leather trunks she would take with her on her journey to Meldenstein.

"I hate them," she whispered to herself. "I like my old faded muslins."

Then she was ashamed at her ingratitude. What girl of her age would not have been delighted to own such a fabulous trousseau? What bride-to-be would not have been excited by her magnificent white satin wedding dress trimmed with real Brussels lace, with a long train edged with ermine, and a tiara which was almost like a crown to uphold the ancient fragility of the family lace veil?

The tiara had arrived only that afternoon in the keeping of Baroness von Furstendruck, who was to be her escort to Meldenstein, not only as a chaperon but also to instruct her in some of the many ceremonies in which she must take part on arrival.

The Baroness was a woman of fifty. Camilla had felt afraid of her until she had discovered the Baroness was an inveterate chatterbox, only too willing to instruct her in many details of her new life.

"You will make a beautiful bride, my dear," the Baroness said. "His Serene Highness will be proud of you, and the people of Meldenstein will love you."

Her words had slightly warmed the chill that seemed to Camilla to be creeping all over her at the thought of what lay ahead, but what was worse than anything else was the thought that now, at the very last moment, her mother and father might not be able to accompany her.

Lady Lambourn was not well. The doctor had been called the previous week and had come daily, but reports of her progress had not been as encouraging as Sir Horace and Camilla had hoped. He was with Lady Lambourn now. As the door opened behind Camilla, she turned quickly, expecting to see the local physician. Instead it was her father who came into the room. She ran towards him.

"How is Mama?" she asked. "I have been waiting so apprehensively to hear the doctor's verdict."

"I fear I have no good tidings," her father replied. "Dr. Phillips wishes to convey your mother to London as soon as possible to consult one of the Royal physicians who, he

informs me, is most experienced in distur-
bances of the heart."

"Heart?" Camilla queried. "Then
Mama . . . ?"

"It is not only her legs that have affected
her health," Sir Horace explained, "it is
something far more serious. Her heart has
never been strong, and now Dr. Phillips is, I
fear, extremely concerned about her condition."

"Oh, Papa, I cannot bear it!" Camilla
cried. "Perhaps I can stay and come with
you to London."

"That is something which would distress
your mother and me more then anything
else," Sir Horace replied. "No, my dear,
there is no question of postponing the wedding. All the plans have been made, and I
am quite certain that in Meldenstein the
flags are already flying in honour of your arrival. You must not disappoint your future
husband."

"But, Papa, how could I be married wor-
rying all the time about Mama?"

Sir Horace's face hardened.

"You will learn, my dear," he said sternly,
"that in our lives duty comes before anything else. That is the position in society
into which we have been born. In the
theatre they have a saying, 'The curtain

must rise'. That means however distressed or even ill a play-actor may be, he will still give his best performance to the public. His private life must not encroach on his public image. It is the same where we are concerned."

"It is so hard, Papa," Camilla murmured, and she was not far from tears. "I cannot bear to think of dear Mama suffering."

"She would suffer far more," Sir Horace declared, "if she thought you were not doing what was right and what was expected of you. The Prince is waiting, Camilla, and tomorrow you leave for Meldenstein."

He spoke harshly, almost as if he was afraid Camilla would rebel against him, but there was no rebellion left in her. Instead she covered her face with her hands, and after a moment Sir Horace put his hand gently on her head.

"You are going to be a person of great import, my dear," he said, not without a note of quiet satisfaction in his voice. "The days of irresponsible childhood are over, and your Mama and I will, I know, be exceeding proud of you."

"I hope so, Papa," Camilla managed to say, her voice choked with tears.

As if he was suddenly impatient of her weakness, Sir Horace walked across the room and picked up a piece of paper from the secretaire.

"I have here," he said, "a list I have made of Meldenstein customs and the protocol at the Palace. I wish you to read it carefully. I am well aware you are entering a new life, of which you are lamentably ignorant, but you have always been intelligent and by applying yourself and listening to my instructions, there will be no need for you to seem in any way gauche or embarrassed."

Camilla drew a small handkerchief from her waistband.

"Thank you, Papa," she said as she wiped her eyes.

"Dinner will be in an hour's time," Sir Horace remarked, drawing his gold watch from his waistcoat pocket. "I am hoping that our other guest will not be late."

"What other guest?" Camilla asked. "Is someone else coming?"

"I told you about him two days ago," Sir Horace replied with a note of rebuke in his voice. "I rather fancied you were not listening, Camilla, when I read aloud the letter from Her Highness, and now it seems I was correct in my assumption."

"I am sorry, Papa, there were so many things to take in."

"The Princess has arranged that you will

not only be chaperoned by the Baroness but also accompanied by her nephew, Captain Hugo Cheverly. It is, I think an expression of solicitude and consideration with which she regards you that she has taken the trouble to choose an English escort. You should be grateful, Camilla."

"I am," Camilla answered obediently.

She wiped her eyes resolutely and slipped the handkerchief back under the blue sash which encircled her tiny waist and which, worn over a new, fresh muslin fashioned by a master couturier, became her greatly.

"You do not seem very interested in this gentleman who will be in your company for nearly a week," Sir Horace said with raised eyebrows.

"I beg your pardon, Papa," Camilla apologised, forcing herself to give him her attention. "Tell me about him."

"He is, as I have already said, a nephew of the Princess. His father, Lord Edward Cheverly, was the youngest son of the fourth Duke of Alveston. A charming man, I remember him well. He died just before the war broke out and, I believe, his wife predeceased him by some years."

Sir Horace paused, and Camilla, realising something was expected of her, said:

"How interesting, Papa."

"His son, the young man who is coming here tonight, has, I believe, a good war record," Sir Horace continued. "He was certainly in a regiment which did well on the Peninsula and at Waterloo. I have not met him, but I have heard that he is popular. You will, of course, Camilla, be very careful what you say in front of him and, of course, to the Baroness. You will be quite sure that everything about us will be reported to Meldenstein."

"I will be careful, Papa," Camilla promised.

"I have, as you know," Sir Horace continued, "contrived with patience and ingenuity to ensure that this evening goes off smoothly. I would not wish the Prince, for your sake apart from my own, to think he was marrying into an impoverished family. It may be a great honour that he has chosen you, Camilla — I am not saying it is not — but at the same time we are of noble blood and can hold our heads proudly. I think that what I have arranged this evening should impress both our guests."

"You have, indeed, been splendid, Papa," Camilla said quickly. "No one else could have had so much of the house repaired at such unprecedented speed, and indeed, with the windows painted and the ceilings replaced, it really does look as it did when I was a child."

"I think the workmen have done a good job," Sir Horace agreed. "Of course, there are many things to be done in other parts of the house, but they will not be apparent this evening."

"The gardens too look beautiful," Camilla said, "and it is a joy to see men working in the fields again."

"I am convinced that our new farm bailiff is worth his weight in gold," Sir Horace said. "He is an expensive man, and I have had to promise to carry out many improvements to this house, but I think he will be worth it."

"I am sure he will, Papa," Camilla agreed.

"And now there is talk — only talk, mind you," Sir Horace continued, "that those of us who have invested money in France will get some return for our investment. If this happens I shall be the happiest man in the world."

"Oh, I am so glad, Papa!" Camilla cried, clasping her hands together. "You mean you will be rich again?"

"Not rich," Sir Horace smiled, "but I am sure that, if with your help we can tide ourselves over the next year or so, we will at least not be in danger of starving or going to the debtors' prison."

"I am positive that will be possible," Camilla assured him. "I mean . . . you know, Papa, that anything I have is yours."

Sir Horace, looking first towards the door as if he thought someone was listening, came forward to take Camilla's hand in his.

"My child," he said, and his voice was moved. "I knew I could rely on you. It is not something we should wish to talk about, is it? Nevertheless, your assistance for the next twelve months will make all the difference to your mama and me."

"You know I will help you, Papa. As soon as the money is in my hands I will send you whatever can be despatched without arousing comment."

"There is no need for haste," Sir Horace said, "there is a great deal left of the ten thousand pounds which von Helm entrusted to me for your trousseau. I would not have the Prince or his mother think that we have been cheese-paring where you are concerned. Nevertheless, Camilla, there are moneys in the bank to tide us over the next few months."

Camilla reached up and kissed her father's cheek.

"You know that I will do anything in my power to make you both happy."

Sir Horace held her close for a moment and then said:

"I must go and see to the wines. Do not delay in changing your gown for dinner, Camilla, you must be waiting to receive our guest."

"Yes, of course, Papa," Camilla said dutifully. "I will go upstairs immediately."

Sir Horace went from the room, but Camilla lingered. She turned again to the window. The sun was sinking in a blaze of glory behind the trees, the sky was translucent. In the great elm trees in the park the rooks were going to roost. It was all very quiet and peaceful, and yet Camilla felt as though her body was torn tumultuously.

She wanted to cry out, to scream that she could not go away and leave all she loved for a strange land and a man she had never seen.

"We all want to marry the man of our dreams!"

She could hear her mother's soft voice saying the words and she knew that this was the moment when she said good-bye not only to her home but to her dreams.

It had been a ridiculous, nonsensical notion, she told herself, and yet she always believed she would meet again the man she had seen that day, nearly six years ago, when she had gone with her father to a race-meeting which had taken place some three miles from their home.

One of the famous regiments, she had forgotten which, had been in camp in the open countryside outside London, and they had organised some horse-races between themselves and the local gentry. News of it had been carried to the Prince of Wales, who announced his intention of attending.

This had caused a great flutter amongst the country families, and everyone who had received an invitation from the Colonel commanding the troops had set off in their coaches and open carriages. The ladies were dressed in their best gowns and gaily trimmed bonnets, and the children who accompanied them were almost as excited as Camilla, jumping up and down and asking innumerable questions, until finally they came in sight of the course.

Camilla could remember it so well. The mass of white tents; the larger ones where the Prince and his guests were to be entertained; the regimental flags fluttering in the breeze; the red coats of the soldiers; the horses being paraded in front of the spectators.

She was not much interested in the glamourous women with their colourful dresses, or the young bucks with their top-hats worn at a rakish angle, who made outrageously extravagant bets and kept the Prince of Wales continuously amused.

Soon she wandered away to inspect the horses, and she saw one that she liked more than any of the others — a spirited black stallion that was letting fly his heels and behaving in so playful a manner that his groom had difficulty in holding him.

When the riders came into the paddock to mount, she saw that the stallion she fancied was being ridden by a tall, handsome young man, who, once he was mounted, seemed part of the horse. She knew vaguely that this was a regimental race and the most important event of the day. She noted that all the other riders were laughing and joking with each other as they rode down the course.

"What price Apollo?" she heard the rider of the black stallion shout to a bookie.

"Only two to one, sir," he answered, "when you're a'riding him!"

"You old crook!" was the reply. "But put me on ten jimmy o'goblins."

"You will lose your money!" another rider — an older man — remarked. "Firefly will walk it."

"Bet you a monkey you are wrong!" was

the confident retort, but Camilla did not hear the reply.

She stood watching as the horses reached the starting place. Then as the race began and they thundered past her, she knew that she wanted the black stallion to win more than she had wanted anything else in her life before.

It was a steeplechase, and new fences had been erected, besides hedges that were natural to the fields over which they rode. It was a long race, but it was possible to see the riders almost the whole way round the course, and even when they were far away Camilla could pick out the bright blue coat of the gentleman riding Apollo.

He was lying about third, she noted, until they were three-quarters of the way round the course. Horses had fallen at some of the fences, but the black stallion took them like a bird in flight, until there was only the last half-mile to go. It was then Camilla saw him gradually creeping up on the two horses ahead of him. Apollo drew nearer and nearer, but when he passed the first horse the second was well out in front.

"Come on," she whispered, "come on! You can do it, I know you can do it."

She almost felt as though she was riding the stallion herself. She could feel it moving forwards at the sound of her voice, responding to her touch. The leading horses took the last fence together and she saw one fall. For a moment she thought it was Apollo, but then she saw he was well over, moving smoothly into the last gallop. As he passed the winning post, amid the cheers of the watching crowd, his rider, low on his neck, had a broad smile on his lips.

"He has won! He has won!" Camilla exclaimed. She felt as though she had achieved a victory.

The stallion had been turned and was now being led past the distinguished guests. The rider took off his hat respectfully to the Prince, bowing his acknowledgment of the spectators' applause.

"Well done! Good ride!" an old man near Camilla exclaimed, and added: "I've lost a packet, damn it, but I cannot help admiring the way that young fellow rides."

How many times, Camilla wondered now, had she relived those moments when she strained every nerve in her body urging the black stallion to victory. She had only to shut her eyes to see the smile of the rider as he passed the winning post, and the gay satisfaction in his face as he lifted his hat to the Prince of Wales.

As she grew older in her dreams he was

often at her side. She told herself it was but the musings of a child and something she should forget, and yet when she imagined the man who would some day capture her heart, he always wore the smiling countenance of the gentleman riding the black stallion.

"Good-bye to him too," she though whimsically to herself as she looked out into the garden. "Tomorrow I start anew, just as though the whole eighteen years of my life had been scrubbed clean from a slate. Everything will be different, and if I am sensible I will look forward to it and try not to look back."

It was not going to be easy, she thought with a pain in her heart that was almost physical. Her eyes lingered once again on the bushes where she had hidden so often from her governess at lesson time; the trees she had climbed, for which she had been punished for behaving like a tomboy; and the fountain where with baby fingers she had tried to catch her first goldfish.

There in the distance was the walk into the shrubbery — she could see the entrance to it clearly from the window — where she had gone when she wanted to be alone, where she had slipped away to dream her dreams, and where she had found sanctuary when life became too difficult for her, when she was unhappy, lonely or afraid.

The clock in the hall struck the half past the hour! With a start Camilla realised that it was getting late. Her father had told her to be ready in good time. She took one last look at the sunset, golden and red, which looked as though the horizon was brilliant with a promise for the future.

"I will do what is right!" Camilla said.

She spoke the words aloud, as if making a vow for herself, and then started when behind her she heard the door open and the butler's voice announce in stentorian tones:

"Captain Hugo Cheverly, Miss Camilla."

She turned quickly. For a moment she felt she must be dreaming, still living again in one of those fantasies which at times had seemed more real than reality. Then she knew it was the truth — he was there, the man of whom she had dreamt, the man whom she had remembered ever since she had seen him riding a black stallion to victory.

She felt her heart give a little leap of excitement, but as she moved towards him and looked up into his face, she saw with surprise that he was looking at her with a strange expression in his eyes, which she could only describe to herself as one of contempt. . . .

Hugo Cheverly had arrived at the Lambourns' house in an extremely bad temper. For one thing he was late, and had been forced to hurry unduly the horses he was tooling in his High-Perch Phaeton. If there was something he disliked above all others, it was to overdrive his horseflesh, and it was no consolation to know he had no one but himself to blame.

He had not meant to linger with Anastasia, but as usual she had tempted him to do what he knew only too well was an indiscretion, and he had been too bewitched to resist her.

"Why must you go?" she pouted. "We have been so happy these last weeks! Now you must go away and heaven knows what may have happened before you return."

"I cannot refuse to escort this female to Meldenstein," he had replied. "My aunt has particularly requested it of me. It is the least I can do for her when, after my mother died, she did everything in her power to comfort and care for me."

"But Meldenstein is such a long way to travel," Anastasia persisted, "and you have only just returned to England."

"That was your fault," Hugo said.

Anastasia raised herself on her elbow and bending over kissed her lover as he lay comfortably against the lace-edged pillows of her bed.

"I shall miss you," she whispered, "hurry back — hurry — hurry."

He reached out his arm to pull her close.

"I may not come back."

"You will, you will!" she cried. "I am a witch, as you have told me so often, and now I cast a spell upon you — a spell you can never break — that when I call you will come."

He laughed and kissed her possessively, feeling the softness of her gardenia-soft skin beneath his hands, seeing the passion in her slanting eyes, the hunger on her parted lips.

"You are insatiable, Anastasia," he said. "A man has to be strong to love you, and even the strongest must have a holiday sometimes from your demands."

"And suppose I will not let you go?" Anastasia asked.

"Then for once your spell will not be potent enough," Hugo answered, "because I am going now."

He kissed her again and would have disentangled himself from her arms, but she held him closely.

"My big, strong, marvellous lover," she

said. "You are everything that I want in a man, how can I let you go to another woman? I shall be jealous of her."

"That is hardly necessary," Hugo remarked. "She is to be the bride of the Prince of Meldenstein, as you well know."

"She is lucky — he is very rich."

Even as Anastasia spoke she realised she had made a mistake. Hugo's whole body stiffened, and now quite firmly he disengaged himself from her clinging arms and rose from the bed.

"That is all women think about, is it not?" he asked coldly.

"Oh, Hu-go, I did not mean it," Anastasia said. "Now you are in one of your miffs. Why, why must you be so touchy about money? You are everything that any woman could ask for."

"Except that I am poor," Hugo answered, dressing himself swiftly with the meticulous care of a man who is used to robing himself without the assistance of a valet.

"It is of no consequence," Anastasia retorted. "If you cannot pay for a woman's comfort — there is always someone who can."

"To whom she should owe her allegiance," Hugo said, pulling on his polished Hessians over the skin-tight knitted pantaloons which Beau Brummel had made so fashionable.

"Bah! You are so conventional," Anastasia complained, patting up pillows behind her and lying against them so that her long, dark hair cascaded over her white shoulders. "In bed it does not matter whether you have any gold in your pockets."

"A sentiment," Hugo remarked, "which would be more acute if you added to whose bed you were referring."

Anastasia laughed.

"You always have an answer, my Hu-go. You are so bitter and yet I think in your heart you love me just a little."

"In my heart I have many hard words for you," Hugo replied, "but it is quite useless for me to tell you what they are. For one thing you would not listen, and for another you would not believe me. So long as your beauty survives, Anastasia, you will do your damnedest to tie men's lives into knots, and the devil take it you will succeed! I have called you a witch — it is a fitting word for you."

"I love your compliments," Anastasia smiled. "I see you are ready. Come and kiss me good-bye."

That, Hugo reflected as he drove at a breakneck speed, was where he had made his mistake. He bent down to kiss her, and then her arms were round his neck and her body was like a pearl against the soft silkiness of the sheets and the darkness of her hair. Witch-like she had tempted him once again, and he had been unable to resist her.

"God! I am a fool!" Hugo Cheverly said beneath his breath as he whipped up his horses, and realised that to be late would augur ill for the impression of responsibility he must create as guardian of the future Princess of Meldenstein.

"Fool! Fool!"

The wheels of the High-Perch Phaeton seemed to be crying as they spun over the dusty roads, and he could hear Lady Jersey's voice saying much the same thing.

"You are behaving like a fool, my dear boy. Wiltshire is bound to hear about it sooner or later. The whole of London is talking."

"They should have something better to chatter about," Hugo said surlily.

"What could be a more delicious titbit," Lady Jersey asked, "than a liaison between the wife of one of our richest Peers — who has antagonised the women by her beauty and her flaunting of the conventions — and the most handsome young man in the Beau Ton?"

"And the most impecunious," Hugo added.

"I agree it is a pity you have no money," Lady Jersey went on, "but if you had been warm in the pocket you would have been married by now, and I can assure you that if Lady Wiltshire has made you unhappy in the past, it is nothing to the misery you would have suffered had you been her husband."

For a moment Hugo had been prepared to repudiate such an idea, and then his sense of honesty had forced him to match the frankness which was so characteristic of Lady Jersey, and he had grinned at her.

"Perhaps you are right."

"Of course I am right," Lady Jersey snapped, "and the best thing you can do, Hugo, is to leave London quickly. Things were quiet until you returned, but now we are all sitting on a powder-barrel. Wiltshire, with all his preoccupation with horses, is not a man to countenance his wife behaving like a 'bit o' muslin' from the opera."

"Anastasia says he is not interested in her," Hugo said.

Lady Jersey laughed.

"Anastasia!" she exclaimed. "That woman was born with a lie on her lips. Is that what she told you? My poor besotted, enslaved Hugo. M'Lord Wiltshire is crazied about her. He may be old, he may have other interests besides lovemaking — that is to be understood — but Anastasia is his, and if he knew what she was about, he would no more share her with you than allow a crossing-sweeper to race his horse at Newmarket."

Hugo remembered how he had jumped to his feet and felt the breath coming quickly between his lips as he said angrily:

"I cannot believe that is the truth."

"My dear Hugo, do not be so adolescent," Lady Jersey said, "older men can be very competent lovers."

"How old, in fact, is he?"

"His Lordship has not yet reached sixty and is by no means senile," Lady Jersey replied. "Lady Hertingfordbury, who was his mistress for years before he married Anastasia, speaks very highly of his prowess."

Hugo recalled how he had thrown back his head and laughed, he could not help it. It was so like Lady Jersey to say such things. Not one lady of quality would have dared speak of such matters, not even in the intimacy of their boudoir. At the same time he was angrier than he had been for many years. He had shaken Anastasia in his fury until she had gasped for breath.

"It is not true," she had stormed at him, stamping her little foot. "What does that old harridan know of what happens in my private apartments? He is no longer my lover, I tell you. He may love me — that is a very different thing. But in bed I do not notice him!"

"You told me you did not sleep with him," Hugo protested.

For a moment he thought he had disconcerted her, but she had an answer — Anastasia always had an answer — and because she fascinated him he was prepared to believe her falsehoods.

But now he asked himself whether it was worth coming under her spell once again. God! How she had made him suffer in the past. He remembered nights in Portugal when he had lain sleepless, his whole body aching for her. He had yearned for her, hated and loathed her because she preferred to marry a man with money rather than face poverty with him. He had bitten his fingers at the thought of it until they bled. He had thought of her with Wiltshire until he had not believed a man could suffer such agony and remain sane.

At length he had come back to London believing he was now free of her. He did not trust her, he did not respect her, he did not love her — not as love should be between a man and woman — but she could arouse in him a passion which was echoed by a passion within herself, until the desire of their bodies erased every other thought from his mind.

Now the wheels mocked at him, and he felt a weakling; a man so stupid that a woman could twist him round her little finger; a man without pride. He drove faster and faster, hating all women because of their promiscuity, because they wanted only a man's body and would sell their own to the highest bidder.

He had only to think of Anastasia lying in the great soft bed, the scented flower-filled room, her dressing-table covered with jewels, to feel a fury which was almost murderous well up inside him like a leaping fire. Often he thought he might kill her. He had only to put his hands round her long white throat and then she would never again exercise such mastery over him, he would no longer dance to the time she played.

"God help me, I'm as mad as Bedlam," he said aloud, and then remembered the groom was sitting behind him.

He turned the last words into an oath, and once again he whipped up the horses.

He was on time, due to superb driving, but it was in no good mood that Hugo Cheverly crossed the threshold of Sir Horace Lambourn's house, to be shown by the butler into the Salon.

A young girl was its only occupant. He noticed that she was fair and that she was very tiny, before she turned to face him, and he saw that she was extraordinarily beautiful. And then he perceived in her eyes a startled astonishment which could not, he thought, be possibly accounted for by his quite ordinary, if dusty appearance.

4

"Her Highness said to me, 'We must find someone beautiful, well-bred and intelligent to help Prince Hedwig rule over Meldenstein,' " the Baroness related, talking quickly and gesticulating with her hands as she spoke, "and then Her Highness exclaimed, 'I have thought of just the right person, the daughter of my old friend and flirt, Sir Horace Lambourn! I remember Camilla as a child, she was an entrancing creature.' "

The Baroness gave a little laugh.

"And so you must see, my dear Miss Lambourn, that is how great events take place in Royal circles — just a private conversation between Her Highness and myself and all the pageantry of an historic and spectacular marriage begins."

Camilla did not answer. The Baroness had been talking ever since they left home, and Camilla, intent on her own thoughts, had hardly heard what was being said.

At first it had been hard to fight against

the tears which threatened to overwhelm her. It had been agonising to say good-bye to her mother, to wonder as she kissed her pale soft cheek if she would ever see her alive again.

"Take care of yourself, my dearest," Lady Lambourn said, her voice a little hoarse, as Camilla realised, from pain. "I feel so help-less letting you go alone. If only Papa and I could be with you! But you must be brave, my dear one, and try to find real happiness with this charming, intelligent Prince, who I know will grow to love you deeply."

Camilla bit back the words which came to her lips, knowing she must not say anything to distress or upset her mother. But she wondered, as she had wondered so often these past weeks, why anyone should assume that the Prince would love her, or she the Prince. It was a *mariage de convenance* and she longed once again to cry out that she could not do it, she could not go through with it!

Her nervous anticipation of that day which lay ahead had not been helped by the attitude of Captain Hugo Cheverly. Watching him during dinner the night before, Camilla had thought he might have been trying purposely to make her worried about what lay ahead.

There was something in his indifference to what was going on around him which showed too clearly that he was bored with the task he had been forced to undertake of conveying her to Meldenstein. He was also, Camilla thought, singularly unimpressed with the preparations which had been made for him with such forethought.

"Must you really go to such trouble, Papa?" she had asked her father half a dozen times when she found Sir Horace had not only engaged a special chef to prepare the evening meal, but had also contrived that there should be many extra servants in the house and in the stable.

Boys from the village had been engaged for the evening, the more presentable of the younger gardeners were brought into the house and the old liveries, which had lain in the attic ever since anyone could remember, were brought down, sponged, pressed, their buttons polished, and utilised for the new flunkeys. Their duties, as far as Camilla could see, were just to stand about and give an extravagant *ton* to the establishment.

"I know you do not want us to appear abjectly poverty-stricken, Papa," she went on as he did not answer, "but surely it is unnecessary for the Baroness and Captain Cheverly to think us as rich as Croesus. No one but the gentleman in question would employ so many footmen. And what are they supposed to do when we are not enjoying the company of such distinguished guests?"

Sir Horace smiled at her.

"I may perhaps have inadvertently given the impression that we entertain a great deal," he answered. "Ex-Ambassadors often play a part in government hospitality, and it would have been an understandable mistake if the Prime Minister of Meldenstein thought that the Court of St. James's looked on me as one of their hosts."

Camilla laughed.

"Papa, you are an old humbug!" she cried. "I really believe that you enjoy theatricals for their own sake. Perhaps it is a good thing you are not coming to Meldenstein! I swear you would have disrupted all their carefully considered plans by reorganising the whole marriage ceremony."

"I doubt if I should find any flaws in the Princess's arrangements," Sir Horace smiled. "She is a woman of tremendous ability — I admire her greatly. I cannot believe that you will not grow to love her as I do."

"I hope so, Papa," Camilla had said dutifully, but she could not help wondering if an over-efficient mother-in-law was not something which every bride dreaded.

"Had the Prince no say in what happens?" she wondered. "He is certainly old enough to have a mind of his own!"

It was difficult for her to discover anything about the Prince. Sir Horace had only known His Serene Highness in his youth before the war. He spoke of him warmly as a brilliant, intelligent, charming young man; but whatever he had been like she felt a father in such circumstances would have painted his future son-in-law in glowing colours.

Camilla had thought to ask Captain Cheverly about the Prince, but that was obviously impossible. He was not the sort of man, she decided, with whom one could have an intimate conversation. Instinctively she resented the manner in which when she did address him he condescended to reply.

"You must tell my daughter about Meldenstein," Sir Horace said affably at dinner after Soup à la Reine had been followed by boiled carp covered with Italian sauce, chickens au Tarragon served with a glazed ham, raised mutton pie and pigeons turned on the spit. The second course had included a Rhenish cream, a plum cake, a red jelly served with early strawberries and mushrooms on toast which Camilla had picked in the fields early that morning.

"I could write a book on the delights of that beautiful country," Sir Horace continued, "but then I am prejudiced. The years I spent there were the happiest of my life. But, of course, I am old and out of date. Tell my daughter about the place from a young person's point of view."

Captain Cheverly had not looked up from the pear he was peeling with deliberate precision.

"What does she want to know?" he asked, and his cold, somewhat distant voice made Camilla feel as though a chill wind blew through the dining-room.

She could not imagine why he could not address her directly instead of speaking to her through her father as though she was a child or half-witted.

"Well, of course, she will want to know everything there is to know," Sir Horace smiled. "Tell us about Prince Hedwig. It must have been a terrible ordeal for him to be abroad all those years when his country was overrun by Napoleon."

There was a pause before Captain Cheverly had agreed it must indeed have put His Serene Highness in a difficult position.

87

"The Prince was in good health when he returned?" Sir Horace enquired.

"I believe so."

"You did not see him?" Sir Horace asked.

"I saw His Serene Highness for a few minutes immediately on his arrival in Meldenstein," Captain Cheverly answered. "It was soon after the cessation of hostilities, and my regiment was passing through the country. We were received by the people with much enthusiasm. My aunt was naturally deeply relieved that Europe was no longer under the heel of a tyrant."

"Yes, of course," Sir Horace ejaculated. "I thought often of the Princess and what she must have suffered when it seemed that Napoleon was all-triumphant. I knew too that the finances of Meldenstein depended wholly on a British victory."

"Money being of tremendous importance to a State as well as to individuals!" Captain Cheverly said with a twist of his lips. "That Meldenstein is still rich is undoubtably another good reason for the extravagant jubilation of the forthcoming nuptials."

The way he spoke made Camilla glance at him in surprise.

"Why should he be so bitter?" she asked herself. "What has happened to make him appear not only cynical but almost antagonistic to the whole idea of my marriage?"

Later, when the gentlemen came from the dining-room into the Salon, Sir Horace went upstairs to see his wife, and Camilla was left alone with the Baroness and Captain Cheverly. As he stood in front of the mantelshelf she could not help noticing how distinguished he looked. His coat, obviously cut by a master-hand, appeared to be moulded to his form, the points of his collar were as stiff as starch could make them, and his neckcloth arranged in the intricate folds of the "Mathematical", which Gervase had once tried to cultivate, was perfection. For all his elegance there was a suggestion of strength about him which made the man triumph over the dandy.

"I have been telling Miss Lambourn how beautiful Meldenstein will be at the time of the wedding," the Baroness gushed. "There will be flowers everywhere, not only those specially arranged for the ceremonial occasions, but in the window-boxes of everyone's house, in their gardens, in garlands round the heads of our young girls, and on our mountains, which will then be covered with flowers intertwined like the colours of an exquisitely woven carpet."

"You are most poetical, ma'am," Captain Cheverly remarked.

Camilla fancied that he sneered, and also she felt for some unaccountable reason that he was actively disliking her. He turned and looked at her and when he did she was certain she saw again the contempt in his eyes which had been so obvious at the first moment of his arrival.

What was wrong? What had she done? Why did he despise her? The questions kept presenting and re-presenting themselves to her all through the night, when she had lain awake unable to sleep at the thought of the morrow. She tried to tell herself she was just imagining things, that Captain Cheverly was just a very disagreeable young man, spoilt and perhaps annoyed that he should be sent on such a mission when he would rather be enjoying the gaieties and dissipations of London society.

"That must be the explanation," she thought, for there could be no other.

She remembered how often his face had haunted her since she saw him winning the race on his black stallion, and she told herself that dreams should never become reality because they could only bring disillusionment.

There had, however, been little time to think of Captain Cheverly when dawn came. Camilla had dressed quickly to have a last moment in which to say good-bye to everything she knew and loved. She went round the garden, stood for a long time looking at the outside of the house, and finally went in to say her last farewell to her mother.

The travelling coach was waiting when she came downstairs, a very expensive, elaborate vehicle which her father had secured from London.

"It is fortunate we are not buying it!" Camilla thought.

It would have been of little use in the future, except to convey her mother to Bath, so it had been hired for a month with the four well-matched roans which drew it at a spanking pace.

The coach was well sprung, and they moved swiftly over the dusty roads. They were followed by a luggage-wagon containing the Baroness's abigail and the young girl called Rose whom Camilla had chosen to accompany her to Meldenstein. Lady Lambourn had wished her to engage a much older woman, but Camilla had insisted that she have someone young.

Rose, warm-hearted and apple-cheeked, had come to the house only in the last few weeks, but had already proved herself not only an excellent housemaid but a quite competent lady's-maid. She liked sewing and had a natural aptitude for handling gowns, and Camilla felt she would like to have her with her.

"I must have someone I can speak to about home," she said, when Lady Lambourn protested at her choice. "Rose, who comes from a most respectable family, has lived in the village all her life, she knows everyone I know. I can talk to her of places and people without having to make explanations. I could not bear to take with me a stranger to live amongst other strangers."

Lady Lambourn had capitulated, and Camilla had her way. Seeing Rose neatly and demurely dressed in black with a black straw bonnet, Camilla did not regret her choice.

The Baroness's lady's-maid was old and obviously disagreeable. Camilla thought it would have been cold comfort to go abroad with someone of whom she stood as much in awe as the people she was going to meet in a new country.

Besides the coach in which she and the Baroness were travelling and the luggage-wagon, Camilla was amused to see at the front door the High-Perch Phaeton in which Captain Cheverly had come down from London.

"You are driving alone?" she heard her father ask somewhat in surprise.

"I thought it best to go ahead," Captain Cheverly replied. "In that way we shall save time at posting-inns and other places where we have to stop. It is only as far as Dover, of course, and when we reach His Supreme Highness's yacht my phaeton will be dispatched to London and I will send your travelling-coach and the luggage-wagon back here."

"That will be most obliging of you," Sir Horace said as he turned to say good-bye to Camilla.

Her eyes were too misty for her to be able to look back at the house as they sped through the drive gates. She also missed the village with its duck-pond, its open green on which stood the stocks, and the small grey church in which she had been christened.

But after a time she was able to look out through the windows to see the hamlets through which they passed, and wished that she was out in the sunshine rather then being enclosed in the stuffiness of the coach. She saw Captain Cheverly pass in his High-Perch Phaeton, and even though she did not wish to be beside him, she would have liked to be out in the air. It was annoying that he kept returning to her thoughts, and she knew that womanlike she would never rest until she knew exactly why his attitude towards her was so unfriendly.

They had left early owing to the distance they must travel to reach Dover. Camilla was therefore both hungry and thirsty by the time the hot sun told them it was noon, and they drew up at a coaching inn.

The first thing they saw in the yard was Captain Cheverly's High-Perch Phaeton and his horses being rubbed down and watered under the instructions of his groom. The innkeeper's wife took the Baroness and Camilla upstairs to a comfortable bedroom where they could wash off the dust of their journey, bringing them hot water and towels smelling of lavender to the wash-hand-stand with its brightly ornamented basin and China ewer.

"What a delightful place!" the Baroness exclaimed. "There are indeed some charming inns in England, though sometimes the food is not so good as we find on the Continent."

"I shall enjoy our luncheon, whatever it is like," Camilla smiled. "I am ravenous!"

The Baroness laughed at her. They were both chattering gaily as they went down the stairs and into the private sitting-room where Captain Cheverly had ordered their meal.

He was standing waiting for them with the landlord at his side. He looked extremely elegant and handsome, but Camilla noted with a sudden drop of her spirits that there was the same look of cynical indifference on his face which had been so obvious the night before.

"I have ordered you ladies a cold collation," he said, speaking to the Baroness rather than to Camilla, "but the landlord tells me there is also hot roast leg of pork, lark and oyster pie, and sheep's head if it would please you."

"You must ask Miss Lambourn first what she would choose," the Baroness said, obviously a little embarrassed at his consulting her before the future Princess of Meldenstein.

"Of course, excuse me," Captain Cheverly said. "What are your wishes, Miss Lambourn?"

Camilla suddenly felt she was no longer hungry. It was almost as though his hostility seeped through everything he said to make her feel uncomfortable and on the defensive. Without her being able to pick out any particular act of rudeness at which she could complain, there was a certain atmosphere he created. She turned from him to speak to the landlord, the sunshine glinting through the bow-window on her fair hair, for she had taken off her bonnet upstairs.

She turned her head unexpectedly and caught the Captain by surprise with a different expression in his eyes, something that she was woman enough to recognise instantly as a reluctant admiration. She knew she was not mistaken. She felt suddenly relieved, as though she had found that after all he was but human. Mischievously she thought she would force him into acknowledging her.

"Tell me about London?" she asked him. "Are all the Dandies, the Corinthians, the Non-Pareils and the Bucks as flash-resplendent as ever? Whenever I see one of them I understand why God made the cock pheasant more splendiferous than his drab little hen!"

Hugo Cheverly laughed.

"Can it be, Miss Lambourn, that you are not so impressed by the superiority of upper crust as you should be?" he asked.

"Why should I be bemused by pretentious creatures who spend a morning tying their cravats, and the nights getting foxed!" Camilla retorted.

"You will have to guard your language

when you reach Meldenstein," Hugo Cheverly said, the warning in his voice belied by the twinkle in his eyes. "Well-behaved young females have no knowledge of such words as foxed."

"When they have brothers they do!" Camilla smiled.

Throughout lunch she chatted away, drawing him into the conversation in such a manner that he could not refuse to respond to her gaiety and high spirits. After the first course and a glass of wine, she saw that he was not only amused by her, but also there was no doubt that she interested him.

"Perhaps, after all, he has a secret sorrow," she thought to herself whimsically, and doubled her efforts to make him respond to her sallies.

She thought it wise not to talk of Meldenstein, but to discuss horses — and soon found that here she and Captain Cheverly could meet on a common ground. She told him about the country fairs to which the horse-dealers came from all over the country; she told him how the gypsies would sell off an old horse that was no longer any use, and yet by herbs and secrets all of their own they could make him appear young and spritely just for the occasion.

More than once in her descriptions of

what took place Captain Cheverly threw
back his head and laughed whole-heartedly,
and she thought then that she saw an echo
of the young triumphant rider of Apollo that
she had remembered so vividly for over six
years.

"If you ladies have finished your repast we
must not linger," Captain Cheverly said at
length. "We have still many miles to travel
before we reach Dover."

"Do we sleep on board the yacht tonight?" the Baroness asked.

"Yes, indeed," the Captain replied. "I am
sure you will be far more comfortable than
at the local inn, and besides we may have
either to sail at once or wait for the tide.
That, of course, is for the Captain to decide,
but everything will be far easier for him if we
are already on board."

"Yes, I can see that," the Baroness
agreed, "but oh how I dread the moment
when we must embark! I had a terrible
journey over, I swear I thought not once but
a dozen times the yacht would sink to the
bottom of the sea. When I spoke of it in the
morning the Captain assured me it was but
a mild swell."

They both laughed and Camilla said:

"It will certainly be a new experience for
me. I have never been on the sea, and until I

do so I have no idea if I am a good sailor or a bad one."

The coach was brought to the door, and for a moment Camilla looked wistfully at the High-Perch Phaeton. She wondered what they would say if she asked if she could drive beside the Captain, and then realised that it would certainly be an unconventional act on the part of a future Princess, and that to leave the Baroness alone would in itself be ill-mannered. She therefore meekly stepped into the coach and watched enviously as within half a mile of leaving the inn Captain Cheverly passed them.

He was tooling the reins with great skill, Camilla noticed, and his beaver hat was at a jaunty angle. He looked very much a Corinthian with the yellow wheels of his swifter vehicle carrying him away from them until he was only a faint cloud of dust in the distance.

After the wine consumed at luncheon the Baroness was somnolent, and soon her voice ceased chattering and she fell asleep in her corner of the coach. Camilla stared out at the countryside. All her fears and apprehensions seemed to close in upon her until she found herself praying beneath her breath that things would not be as difficult as she anticipated.

There was one last stop when they changed horses, and this time while she and the Baroness enjoyed a cup of chocolate and some slices of home-made cake, they saw little of Captain Cheverly. He had a quick glass of wine, then disappeared to the stable-yard where apparently there was some dispute over the horses that had been provided, which were not to his entire satisfaction.

Soon they were off again, and now at last Camilla tried to doze a little, while the Baroness made no pretence of not wishing to sleep. It was to avoid, she told Camilla, the continuous rocking of the coach which reminded her all too vividly of the motion of the sea which they would endure later on.

When finally they arrived at Dover it was nearly seven o'clock. The coach drove straight down to the harbour and the Baroness, waking with a jerk, said:

"Are we there? Oh dear, is my bonnet straight? I forgot to tell you that there will doubtless be a short ceremony as the Mayor bids you farewell."

"The Mayor!" Camilla exclaimed.

"Yes, of course. I should have mentioned it earlier," the Baroness said. "You are a person of importance, my dear, and naturally your own countrymen would like to wish you God speed."

"Gracious!" Camilla exclaimed in a fluster. "I wish you had told me before. Now I do not know what to do. Do I have to say anything?"

"I should not imagine so," the Baroness answered, "just a few gracious thanks. I really do not know what to expect myself, so I can be of little help."

"Is my appearance to your liking?"

Camilla turned an anxious face towards the older woman. Her eyes were very large and a little frightened under a most becoming high-crowned bonnet of chipped straw trimmed with blue forget-me-nots to match the blue of her travelling coat.

"You look charming," the Baroness said, her voice warm and sincere.

Camilla tried not to look nervous as she stepped out from the coach. With a sense of relief she saw that Captain Cheverly was already there. When he gave her his hand he said in a low voice:

"The one with the necklace is the Mayor."

Though it made her want to laugh, she managed an entrancing smile as the Mayor of Dover, resplendent in his red robes and gold chain of office, delivered a long and somewhat pompous speech — the theme being that England's loss would be Meldenstein's gain.

Camilla tried to listen attentively. The breeze was blowing from the sea and she could not help thinking, as it blew the fur edging of the Mayor's and the Aldermen's robes, that it made them look rather like furry pussy-cats. She noticed that many women in the crowd were having difficulty in preventing their headgear being blown out to sea. She was thankful that her own bonnet was tied with blue satin ribbons under her chin, and she wondered how many such addresses she would have to listen to before she was finally married. The thought was depressing, and then, as the Mayor finished, she heard Captain Cheverly whisper "Say thank you!"

"I thank you, Mister Mayor," Camilla said obediently, "for your most kind and gracious address. I am very touched at all you have said, and I shall remember your words long after I have left these shores. I shall convey to my future husband and to all the citizens of Meldenstein your good wishes and kind thoughts of them."

There was a burst of applause as she finished, and then Camilla, instinctively doing the right thing, walked forward to shake the Mayor and the Aldermen by the hand. They were obviously delighted at her gesture and they cheered her wholeheartedly as Captain Cheverly led her towards the yacht.

It was then that she saw the first time the magnificent ship which, dressed in flags and bedecked with garlands of flowers, had been sent to convey her to her future country. The Captain met them at the top of the gangplank, a good-looking, elderly man wearing what seemed to Camilla a very elaborate, over-decorated uniform. Some words her father had said many years ago came immediately to her mind.

"Officials of small countries, and the least important Royalty," he said, "always make themselves appear as spectacular as possible. It is one way of commanding attention. Always remember, Camilla, that to make them happy you must be more effusive than you would be to the great and to the strong. And to their Kings and Queens you make a deeper obeisance, simply because they think you might not."

Camilla had laughed at the time and thought it unlikely she would meet the Kings and Queens of any country. Now she remembered his words and forced herself to be even more charming to the Captain and his officers than she might have been had she not set aside her natural shyness to do so.

They were shown below to two large State cabins to be occupied by herself and the Baroness. Camilla saw at once that her own cabin was larger than that of her companion. It was also decorated with flowers, and she was relieved to see that Rose was there already with some of her clothes unpacked.

She had thought it harsh when she had been told that there would be no rest for the occupants in the luggage wagon at any of the posting places *en route*. They had changed horses and gone straight on, and if the lady's-maids and the coachmen wished to eat, they must eat on the way. But now she was glad, and as soon as the door of the cabin closed behind her, Camilla ran across and put her arms round Rose and gave her a little hug.

"I am so glad to see you!" she said. "Are you very tired after the journey? I was not expecting the Mayor to be waiting for me on the quay, I do hope I said what was correct and pleasurable. What a wonderful yacht. it must be as big as a battleship."

Rose chatted back, and for a moment they were two young girls gossiping away over what had happened, forgetting everything in the excitement of a new adventure. Then Camilla realised it was late and she must change for dinner.

When she went to the saloon it was to find everyone waiting for her — The Captain, his Chief Lieutenant, the Baroness and Captain Cheverly — and she realised she was commanding a great deal more attention than she had ever done in her life before.

Everyone stood, including the Baroness, until she was seated, they bowed when they spoke to her, and the whole meal would have been extremely stilted had not Camilla, hardly realising what she was doing, directed an appealing glance at Captain Cheverly as the Captain of the ship stuttered and floundered in broken English in an effort to pay her fulsome compliments.

As if he realised how embarrassing it was, Captain Cheverly started a discussion about the sea, the tides and marine life. Soon, to her relief, Camilla was almost forgotten and she could enjoy the excellent food which, hungry though she was, soon proved superabundant for her needs. More and more dishes were brought to the table by attentive stewards until at last Camilla exclaimed:

"I declare, Captain, if you always eat like this in Meldenstein I shall become as fat as a prize ox."

"We are indeed gratified that we have

been able to please you, ma'am," the Captain replied.

When dinner was finished he said:

"Perhaps you will be kind enough, ma'am, to excuse me. It will be full tide within the hour and the sooner we can get under way the better. As the yacht is so large we can only set sail when the tide is in, and I have my instructions to proceed to Meldenstein with all possible speed."

"Then I will say goodnight, Captain," Camilla smiled, "and thank you."

She held out her hand, not certain if that was correct, and he bowed over her fingers before he withdrew from the cabin.

"If the ship is going to move I must get to bed at once," the Baroness said in agitation. "Would you like me to see you to the door of your cabin?"

"No, I can find my own way, thank you," Camilla replied. "I hope you sleep well."

"I must be frank with you and admit that I will take a little laudanum," the Baroness said. "I only hope that you will not need me in the night."

"No, I am sure that I shall sleep peacefully," Camilla answered. "Goodnight, and thank you."

To Camilla's astonishment the Baroness dropped her a little curtsy, then went from the room. As the door closed she looked at Captain Cheverly, the surprise still in her face.

"Will they curtsy to me?" she asked. "I had not thought of that."

"The Baroness is starting as soon as you are on the soil of Meldenstein," Hugo Cheverly explained. "That is correct, and you will soon get used to it."

"I suppose so," Camilla said doubtfully. "It seems wrong somehow that anyone should curtsy to me, since I am of no importance. I have always thought it was a gesture only accorded to those of Royal blood."

"You forget you will be Royal when you are married," Hugo Cheverly said. "A wife takes her husband's status."

Camilla moved across the cabin. The ceiling was low and when Hugo Cheverly rose he had to be careful that his head did not strike the oak beams. But she was so small that she could move freely without fear of hurting herself. She went to a porthole to look out at the darkening sea.

"The waves are white-crested," she said. "Will our passage be rough?"

"Not rough enough to trouble anyone but the Baroness," Hugo Cheverly replied.

There was a little pause and then Camilla asked how soon they would arrive.

"We shall be in Antwerp early to-morrow," Hugo Cheverly answered. "That is if the wind blows in the right direction."

"And then?"

"We have a quite long journey to Meldenstein. We shall push the horses to the uttermost. I trust you will not find it too tiring."

She did not answer and after a moment he said:

"May I congratulate you on the excellent manner in which you performed your first ceremony this evening. I can see that the Prince has chosen exactly the right bride, who will perform her duties admirably."

"The Prince has chosen?" Camilla echoed turning round. "I thought it was his mother who chose me. Had he any say in the matter?"

There was a sharpness in her voice which made Hugo Cheverly hesitate before he replied, and then his answer was unexpected.

"Does it matter whose suggestion it was?" he enquired.

"No, I suppose not," Camilla admitted, "but if things go wrong someone will be blamed. I just wondered who it would be."

"If things go wrong?" Hugo Cheverly

queried. "What could go wrong? As I have already told you, you are the perfect choice, a girl with both beauty and brains. What Prince could ask for more? These small European Royalty do not usually pull off such an advantageous deal, I can assure you."

"You talk as though I were a piece of merchandise," Camilla said angrily.

There was a spark in her eyes, and she thought she saw a ghost of a smile on his lips before he replied suavely:

"If that is the impression I conveyed I must, of course, apologise. I meant what I said as a compliment."

"I do not want you to apologise," Camilla replied. "I beg your pardon. I should not have spoken as I did. It is just that I . . ."

She stopped suddenly and turned again to the porthole. How could she tell this young man that she was afraid, that she wished now, even at the last moment, that she could run away, that she could go home, that she need not go through with all that lay ahead — the pomp, the ceremony, and most of all the moment when she would meet this stranger, this man to whom she was to be married?

"I assure you, Miss Lambourn," Hugo Cheverly was saying behind her, "that everything will proceed as smoothly as possible. I quite realise that it will all seem strange to you; for after all you will have a position of great import in Meldenstein, one of authority and one which commands great respect."

"And do you think they will . . . grow fond . . . of me?" Camilla's voice was so low that he could hardly hear the words.

"Of course," he said quickly.

"You answer too glibly," she said accusingly, turning round once again. "Do you really think the people will like me, that . . . he will . . . like me too?"

It was the cry of a child, and yet Hugo Cheverly's face darkened and his eyes were hard.

"His Serene Highness will, I am convinced, be overjoyed with the attractions of his English bride," he said positively, "And you, Miss Lambourn, will get exactly what you wanted. That, surely, is all that matters."

The tone of his voice seemed suddenly to sharpen, and abruptly he turned and went out of the cabin, slamming the door behind him.

Camilla stood staring at the closed door. She could hear his footsteps fading away into the distance and she thought despairingly that while she had believed for a moment that he might be her friend, he had proved, after all, only to be an enemy — he hated her, she was sure of it.

5

Camilla awoke to find the ship was pitching quite uncomfortably, and as soon as Rose had called her she asked her to knock at the door of the Baroness's cabin and see how that lady was faring. Rose returned with a message that the Baroness felt extremely ill and sent her apologies that she would not be able to make an appearance until the sea had subsided.

Camilla was not worried, for she really preferred to be alone than to listen to the Baroness's endless chatter about the marvels of Meldenstein and the virtues of the Princess, for whom she apparently had an almost schoolgirl devotion.

She rose, dressed herself with Rose's assistance and sat down to write to her mother. She found it difficult as the yacht pitched and tossed to form the words clearly on the thick parchment writing-paper embossed with the Meldenstein coat of arms surmounted by a crown. Camilla thought her mother would be impressed by the latter if nothing else, and she was careful not to let any of her homesickness or anxiety about what lay ahead creep into her simple narrative of what had occurred on the journey. She managed to speak warmly of the Baroness, but felt there was nothing she could say about Captain Cheverly.

She found her thoughts continually turning to him, and she told herself a little wistfully that she had little understanding of the gay young blades she had seen on her visit to London, and with whom she had enjoyed a very slight acquaintance.

Captain Cheverly, she decided, was typical of the dashing Bucks who surrounded the Regent, who drank in White's Club, gambled at Wattiers, raced at Newmarket, learnt the art of boxing from 'Gentleman Jackson' and tooled or rode their horses in a masterly manner which could not fail to evoke admiration.

Admiring a man for his horsemanship was quite a different thing from being friends with him, she decided. The best thing for her peace of mind would be to see Captain Cheverly as little as possible — this cynical, bored Non-Pareil who made her somehow uneasy whenever she was in his presence.

At the same time she could not resist the challenge that he offered, and she was, in fact, extremely disappointed to find when luncheon was served that she was eating alone in the saloon. The food was delicious; at the same time she felt rather lonely with only the attentive stewards to serve her. Finally, unable to repress her curiosity, she questioned the chief steward, who spoke a little English.

"Where is the ship's Captain?" Camilla enquired.

"He on bridge, Madame. He stay bridge all voyage."

"And have you any knowledge of the whereabouts of Captain Hugo Cheverly?"

"He with Captain. He like storm and bad weather."

When luncheon was finished Camilla sent Rose to fetch her travelling-cloak. It was the one garment she had brought with her which was not new; but she had worn it very little, having bought it for driving when the weather was cold and when unconventionally she preferred to sit outside rather than in the enclosed comfort of the interior of a vehicle, something which had continually brought her into conflict with her mother.

"It is not seemly, Camilla, for a lady to ride on the box of a coach."

"I know, Mama, but who will see me?"

"It is not a question of being seen,

Camilla. A well-bred girl should behave with circumspection, even when alone."

"Yes, Mama," Camilla had agreed, but nevertheless she had continued to sit outside, the wind blowing her hair around her face, until even her father declared she looked "a sad romp".

The cloak was made of warm, thick, emerald green wool, the attached hood with which she could cover her head was edged with fur, and it made her face look very small and her eyes very large. Holding it tightly round her she stepped outside on deck.

The wind almost took her breath away; then slithering across the wet planks she managed to reach the rail and to hold on to it tightly. They were moving at a tremendous pace with the wind behind them, the sails billowing out, the bows covered in spray as the yacht cut through the waves.

Camilla felt a sudden exhilaration take hold of her. This was exciting, this was something she had never known before, and she loved it. Every few minutes there was a sudden hard slap as a wave broke the onrush of the ship and made the whole vessel shiver. Then they were off again, running before the storm, the ropes creaking, the sailors shouting above the noise of their passage. She felt the wind whip the curls against her cheeks, there was the taste of salt on her lips. Suddenly she heard a familiar voice saying disapprovingly:

"What are you doing here, Miss Lambourn? You must go below immediately."

She turned her head to laugh up at Captain Cheverly. He too was windswept, his carefully arranged hair in disorder, his many-tiered overcoat tightly buttoned round his neck, the tassels on his polished Hessian boots swinging with the movement of the ship.

"It is wonderful!" she cried. "I never knew the sea would be like this."

"It is dangerous for you to be on deck," he warned her, but the words were almost automatic as he observed her flushed cheeks and sparkling eyes.

"Now I understand why Gervase wished to be a sailor," she shouted, knowing it was hard for him to hear her above the flap of the sails and the rush of the water beneath them.

"Gervase?" he questioned.

"My brother," she explained. "He is somewhere at sea. Oh, I wish I were with him! I only want to stay like this for ever, going round the world and back again."

She thought he smiled at her enthusiasm before he said:

"If you fell overboard in this sea it would be almost impossible to save you."

"I will not fall," she promised, then added with a little laugh: "It would be awkward for you, would it not, to have to admit that you lost your package of merchandise overboard before you could deliver it."

"Very awkward," he agreed in an amused tone.

An unexpectedly big wave made the ship lurch. Camilla staggered, and found Hugo Cheverly's arm around her.

"For God's sake be careful," he admonished.

"For your sake or for mine?" she teased.

She did not know why the buffeting of the wind seemed to have swept away her shyness and reserve where he was concerned. She was no longer afraid of him, only determined to see if she could erase the look of cynicism and indifference in his face.

"For your own," he answered, "and for those who are expecting you."

For once the thought of what lay ahead did not depress her.

"Perhaps we shall never get there," she said. "Perhaps this is a magical ride into some unknown, enchanted sea where our souls will cruise for ever in the sunshine of happiness."

She spoke her fantasies aloud, half forgetting who was listening, and then heard him replying almost roughly:

"It is your bridegroom who is waiting for you."

She knew he was deliberately trying to crush her exhilaration, but he did not succeed. Instead she laughed at him.

"You are as gloomy as a Good Friday sermon!" she cried. "Why did they not send me someone gay as an escort? Whatever lies ahead, you cannot take this away from me."

A burst of wind blew the hood from her head so that it fell back on to her shoulders, and now her hair, golden as the spring corn, was first blowing wildly around her face, then swept back from her white forehead to show the exquisite line of her tiny straight nose and the shell-like perfection of her little ears.

She knew without even glancing at him that Hugo Cheverly was looking at her. She thought it was with disapproval that the sailors and officers aboard should see her so dishevelled, but she did not care.

"This is my last moment of freedom," she told herself, and she felt that she was like a bird flying over the water, rising and

118

swooping at will, untrammelled, uncaged.

And then, when she was just about to speak again to the man beside her, she saw one of the younger officers come hurrying down from the bridge.

"The Captain's compliments, ma'am, and he begs you to go below. The weather is getting worse, and as he is responsible for your safety he cannot risk the danger of your remaining on deck."

Camilla hesitated, but she heard Hugo Cheverly say in a low voice:

"You cannot refuse his request."

"Please thank the Captain for his consideration," Camilla said, "and tell him that I am grateful to him for his thoughts for my safety."

She tried to leave the rail but found it impossible to move. Then Hugo Cheverly's arms were round her and she was thankful for his strength as he helped her move precariously towards the steps which they must descend to reach the cabins. She clutched at the balustrade when they got out of the wind and he released her. She raised her face to his.

"It is not fair," she protested, "I was enjoying myself so much."

"I told you it was safe," he answered as he followed her below and held open the door for her to enter the saloon.

It was extremely difficult to walk at the angle at which the ship was lying over, and Camilla sank quickly down into a chair which was battened to the floor. She was conscious now of her salt-sprayed, untidy hair, and put her hands up to her head to restore the curls to some sort of order. Captain Cheverly seated himself opposite her.

"I have never before known a female who enjoyed the sea."

"There is always something exciting about water," Camilla answered. "My brother and I, when we were children, used to spend a great deal of time boating on the river near our home and bathing in the lake, although it was strictly forbidden."

"Do you always do things you are told not to?" Hugo Cheverly asked.

He noticed for the first time the dimples which showed in her cheeks when she was amused.

"Would you have me a drab little mouse with no spirit?" she asked. "Perhaps that is what you expect country girls to be like!"

"I have scarce knowledge of them," Hugo Cheverly replied.

"And, of course, you would much rather have escorted a young lady of fashion," Camilla joked, "ready to swoon at the first wave, and terrified lest a breath of wind disturbed her carefully arranged coiffure."

Hugo Cheverly laughed.

"Is that your idea of a lady *à la mode?*"

"I have met them," Camilla replied, "and a more spineless lot it would be hard to imagine. When I went to London I could not find a girl who would ride with me, unless it was on a fat old carriage-horse, which she knew was as safe as trundling along the Row in a wheelchair."

"You are too small to ride anything but a child's pony," Hugo Cheverly remarked, and saw the flash in her eyes as she replied:

"I can ride the most spirited horseflesh and school them over jumps."

She saw his smile and added quickly:

"You are just trying to gammon me into losing my temper. When we have the opportunity I will race you on even mounts. I might even beat your Apollo, if you still have him."

"Apollo! What do you know of Apollo?" Hugo Cheverly asked sharply.

Realising she had inadvertently given herself away, Camilla felt the blood rise in her cheeks.

"I . . . just . . . heard that you had a . . . horse of that name," she answered.

"You are prevaricating," he said accusingly. "Tell me the truth! How did you know about Apollo?"

"I saw you win a race on him over six years ago," Camilla confessed. "You came in first, when everyone was expecting another horse to win. I cannot recall its name. Yes, I do . . . it was Firefly."

"I remember the occasion well," Hugo Cheverly smiled. "So you were there? You would only have been a child."

"It was my thirteenth-birthday treat," Camilla told him.

"So that was why you looked so surprised when you first saw me," he said slowly. "I could not understand the astonishment in your face."

"I never thought I would see you again," Camilla said.

"So you remembered me," he said. "Is it not rather strange that out of all the races you must have watched that afternoon, you should remember me?"

"I wanted Apollo to win," she said hastily.

"Yes, of course," Hugo Cheverly agreed, but his eyes were on her face. "He was a magnificent horse, but actually that was his last race. He was put out to grass and has, I am told, sired several stallions almost as good as himself."

"You were told?" Camilla said quickly.

"You mean you did not keep him?"

"I could not afford to," Hugo Cheverly confessed. "My regiment was posted abroad and I could not pay Apollo's keep while I was away. So I sold him to a friend, someone I could trust, someone who would look after him. But I hated to see him go."

"It must have hurt you terribly," Camilla said in a low voice. "When one owns a horse like Apollo he becomes a part of one."

"That is true," Hugo Cheverly agreed, and added: "Strange that you should remember Apollo. I often think of that race myself."

"So do I," Camilla admitted without thinking. "I thought you had fallen at the last fence. For a moment I could not look, but when I saw you were safely over, I knew you would win."

"You really wanted me to win, did you not?" Hugo Cheverly asked in a deep voice.

"I prayed that you would do so," Camilla replied simply. "I wanted it so badly I felt as though I was riding Apollo myself."

She spoke passionately and then realised that she had said too much. Her eyes dropped, her eyelashes brushed against her cheek.

"Of course, I was only a child at the time."

"But you remembered me as well as Apollo," Hugo Cheverly persisted, "and you did not expect to see me walk into your Drawing-Room."

"No, of course not," Camilla answered. "I . . . I think I should return to my cabin and tidy my hair."

She made as though to rise from the chair, and then somehow it was difficult to leave. She wanted to stay, and yet the silence which had fallen between them was uneasy.

"Where is the Baroness?" Hugo Cheverly asked, as if he too was suddenly conscious that they were alone together.

"She was ill all night," Camilla explained. "Today she is too indisposed to leave her cabin."

"Tiresome woman!" Hugo Cheverly exclaimed sharply. "She should be with you, you should not be left alone."

"I do not mind," Camilla answered, "although it was extremely dreary having no one with me at luncheon-time."

"I would have come down had I realised," Hugo Cheverly said, then added: "No, of course not! It would not be correct for us to eat together unchaperoned."

"Must I have dinner also alone?" Camilla asked. There was a moment's silence and their eyes met. "You well know it would offend the conventions," he said a trifle lamely.

"And who is to know or to care?" Camilla asked. "For a moment, surely, we are between two authorities — those we have left behind in England and those who are waiting for us on the other side. We can make our own laws."

"I am here to protect, not to compromise you," Hugo Cheverly said.

"Would it really be so irretrievably compromising if you dined with me?" Camilla asked.

"I think I would be wise in declining such an invitation," he replied.

"Supposing it were a command?" Camilla enquired. "You have told me that in a few days' time I shall possess great authority. Of course I would not be able to command a British subject to do anything he did not wish to do, but would he not find it difficult to refuse if he were a guest in a foreign country."

Hugo Cheverly's lips twisted in a smile that was neither cynical nor bored.

"I can see you intend to get your own way in life," he said. "Very well, ma'am, command me and I will obey."

"I would rather ask you," Camilla said softly. "Captain Cheverly, sir, the late owner of a very wonderful black stallion called Apollo, will you dine with me?"

She had meant to speak jokingly, but somehow her voice became serious and appealing, and now their eyes met and it seemed to her for a moment as though the cabin swung dizzily around them.

"I am convinced I am making a mistake," Hugo Cheverly replied, "but I have the greatest pleasure, ma'am, in accepting your invitation to dinner."

"That will be wonderful!" Camilla exclaimed, and was not aware of how her delight lit up her eyes.

She rose to go to her cabin, but the ship lurched and she lost her balance. She would have fallen had not Hugo Cheverly caught her in his arms. For a moment her head was against his shoulder and she laughed up at him, amused by her helplessness. Then, as their eyes met, she drew in her breath sharply.

It seemed as if they were both spellbound, unable to move or speak, only conscious that something indefinable passed between them, something which made Camilla say hesitatingly:

"I must . . . go . . ."

She reached her cabin with difficulty and lay down on her bunk. For the next hour the storm seemed to get worse, and then slowly it abated. Though it was still rough, she could, however, move around without clinging desperately to the walls and the furniture, and by the time there was a knock on the door to announce that dinner was ready, she had managed to change and Rose had rearranged her hair.

She had told her maid to unpack one of her prettiest new gowns, and looking at herself in a small mirror which reflected only a small part of her at a time, she knew it was vastly becoming.

As the dress was made of the finest gauze sprigged with blue flowers, she carried over her arm in case she was chilled a wrap of Nile blue velvet lined with white swansdown. She was aware she looked more elegant than she had ever appeared in her life before, and somehow, though she would not admit it, she knew it was important that she should see again that quick, irrepressible look of admiration in Hugo Cheverly's eyes.

He had a grim and disdainful air about him when she entered the saloon to find him waiting for her, but to her relief his expression changed at her appearance and he took her hand and raised it conventionally to his lips.

"Your servant, ma'am."

She dropped him a curtsy, but as the ship rolled she staggered and her laughter broke the ice.

"What has it been like on deck?" she asked. "I longed to go up and look for myself, but I dare not provoke your disapproval or the Captain's."

"The wind is dropping now, it should be calm by tomorrow morning."

"I thought we were to arrive this evening?" Camilla asked.

"We were blown miles off course," he replied. "So the Captain has decided to bring her slowly into port on the dawn watch. When you awake you will find yourself in Europe."

"I am glad we could dine on board tonight," Camilla said simply as they seated themselves at the table and the stewards brought the first of a long series of unusual dishes for their delectation.

They talked about Apollo and Hugo Cheverly's years in the Army; about Gervase and how he had always preferred the sea. Camilla managed to make Hugo Cheverly laugh again and again, and it was only when finally the table was cleared and the stewards left the cabin that a sudden silence fell between them.

"That is the first time I have ever dined alone with a man," Camilla said unexpectedly. She was following her own train of thought and was almost unaware she had spoken aloud. "It is far easier to talk with one person rather than with half a dozen or more."

"Surely that depends on the person," Hugo Cheverly said.

"I suppose it does," Camilla answered, "but as I have had no experience of anyone else save yourself, it is difficult to judge."

"You must not tell anyone we have dined alone like this," Hugo Cheverly said quietly. "It is essential that there should not be a breath of criticism about your behaviour."

"A depressing thought, is it not?" Camilla remarked. "From now on I must go through life remembering that whatever I do there will be eyes to watch; whatever I say there will be ears to hear. Oh dear, if only I could have remained at home and just been Miss Nobody!"

"That was surely up to you," Hugo Cheverly said.

She knew from the change in his voice that now he was disliking her once again, and she could have cried out in her disappointment.

"That reminds me," he said stiffly, "and it

was remiss of me not to have thought of it before. There is a package for you."

"A package for me!" Camilla exclaimed. "Why was I not given it sooner?"

"I am afraid I am to blame," Hugo Cheverly replied coldly. "The Captain entrusted it to me last night and with the rising storm it escaped my memory."

As he spoke he fetched from a side-table a large package, which was done up with several impressive-looking seals. He placed it in Camilla's lap, and sitting down again he stretched out his hand for the glass of brandy which had been set beside him.

Camilla after staring at the parcel for a moment tried to open it, but her small fingers were not strong enough to break the seals. After a short struggle she passed it to the man watching her.

"Will you not open it for me," she asked, "or would you rather I rang for a steward?"

"I will do it," he said sharply, and with hands that seemed to her unnecessarily rough he pulled the paper aside to reveal a blue leather case embossed with a crown. This he lifted with what seemed to Camilla a mock reverence and handed it to her, throwing the seal-covered packaging on the floor.

Uncomfortably conscious of his eyes

watching her, she raised the lid and gave a little gasp of astonishment. Inside was a magnificent diamond necklace, earrings and bracelet. They had been designed as a matched set and lay displayed on white velvet, while attached to the lid of the box was a card which read — *To my Bride. Hedwig of Meldenstein.*

"A pretty bauble," Hugo Cheverly commented before Camilla could speak, "and one which will become you mightily in your new station in life. With diamonds round your neck, encircling your wrist and dangling from your ears, you will find that the wind and your enchanted ocean is an illusion well lost. The substance is, I assure you, far more satisfactory than the shadow."

Camilla shut the box to with an impetuous hand. She felt that the brief, three-word message was somehow a poor welcome from a future husband. It would have been easy for him to write her a letter, to pen a few words of welcome saying he was looking forward to meeting her. The jewels were magnificent; but the diamonds were cold, and suddenly she shivered.

"Are you not going to put them on?" Hugo Cheverly asked sneeringly. "Surely no woman can resist the look of herself in diamonds, especially diamonds such as these."

"I am not particularly interested in jewels," Camilla said. "I thought perhaps there would be something else."

"Something else? What do you mean?" he enquired.

"Was that all the Captain gave you?" she asked.

"What more did you expect?"

"I thought there might have been a letter."

There was a moment's silence before Hugo Cheverly bent forward in the chair in which he was sitting.

"Camilla," he said in a low voice, and neither of them realised that he had used her Christian name, "why are you doing this? You are not suited for the life you have chosen — you are too young, too sensitive, too vulnerable. Change your mind now before it is too late. If you wish I will turn the yacht round. I will make some excuse. I will say you are ill and have to return, but do not go on with this foolishness. It is wrong for you — you know it is."

Camilla stared at him. She felt as if he looked into her heart and saw the fear and the darkness she was hiding even from herself. Then, with an almost superhuman effort, she forced her eyes away from him.

"No . . . I . . . I cannot go . . . back," she

132

whispered. "Of course I must . . . go on as
. . . arranged."

"You need not do it, you know you need
not," Hugo Cheverly said insistently. "It is
not too late, Camilla, but by tomorrow
morning it will be. Tell me to take you back.
I will find a reason, only tell me to do so."

Just for a moment Camilla felt she must
give him the answer for which he was
pleading. She would do as he asked and
return home to everything she loved — then
she remembered. Her father and mother
were depending on her, in fact, only she
could save them.

"I cannot," she murmured, and her voice
was so low that he could hardly hear it, "I
must . . . go on."

"But why, for what reason?" he asked.
"Can it really be that you want the position,
the wealth, the power all that much? You
have so much already, do you really need
more?"

Her lips opened and Camilla thought she
would tell him the truth, explain that her
parents were penniless and on the verge of
being taken to the debtors' prison. Then she
remembered her father's warning that everything she said in front of the Baroness
and Captain Cheverly would be reported in
Meldenstein. She would appear as the

beggarmaid and that, she knew, would be the last humiliation of all.

"No," she cried, "no, you must not speak to me like this! I have made my . . . choice. I am going to Meldenstein to marry . . . the Prince."

As she spoke she sprang to her feet, and the leather case containing the diamonds fell with a crash to the floor. It opened and the jewels spilled out, lying there glittering and glimmering in the light of the lanterns. An omen, it seemed to Camilla, of the brilliance but coldness of her life that lay ahead.

Hugo Cheverly rose too.

"Yes, you have chosen," he said in a loud voice, "and how wise and sensible you are. You almost deceived me with your talk of enchanted seas, of escaping to a new freedom. Young you may be, but you are like all women wise in the ways of the world. It is wealth that counts more than anything else. I congratulate you, ma'am, you will make an exemplary princess."

His bitter tone of voice and this undisguised sneer were almost intolerable. She felt as though he had struck at her and left her bleeding.

With a little sob which she could not

choke down she turned and ran blindly from the cabin, leaving him standing there looking after her, the diamonds at his feet.

6

Camilla came on deck conscious that while her new gown and high-crowned bonnet trimmed with ostrich feather tips were becoming, her face was pale and she had lines under her eyes. She had cried herself to sleep the night before, feeling homesick and at the same time in the depths of a despondency. But she would not admit to herself that this could be entirely attributed to her passage of words with Hugo Cheverly.

She had woken feeling heavy-eyed, and common sense had told her she was making a mountain out of a molehill. What did it matter what an obscure Englishman thought? He had merely been sent as an escort to convey her to her prospective bridegroom, and his manner towards her had been reprehensible from the first moment they had met.

She could not believe that her future husband would countenance such an attitude from someone who was not even a citizen of Meldenstein. At the same time she knew that she would not tell the Prince what had occurred, but merely, she told herself, that in the future she would ignore Captain Cheverly and force herself not to be perturbed by his quite unreasonable attitude towards her.

"What right has he," she asked herself, "to try to persuade me not to go through with the marriage, or to turn back when once I had made up my mind that I would marry the Prince?"

Of course, her brain told her, Hugo Cheverly was not to know the very dire circumstances in which her father and mother found themselves. He had only seen the house bedecked with liveried flunkeys and had eaten as good a dinner as he could have enjoyed in any of the great mansions in London. In fact, as Sir Horace had intended, he had received an impression of wealth which could give him no inkling of what lay beneath the surface.

Yet even this, Camilla thought, did not excuse the manner in which he had raged at her, the dark contempt in his eyes or the sneering expression on his face.

"I shall ignore him for the rest of the journey," Camilla promised herself, and yet when she stepped on deck she found herself feeling an almost ridiculous sense of relief when she saw him there waiting for her.

He was magnificently dressed in full regimentals. She had not seen him in uniform before and she could not help thinking how well they became him and how elegant a couple they must look as he handed her down the gangplank on to the quay where, as the Baroness had already warned her, a deputation of citizens, headed by the Mayor, were waiting for her arrival.

There was also an agitated young Consul from the British Embassy full of abject apologies because the Ambassador was away, and carrying a large, cumbersome wedding present. He pressed this into Camilla's arms, who, after expressing her gratitude, handed it to the Baroness, who passed it to a naval officer, who gave it to a rating, who, after various attempts to be rid of it, forced it on a protesting Rose.

"Here, Mister Impertinence. I've got me arms full without acarrying your by-blow," Camilla heard her say aggressively.

She could not repress a little giggle, felt Hugo Cheverly's arm shake and knew that he too was amused.

The Mayor began his address, which Camilla guessed conveyed very much the same sentiments as the one she had heard from the Mayor of Dover, only this time she could not understand a word that was being said. A pretty child dressed in Dutch national costume with wooden sabots stepped forward to present her with a bouquet of pink tulips which, she felt, blended well with the pale leaf-green crepe of her new gown.

She was glad that the Baroness had warned her to put on something truly elegant; for there was a large crowd and she felt that the cheers that greeted her appearance was at least in part a tribute to her gown. Truly elegant, it had little puffed sleeves embroidered with pink silk which matched the three frills round the hem of the skirt and ribbons which were tied under her chin.

Camilla was proud that being English she was creating a favourable impression as soon as she stepped on foreign soil, and she could not help stealing a glance under her eyelashes at Captain Cheverly to see if there was a hint of admiration in his eyes.

Quite unaccountably, as she saw he was looking grave, the lines of cynicism round his mouth strongly pronounced, she felt her spirits sink. Despite all her resolutions that he should not upset her, she faltered in her reply to the Mayor, and her words did not come so fluently as they had on leaving Dover.

Nevertheless there was loud applause

when she finished speaking. Holding her bouquet with one hand and the other resting lightly on Captain Cheverly's arm, she proceeded down the dockside amid the waving crowds to where she could see a coach was waiting.

It was the largest and most impressive vehicle Camilla had ever beheld, drawn by four perfectly matched horses, their silver bridles glinting in the sunshine, the feather fronds which ornamented their foreheads fluttering in the breeze. There were two coachmen in scarlet and gold-braided livery on the box, with two footmen standing behind. There were four outriders, a baggage wagon and a four-in-hand which was almost as important-looking as the coach. There was also, Camilla noticed, an unmounted horse standing near being held by a groom.

She could see it was a spirited animal with a touch of Arab in it, and she guessed that it was waiting for Captain Cheverly. Once again he would not accompany herself and the Baroness in the coach.

As Camilla reached the coach the cheering grew louder, and Hugo Cheverly spoke to her for the first time since she had appeared on deck.

"The peasants would undoubtedly appreciate it if you would be obliging enough to turn round and wave to them, Miss Lambourn," he said formally.

His voice was low, but she thought she heard the sneering note in it. Her cheeks flushed as she obeyed him, taking her hand from his arm and waving to the crowds again and again before finally she stepped into the coach, followed by the Baroness.

The footman shut the door and almost immediately they were off, Camilla bending forward for a last glimpse of the Dutch people who had given her such a spontaneous welcome. She only wished she could feel more elated by it, but instead her eyes went from the quay across the harbour to where the sea was very blue beneath the clear sky.

She had crossed the Channel. Only a ship could carry her back to England and to her father and mother, and she knew it would be a long time before there was any chance of her being able to embark in one.

The coach had now taken her out of sight of the Quay, and after a quick glance at the houses, which were quite unlike any she had ever seen before, and the canal they were crossing by a narrow bridge, Camilla sank back and turned to the Baroness.

"How are you this morning?" she asked. Then a look at the Baroness's face made her exclaim hastily: "But you are in ill health, you should not have come!"

"I shall be all right presently," the Baroness answered in a weak voice. "It is this terrible sickness, but now we are on shore I am convinced the nausea will pass."

"You are not well enough to travel," Camilla insisted. "I blame myself for not having come to visit you this morning. Rose took an unwarrantable time arranging my hair and I was afraid of being late. Why did you not send for me? We could at least have rested here for today."

"How could I upset all the plans which had already been made?" the Baroness asked. "My health will, I anticipate, improve as the day progresses. Captain Cheverly was most considerate and insisted on my having a small glass of brandy before I left. Otherwise I doubt if I could have walked the length of the gangplank."

"Oh, I am so sorry!" Camilla exclaimed again. "It is humiliating to suffer so inordinately from seasickness, but I have always heard tell that once one is on firm ground the recovery is swift."

"I pray that is so," the Baroness said, closing her yes and looking still so white and exhausted that Camilla wondered whether she should stop the coach and insist that they go to a hostelry until the Baroness was stronger.

She looked out of the window anxiously, wondering it would be best to discuss the matter with Hugo Cheverly. While she could see the outriders jingling along beside them, there was no sign of the other horse, and she guessed that the Captain had already taken the opportunity to ride ahead of them, bored by the thought of moving slowly on such a spirited mount.

"It is most inconsiderate of him," Camilla thought angrily, but she realised that it was unlikely that he would have acceded to her request that they should disorganise the arrangements by staying in Amsterdam.

She was well aware that every part of their journey was planned in advance, and Rose had brought her a memorandum with her morning chocolate.

9.5 of the clock — *Disembark at Amsterdam, reception by the Mayor and Aldermen.*

9.15 a.m. — *Leave for Zutnegen where luncheon has been arranged at an inn.*

She read on to find they were due at the inn at the hour of noon, and she was relieved to see they were also staying at another inn that night.

"Fräulein Johann says we may not be in goose-feather comfort this evening," Rose volunteered, "but we can be sure that tomorrow everything will be as posh as polish."

"Who is Fräulein Johann?" Camilla enquired, smiling at Rose's newly acquired manner of speech.

"The abigail to the Baroness," Rose replied. "A miserable creature, miss, only thinking about her own comfort and complaining that everything she eats gives her indigestion. She hates the sea, even though her stomach is as strong as a boar's and she was not sick. She also found a dozen things wrong with the cabin we were asleeping in. I thought it were real cosy, I did really."

"I expect Fräulein Johann lives at Meldenstein," Camilla said.

"She would soon see to it if she did not," Rose answered scornfully. "Why, the way she talks about some of the places where she has stayed with her mistress, you would think that most of them were nothing better than pigsties! She told me, miss, that the Princess tried hard to find a princely Palace or a castle for you to stay in tonight, but they were too far off the route. So we must be accommodated in a common inn."

"I, personally, am very relieved," Camilla declared, thinking that to have to suffer the acquaintance of strange people after a long journey and to make herself pleasant to them would be exhausting.

"Tomorrow night we are to be the guests of some high-sounding nobleman," Rose announced. "I can't pronounce his name or that of his country. Fräulein Johann says his palace is magnificent, but nothing compared with the Palace of Meldenstein!"

"What did she tell you about Meldenstein?" Camilla asked curiously.

"Oh, to hear her talk, miss, you would think Meldenstein was more important than England," Rose said scornfully. "But the Captain's valet, Mister Harpen, is English and says it is only a small country and of little real consequence."

Camilla burst out laughing.

"Well, you have certainly heard diverse points of view!"

"Personally I would rather believe Mister Harpen," Rose went on. "He's a real nice man, miss, and says he is too old to be taken in by them foreigners. He never did approve of an Englishwoman marrying one of them."

Rose spoke without thinking, then put her fingers up to her mouth.

"Oh, I'm sorry, miss, I did not mean to say that. I should not have repeated it."

"You can say what you like to me, Rose," Camilla said, "and do not be afraid that I shall be offended at anything you tell me. I wanted you to come with me simply so that I could have someone who would be frank and open, someone with whom I could talk without having to be careful of what I said."

"Well, me mother always did say me tongue ran away with me," Rose replied, "so you will have to forgive me, miss, if I speaks out of turn. Mister Harpen has been to Meldenstein before, and of course I asked him what he thought about it and what the people were like."

"What did he say?" Camilla enquired.

"He said they're pleasant enough and friendly," Rose answered. "He said the Princess ruled the place when he was there like a queen. Real masterful, he says, she was and no nonsense. But then, of course, she's English, and Mister Harpen thinks anything English is right and tight."

"And what did he say about the Prince?" Camilla asked. She was beginning to realise who was responsible for Rose's unexpected vocabulary.

She knew that her mother would think it reprehensible of her to be gossiping with the servants, but she told herself that Rose was the exception. There was a little pause, and to Camilla's astonishment she could see that the young maid was looking embarrassed.

"Mister Harpen didn't say much about the Prince, miss," she muttered finally.

It was with a little feeling of apprehension that Camilla guessed Rose was hiding something from her. While she wondered whether she should force the issue and persuade Rose to tell her what she had heard, the maid added quickly, as though anxious to get away from the subject:

"Mister Harpen hasn't met His Supreme Highness, and anyway he doesn't talk of anyone much except his Master. He just thinks the world of the Captain, as he calls him. And it does sound, miss, as though the gentleman were a real hero when it comes to a battle."

"I think perhaps I had best robe myself, Rose," Camilla said, and to herself her voice sounded cold. "It would be extremely rude to be late for the Mayor."

"Yes indeed, miss. There are already crowds outside. Mister Harpen went ashore early this morning and said they were all agog to get a peep at you."

"People are always curious about brides," Camilla said despondently.

"It is ever so exciting, miss," Rose enthused as she poured a jug of hot water into the basin and stood ready with a soft, white towel while Camilla washed herself.

Camilla wished that she herself felt more excited, and it seemed to her a very woebegone face that stared back at her from the mirror as Rose arranged her hair.

"Mister Harpen says this is nothing to the excitement there will be in Meldenstein," she chattered as she twisted Camilla's golden hair into long shining ringlets which framed her little face, and pinned the rest into a fashionable coil on the top of her head.

"Oh, Rose, I hope the crowds will not be too big!" Camilla cried.

"It'd be insulting if they were not," Rose retorted. "Besides, miss, they'll be glad not only to see you but that their Prince is being wed. Mister Harpen says everyone tried to persuade him to take a wife before the war because the country wanted an heir, and who shall blame them?"

Camilla drew in her breath sharply. She did not want to think what the implications must be for the Prince having an heir. She did not want to think further ahead than the fact that in a few minutes she had a public duty to perform. But she could not help wondering what would have happened this morning if she had agreed to Hugo Cheverly's urging that he turn the yacht round and sail back to England.

"You look real lovely in that gown, miss," she heard Rose's voice say, and roused herself from a reverie without realising that she had let Rose assist her into her new dress and arrange a Bond Street bonnet on her head.

She pulled on long white gloves and picked up her reticule.

"I am ready," she said. "Do not get left behind, Rose, I could not bear it."

"No indeed, miss," Rose smiled, "there's no chance of that. Captain Cheverly was telling Mister Harpen only this morning that he has got to make a real push to get ahead so that you'll be put to no inconvenience by waiting for us. Very ferocious he was about it too. 'Tis not Mister Harpen's fault if the baggage horses can't travel as fast as those harnessed for the quality."

Camilla did not answer. She was thinking that Hugo Cheverly was in a hurry to reach their destination, to hand her over and know that his responsibilities were at an end.

"He will be glad to get rid of me," she whispered beneath her breath, and wondered why she felt no elation at the thought that there would be no need for her to see him again.

Now with the Baroness ill she thought it was extremely inconsiderate of him to have rushed ahead when he might be needed, and she decided it would serve him right if she stopped the coach and kept him waiting at their rendezvous for luncheon wondering what had happened to them.

She almost did so out of a sheer desire to annoy him, and then she remembered that the Baroness would doubtless get into trouble if she delayed the Royal programme which had been made so far in advance. She had heard her mother talk of the stiff protocol which existed for ladies-in-waiting and those in attendance at court.

"The hours they have to stand, poor things!" Lady Lambourn said once when she was telling Camilla of a foreign Court at which her father had been the British Ambassador. "I swear your Papa was often exhausted when he got to bed, not from the amount of work he had done but from being in attendance at one of the many receptions or ceremonies. And as for the ladies-in-waiting, well my heart often bled for them, they looked so tired, with never a chance to sit down for hours and hours."

"Surely the Queen must have realised that?" Camilla asked.

Lady Lambourn laughed.

"Kings and queens abroad seldom trouble about those whose duty it is to serve them," she replied. "It is different in England — I believe Queen Charlotte is most graciously considerate and everyone at Court is devoted to her. Foreigners do not have the same sympathy as we have for those around them. I know Papa has said that the ladies in the Court of Spain often fainted away from sheer exhaustion, and as soon as they were revived they had to go back on duty."

"It sounds inhuman," Camilla exclaimed angrily.

Lady Lambourn only sighed and said:

"Despite all the disadvantages and hardships, lords and ladies — especially the latter — fight for a place in the Royal presence. It means everything to them, and should they be excluded from Court they feel that their very lives are over."

"You did not feel like that, did you Mama?" Camilla asked wide-eyed.

Lady Lambourn smiled.

"I am afraid, darling, I never could believe in the omnipotence of Royalty. I have always felt that whatever people's position in life they still remain men and women — They suffer, they are happy or unhappy, they are worried and anxious exactly like us."

She suddenly laughed and Camilla enquired:

"What is amusing you, Mama, do tell me?"

"I was thinking of something your Papa said once, and although it was true it was very unlike him to say what he did."

"What was it?" Camilla asked.

"When we were in Paris there was a very pompous Statesman who was always talking about the King as though he was a kind of god. He would literally have lain down on the floor and let the King walk all over him had His Majesty wished to do so. He was always lecturing Papa on the Royal prerogative, and I think too he thought that Papa, being British, was not quite humble enough in the Royal presence. He went on and on until one day Papa got incensed with such strictures, and when this Statesman said, 'I am sure, Ambassador, you realise what an exceptional and supreme person we are privileged to find in His Majesty,' your Papa said very quietly, 'I always remember too that, if one stuck a pin in him, he would bleed.' "

Camilla burst out laughing.

"Oh, did Papa really say that?"

"Yes, indeed he did," Lady Lambourn said. "The Statesman was very angry and threatened to report Papa to the Court of St. James's. Finally he thought it would make him look absurd, so he said nothing."

As Camilla now remembered that story, at the same time she felt that the Baroness, with her adoration for the Princess of Meldenstein, would not either be amused or even believe it true. She would sacrifice herself in any way possible for the Royalty she worshipped, and even if the journey killed her, Camilla was certain that she would attempt it.

"Is there anything I can do for you?" Camilla asked as the Baroness groaned.

"The brandy seems to have settled my stomach," she answered, "but my head! I feel as though it were splitting open, and the motion of the coach is almost as bad as being at sea."

She was obviously so distressed that Camilla eventually persuaded her to lie down on the back seat of the carriage while she sat opposite. She soaked her handkerchief in lavender water — which thoughtfully Rose had included in her reticule — and placed it on the Baroness's forehead.

After a time the invalid fell asleep, and Camilla was free once more to indulge herself in her own thoughts and look out of the window at the passing countryside. The horses were travelling at a fine pace and throwing up a lot of dust, but Camilla was determined not to close the window.

When they reached the inn where they were to stop for luncheon, it was to find Captain Cheverly on the doorstep, his watch in his hand, complaining that they were late according to his schedule and asking what had delayed them.

His tone changed, however, when he saw the Baroness, grey in the face and unable to walk without support, being helped from the coach by Camilla. He hurried forward and half carried the unhappy woman into the inn.

"We will take her upstairs," Camilla said to Captain Cheverly, "it will be best for her to lie down. At least while we have luncheon there will be no movement. She still feels as though she were at sea."

It caused quite a commotion getting the Baroness upstairs, placing her on the bed, taking off her bonnet and shoes, while Captain Cheverly sent people hurrying for hot bricks, a glass of cognac, a cold compress.

"He certainly knew what should be done for her comfort," Camilla thought gratefully.

The chambermaids hurried to obey him, and the cognac seemed to come upstairs almost as quickly as he had commanded it.

"You must have some luncheon," Captain Cheverly urged the Baroness. "You will feel better, I promise you, when you have eaten something. So pray make the effort, otherwise it will only be the worse for you this afternoon."

The Baroness gave a little involuntary groan as she sipped the brandy.

"I will stay with you," Camilla said consolingly.

She shook her head.

"No, dear, I would rather be alone," she answered. "I beg of you to go downstairs and enjoy your luncheon. There will be nobody to realise I am not in attendance. But I cannot move. I am afraid I am too indisposed."

Camilla did as the Baroness requested, and downstairs in the private sitting-room to which Hugo Cheverly took her she said:

"The Baroness is really not well enough to travel! I think we would do well to wait here until she feels better."

"You know that is impossible," he answered. "Everything is arranged for your arrival at Meldenstein. It would not go well for the future if you kept the crowds waiting, or indeed changed the plans."

"It is sheer cruelty to make the Baroness travel in such a state of health," Camilla said angrily.

Hugo Cheverly shrugged his shoulders.

"Let us hope she will make an effort to pull herself together," he said.

"You are a monster!" Camilla cried accusingly. "It is medieval torture to force a woman who is really ill to make such a long journey and at such a pace!"

"Those fat, overfed carriage cattle are making a labour of what more spirited blood stock would complete in half the time," he answered. "They are the best in Meldenstein and replacements from the Royal stables await us at every posting inn. It was the wish of Her Highness that you should only spend two nights *en route*."

"It would have been better not to be thrown about on these rough roads like milk in a churn," Camilla retorted. "I am worried about the Baroness. Surely you do not want us to arrive at Meldenstein with a dead body in the coach?"

"No one dies of seasickness," Hugo

Cheverly snapped.

"The Baroness might be the first to do so," Camilla retorted.

Suddenly she realised that they were quarrelling like a pair of schoolchildren.

"Please do not let us quarrel," she said impulsively, forgetting that she was annoyed with him. "I am really worried about the poor woman."

"And I am worried about you," he answered. "You must see my position in this matter; since I have to get you to Meldenstein, can you not imagine what might be said if you arrive a day late with no valid explanation for our lingering on the way?"

Her eyes widened for a moment, and then despite herself she felt her lips twitch.

"They should have sent me someone old, stout-bellied and pompous as an escort," she said.

She knew she had amused him, though for a moment he fought against it. Then he suddenly burst out laughing.

"You are incorrigible," he said. "Yes, I agree, the choice was not a very wise one with our chaperon wilting on our hands and threatening to be too ill to proceed."

"Is it far to where we are staying the night?" Camilla enquired.

"I planned that we should be there about five of the clock," Hugo Cheverly replied, "but if the coach has to go slower because of the Baroness it may be much later. It is tiring for you, but what can I do about it?"

"Nothing," Camilla answered. "I do not mind looking after her. I made her lie down on the seat and it seemed to ease her slightly. What I suggest you do is buy two extra pillows from the landlord. That will make her more comfortable and perhaps she will sleep. I might even give her a spoonful of laudanum."

"I think that is a good idea," Hugo Cheverly agreed. "We cannot leave her behind, you must see that, and tomorrow night we are due in Westerbalden. The Margrave will be your host."

"So that is his title!" Camilla exclaimed. "No wonder Rose could not pronounce it."

He raised his eyebrows. "Rose?"

"My maid. She has found out all the gossip from the Baroness's abigail and your valet."

"The servants always know everything that is happening," Hugo Cheverly said, "that is why we must be so careful. Everything we do on this journey will be repeated in Meldenstein."

Camilla looked suddenly serious.

"I am aware of that," she answered.

The landlord came bustling in with the luncheon that Hugo Cheverly had already ordered. It was well cooked, and although there was far too much, Camilla found that what she did eat was very palatable.

"You look tired," Hugo Cheverly said, a note of solicitude in his voice. "Would it be best if the Baroness's maid attended her? I cannot have you exhausting yourself before your duties really begin."

"No, I am all right," Camilla replied, "I just did not sleep well."

She dropped her eyes as she spoke, not wishing to sound reproachful, and being glad for the moment that he was not actively incensed by her.

"Nor did I," he said unexpectedly. "I went up on deck and watched the Captain bring the ship into harbour. It was not easy, for the storm had given way to a deep swell. But he handled the craft well and we made harbour at almost exactly the time he had predicted."

There was a little pause, and then almost as if the words had been in his mind earlier Captain Cheverly bent forward.

"I must apologise, Miss Lambourn, for what I said to you last night. It was unpardonable of me and I have no excuse for such an outburst. I can only pray your forgiveness."

He spoke conventionally and yet Camilla had the feeling there was something deeper behind his words, some emotion she could not fathom. She raised her eyes, and saw that there was an expression in his face which was very different from his usual cynicism.

For a moment they looked at each other across the table, blue eyes meeting grey, and Camilla knew suddenly that she sought him wordlessly to be her enemy no longer. Then, as she thought he seemed about to acquiesce, he rose hastily to his feet.

"I must ask your permission, Miss Lambourn, to withdraw," he said formally. "We change horses here and I must see the new team are not too fresh for your comfort."

He went from the room without looking at her, and she knew that what he had said was not true but merely an excuse to leave her. Almost unconsciously her hand went out as though she would stop him and his name trembled on her lips. Then he was gone, and she realised that he had not finished his luncheon and his glass of brandy remained untouched. She waited for a moment, thinking he might return, and then she knew he would not do so. Slowly she went upstairs.

The Baroness was a trifle better. Hugo Cheverly had been right in saying that it was best for her to eat, or perhaps the wine had something to do with her improvement. Anyhow there was no difficulty now in getting her on to her feet, although she clutched nervously at the bedpost and declared dizzily that the room was swinging around her. However she managed to walk downstairs without help and in a few minutes they were off again, the Baroness propped up with cushions on the back seat, and soon, after a small teaspoon of laudanum, she fell asleep.

As soon as she was comfortably off, Camilla let down the window and, pulling off her bonnet, allowed the breeze to play amongst her hair. It was pleasant to feel the warmth of the sunshine on her cheeks, and she wished only that she was riding instead of driving and that she had someone to talk to.

She was afraid of her own thoughts. She had the feeling that she was walking along a very narrow plank over a deep abyss, and that at any moment she might slip and plunge into the dark depths of the water beneath. She had the notion that should she do so she would drown in them, not to lose her life but to be submerged in emotions which she dare not question for fear that she should learn the truth.

The afternoon passed incredibly slowly. She realised that Hugo Cheverly had told the coachman to drive as smoothly as possible, but even if they had hurried she had the feeling that the Baroness would not wake, lying almost motionless on the back seat and covered by a luxurious fur rug which Camilla realised had been sent for her comfort. She could not help thinking with a little smile how surprised they might be in Meldenstein if they could see her at the moment, taking a very subservient place to her chaperon who was also ostensibly her lady-in-waiting.

Slowly the hours dragged by until shortly before seven o'clock they finally drew up in the courtyard of an attractive old inn. They had been driving through flat, treeless country ever since they left Amsterdam, but this had now given place to woods in which nestled the inn, which was obviously hundreds of years old. It had an air of hospitality and of welcome which told Camilla at first sight that they would be comfortable.

It was quite difficult to wake the Baroness, and when they did so she was still drowsy from the laudanum and obviously in need of her bed. Camilla handed her over to her abigail who to her relief had already arrived with Rose. Then, when the Baroness had been helped up the stairs, Camilla turned to find Hugo Cheverly at her side.

"I think it would be best if we did not dine together alone," he said in a low voice. "If you will permit me, I will have something sent to your room. I would not wish the servants to think that we in any way outraged the conventions when the Baroness was not in attendance."

"What about luncheon?" Camilla asked. "We were alone then."

"It all happened so swiftly. I was too mutton-headed to think things out," he replied gruffly, "and I cannot help believing, Miss Lambourn, that you will be glad to dispense with my company."

She was surprised at his words, but there was nothing she could do about it. She was only conscious of an inescapable sense of disappointment as obediently she bowed her head and went to her own bedchamber.

There was no point in dressing to eat by herself, so at Rose's suggestion she had a bath and then arrayed in one of the new diaphanous nightgowns Lady Lambourn had bought for her trousseau, she got into bed.

Rose brought in her dinner on a tray, but Camilla was not hungry. She could not help remembering how she had dined alone with Captain Cheverly the night before and how, until they had started to quarrel, they had talked of many things of interest to both of them. She remembered there was so much she wanted to ask him about Apollo and now she thought the opportunity had passed and it was unlikely she would ever be alone with him again, or indeed with any man other than her husband.

She did not know why her spirits felt so low at the thought. She told herself she was tired, and sent away the dinner with two of the dishes untouched.

"If you do not want me any longer, miss," Rose said, "I'm agoing to the stewards' room for my own meal. Shall I come up and see you afterwards?"

"No, do not trouble to do so," Camilla answered, "I expect I shall be asleep. Where are you sleeping?"

"Someway away, miss. There is no bell by which you can reach me."

"Never mind, I am sure I shall not want you," Camilla said with a smile. "Call me in the morning at seven of the clock."

"The Baroness's room is on your right, as you know, miss," Rose told her, "and Cap-

164

tain Cheverly is on your left, so you should be well protected."

Camilla laughed.

"I do not think any of us need protection in this pretty place."

"No indeed, miss," Rose said. "Mister Harpen has offered to take me down into the village if you did not disallow it. He's a very respectable man, miss. I told him I was sure you would not forbid me to go out with him."

"No, I do not forbid you," Camilla replied. "Go and enjoy yourself, Rose, you may not get another opportunity."

"Thank you, miss, I've never had so much fun in all my life," Rose said, and her face was glowing as she shut the door and Camilla was left alone.

She read for a little while, said her prayers, then decided it was time she went to sleep. But strangely she was no longer tired, she felt wide awake, and she was also conscious, restlessly, that the bed was hard.

She remembered her mother had said that when she and Sir Horace used to travel in Europe unless there were feather beds the mattresses would be as hard as boards and she had evolved a clever trick of pulling a pillow into the centre of the bed and lying against it.

The bed in Camilla's bedroom was a large double one. There were four pillows, and she placed one in the centre of the bed and half lay on it, stacking two others behind her head. That was more comfortable, she decided, very much so, and yet she still could not sleep.

She had pulled back the curtains before she went to bed, as she had always done at home, liking to be woken by the sun in the morning when the first rays touched her face. Now on the left-hand side of the window she could see a pale crescent moon creeping up the sky. She realised it was a new moon and felt suddenly afraid because she had seen it through glass.

"It means bad luck!" she thought apprehensively, and then was ashamed of herself for being so childish.

Nevertheless she nodded her head seven times to it and wondered if she should get out of bed and turn her money. It seemed ridiculous, and yet the superstition persisted, and she felt she was desperately in need of good luck.

Smiling at her own childishness she finally got up. There was no need to light a candle — the moon, pale though it was, and the brilliance of the stars, enabled her to find her way to the dressing-table and to take out of the drawer the reticule in which she carried two or three pieces of gold in case she should need them.

She held them in her hand and turned them over, and then once again bowed her head seven times, this time with a deeper obeisance, looking at the moon through the open window and not through the closed casement through which she had seen it first.

"Bring me luck," she whispered, "please bring me luck and . . . happiness."

She put her reticule back on the dressing table and then she thought, as she was out of bed, she would drink a glass of water. Perhaps that would help her to sleep.

The washing-stand was at the far end of the room in a corner. It was in darkness, but Camilla remembered where she had seen an ewer and a glass. She reached the washing-stand, felt for the glass, found it and holding it in her hand reached out for the ewer. As she did so she felt the moonlight in the room was suddenly dimmed. She turned her head and was paralysed into stillness. In the window, silhouetted against the sky, was a man.

Unable to move, unable to make a sound, Camilla saw him creep into the room. Swiftly and completely noiseless he moved towards the bed. Then, as he raised his arm, something glinted evilly, caught in the moonbeams. Camilla saw him strike with all his force and the glass fell with a crash from her nerveless fingers.

Without looking round he moved with an almost incredible speed towards the window, slipped over the sill and was gone. Camilla tried to cry out but found she was unable to make a sound — her voice was strangled in her throat.

7

Camilla stood staring at the window feeling as though she were turned to stone. She struggled to cry for help, but her voice had ceased to obey her commands. Then suddenly sheer terror took hold of her and with an inarticulate cry she pulled open her door and rushed into the passage. Without coherent thought, driven only by a wild desire to find assistance, she flung open the first door she came to.

Hugo Cheverly was seated at a *secretaire*. He had not undressed but had removed his coat, revealing a fine lawn shirt and his cravat, tied in the fashionable "waterfall", undisturbed. Two tapers in pewter candlesticks were burning on the desk at which he was writing.

He looked round as the door was flung open, and seeing Camilla rose hastily to his feet.

"Miss Lambourn!" he exclaimed. "What is amiss?"

Camilla's hand went to her throat.

"A . . . man," she managed to say in a strangled voice, "in . . . in . . . my . . . room."

Hugo Cheverly with a speed which Camilla would not have thought possible, snatched up a pistol which lay on the table beside his bed and took one of the candles in his other hand.

"Wait here," he said sharply.

His usual lazy indifference was gone. Here was a man of action, a man who had his wits about him in any emergency, however unexpected.

"No . . . no!" Camilla stammered desperately, "you . . . cannot . . . leave me . . . alone!"

But already he was out of the room and down the passage towards her bedchamber. Frightened she ran after him and reached it just as he entered through the door she had left open.

He held the candle high, his pistol at the ready. The room, as she well knew, was empty, and after looking around him for a moment he advanced further, followed by Camilla.

"He has . . . gone," she explained, "he went . . . back the way he . . . came through the . . . window when . . . I dropped my . . . glass."

She pointed to where pieces of the tum-

170

bler she had held in her hand lay scattered on the floor, and Hugo Cheverly raised the candle so that he could see them before he set it down on the table beside the bed. As he did so Camilla gave a shrill cry.

"Look! Look!"

Once again Hugo Cheverly followed the direction in which her finger pointed, and there in the centre of the bed he saw the bulge under the bedclothes, made by the pillow against which Camilla had been lying, and plunged deep into the centre of it the hilt of a dagger.

"He . . . meant to . . . kill me," Camilla ejaculated in terms of horror, and then, not knowing what she was doing in her fear, she turned towards Hugo Cheverly and buried her face against his shoulder.

Instinctively his arm went round her. He could feel her whole body trembling.

"It is all right," he said soothingly, "he has gone now."

"But he . . . intended that I should . . . die," Camilla murmured. "Why? Why? What . . . have I . . . done?"

"It can only have been a blunder," Hugo Cheverly said. "The knife must have been intended for someone else — perhaps for me."

"If I had not risen . . . because I wished for

171

a . . . glass of . . . water," Camilla whispered, "it is I . . . who would be lying there . . . dead . . . or dying."

She gave a convulsive sob and pressed herself even closer against him. She felt a comforting sense of security in the broadness of his shoulder against which she was resting, in the strength of his arm supporting her and the knowledge that he would protect her should the murderer, whoever he might be, return.

"You are quite safe now!" Hugo Cheverly assured her. "I promise you that it can only have been an error. A terrifying experience indeed, but you must be brave."

His words seemed to sweep away her panic and suddenly Camilla was conscious of her appearance; of the diaphanous nightgown she wore which revealed rather than concealed her figure; of Hugo Cheverly's heart which she could hear beating against her cheek under the soft linen of his shirt; and the fact that for the first time in her life she was being held closely by a man.

"I . . . I . . . am . . . sorry," she managed to say, and moved so that instantly he released her.

Quickly she picked up a wrap of white silk trimmed with lace, which lay over the end of the bed. With a feeling of embarrassment she slipped her arms into the wide sleeves and pulled it round her, aware that while she did so Hugo Cheverly was not looking at her but was bending forward to pull the dagger from the pillow in which it was embedded.

He drew it forth and Camilla saw that the handle was engraved. The blade was long, thin and evil, and would, she knew, pass easily into any part of the body into which it was thrust. The mere sight of it was enough to recall her terror, but now she had enough control of herself to hold on to the wooden bedstead for support, already ashamed of the manner in which she had clung to Hugo Cheverly.

He turned the dagger over in his hands, examining the marking on the hilt. "A pretty weapon," he said drily. "There are some strange signs engraved on it, but I cannot decipher them."

"The man was Chinese," Camilla said.

At her words his eyes turned to her enquiringly, and she saw by the expression on his face, as well as by the sudden tension in his body, that she had startled him.

"Why do you say Chinese?" he asked.

"He had a pigtail," Camilla answered. "I saw him silhouetted against the sky. There was a pigtail falling from his head at the back."

"You are certain of that?" Hugo Cheverly asked with some urgency.

"Quite, quite certain," Camilla answered. "Why? What does it signify?"

He seemed about to speak and then looked away from her at the dagger he held in his hand.

"It signifies nothing in particular," he answered, but she knew that he was concealing the truth.

He set the dagger down on the bed.

"I must go and see if there is any sign of the man lurking about outside," he said, but his words brought Camilla's terror flooding over her again.

"No, no," she cried, "you cannot leave me . . . alone! I will not . . . be left . . . here."

"You will not be alone," Hugo Cheverly said gently, "I will fetch your maid. Come with me and we will awaken her. I think I know where she is sleeping."

He moved towards the door but Camilla put out her hand to stop him.

"Wait," she said, "do you think it wise?"

"What do you mean?" he enquired.

Camilla forced herself to speak in a more controlled manner as she answered:

"If we awaken Rose and you tell the innkeeper what has occurred, can you not see what a commotion it will cause, what a scandal there will be . . . before I arrive in Meldenstein?"

Hugo Cheverly turned back.

"I did not think of that," he admitted. "Perhaps you are right."

"The man heard me drop the glass," Camilla said. "He must have thought there was someone else in the room; perhaps he believed his mission was fulfilled."

"You mean he imagined he had killed whoever was lying in the bed?" Hugo Cheverly said. "That certainly seems possible."

"I dropped my glass just as he struck," Camilla went on. "If he were flustered he may not have realised that his dagger had pierced not a body but a pillow. He certainly went out through the window with almost incredible swiftness."

She paused, and then added:

"And silently! I think that was what was so horrible about it. He moved so silently, almost as if he were not human."

Hugo Cheverly did not speak, and after a moment she went on:

"That confirms my impression that he was Chinese. Could it not? I am convinced that only someone from the East could have moved like that."

"I think you are very sensible," Hugo Cheverly said gravely. "To start a search-party would be useless. The man would not have waited. He knows that someone saw him, someone who was in the room, and he may easily, as you have already suggested, have thought there were two people here. We shall not find him, however hard we search, and, as you say, it will cause an uproar in the Inn if they realise that there has been an attempt to murder their most distinguished and important guest."

"Up to now I believed I had no enemies," Camilla said almost pathetically.

"It was not you the assailant was after," Hugo Cheverly said positively. "Who knows what feuds and vendettas take place in these isolated country districts? The man has gone. I will keep the dagger and we will say nothing about it."

"We must not mention it to anyone," Camilla insisted, "and especially not to the Baroness."

"No, indeed," Hugo Cheverly agreed. "But I wish to God I could get my hands on the fellow. I would teach him not to frighten women in such a way, or anyone else for that matter!"

"Do not try to find him," Camilla pleaded, "I am convinced that it was all a terrible mistake. We can only hope that he believes that his crime was successful and will not seek to murder some other unhappy, unsuspecting victim."

She walked across the room as she spoke and shut the window.

"Perhaps it was my fault for leaving the window open and the curtains drawn back," she said. "I made it easy for . . . him! But I have always slept with the window open and cannot bear the stuffiness of a closed room."

"There speaks the country maid!" Hugo Cheverly remarked.

She turned to smile at him bravely, and as she did so was suddenly conscious of her appearance. Her hands went to her hair. She had forgotten that it lay hanging over her shoulders, the pale gold waves framing her tiny face. She had no idea how young and lovely she looked with her eyes still dark with fear and her cheeks very pale after the dreadful experience which had left her still trembling a trifle.

"I admire your bravery more than I can say," Hugo Cheverly said in a quiet voice. "Most females would have succumbed to the vapours, having smelling salts held under their nose."

"I assure you I am still very frightened!"

Camilla said. "It is rather lowering, as you can comprehend, to find that someone wishes to dispose of me. It disperses every puffed-up opinion I ever had of myself."

"It was a mistake," Hugo Cheverly said again, almost as though he would convince himself by repeating it. "No one would wish to murder you, indeed what would they gain from it?"

"It might," Camilla said in a low voice, "it might . . . have been an . . . anarchist."

As she spoke she felt herself quiver with fear, and her face was very white and pathetic as she moved towards Hugo Cheverly and said:

"If it were, he will strike again — we may be sure of that — perhaps during the . . . marriage celebrations."

Hugo Cheverly put out his hand and took her cold fingers in his.

"You are not to think of it," he urged, "and I assure you that in Meldenstein things do not happen that way. It is the quietest and most contented country in all Europe. The Royal family are adored by the people."

"My father has spoken of anarchists," Camilla continued. "They belong to no particular country, they have no loyalty, they just wish to kill, to annihilate, to destroy! Oh God! What shall I do!"

"You will be brave!" Hugo Cheverly said, and there was an authority in his voice such as he might have used to a trooper wavering on the eve of battle. "If there is trouble of that sort, which I am utterly convinced there will not be, then, as an English-woman, you will behave in a manner which will help to strengthen and control those who would otherwise be panic-stricken."

"Suppose . . . I am . . . panic-stricken?" Camilla asked in a low voice.

"You will not be," he assured her, "you have too much spirit."

She felt as though his words brought the colour back to her cheeks.

"Perhaps it would be easier to bear if the assault did not come at night . . . so secretly and . . . silently," she murmured.

"Whenever it happens," he said, "you will have the courage to face it, I am sure of that."

"I wish . . . I could believe . . . you," she said tremulously.

Conscious that he still held her hand and that she seemed to draw some strength and magnetism from his touch, she raised her eyes to his and saw that he was looking down at her with a kindliness and compassion she had never before seen in his expression.

"I shall try . . . to do what is . . . expected

of . . . me," she said in a very small voice.

"I was sure of that," he answered. "It may not always be easy, but you will not fail."

His words made her lift her chin a little higher and he knew that he had reawakened her pride and now she was in control of her emotions.

"You must rest," he said, "you have a long day ahead of you tomorrow and I would not have you over-tired."

He had relinquished her hand, but now Camilla clutched at his arm.

"I cannot . . ." she stammered. "Whatever . . . you may think . . . of me . . . I cannot . . . sleep in this . . . room . . . tonight."

"No, of course not," he said soothingly. "I suggest that you move into my bed-chamber. I will bolt and bar the window and I will sit outside the door. If anything unto-ward happens — and I assure you it is the most unlikely thing in the world — then you have but to cry out. My pistol will be in my hand, there will be no delay and, I assure you, no danger to yourself."

"But you also need your sleep," Camilla objected.

He smiled at that.

"When we were campaigning on the Peninsula," he said, "I often went for nights without sleep or rest. I assure you that for me to stay awake is no hardship, and the chair in which I shall be sitting will be very much more comfortable than the hard ground to which I am accustomed."

"Are you really sure you do not mind doing this?" Camilla asked. "If you would prefer it we will awaken Rose. I am sure I can swear her to secrecy and she would not talk."

Camilla sounded doubtful even as she spoke. She knew that Rose was a chatterbox, and the fact that there had been an attempt to murder her mistress was too thrilling a story not to be repeated, exaggerated and exclaimed over.

Hugo Cheverly shook his head.

"Your first idea that it would be a secret between you and me is far the best one. Rose would talk and so indeed would the Baroness. When it is dawn and people will soon be arising and moving about the Inn, then I will awaken you and you can go back to your own room. In the meantime, while it is dark, you will be safe — for I shall be on guard."

"Thank you," Camilla said, "I am grateful — very grateful."

She moved towards the door, but could not resist a backward glance at the bed, which made her shudder. The position of the pillow under the bedclothes still gave the impression of a body, and once again she thought that she might have been lying there, that she might at this moment have been dead.

As if he read her thoughts she heard Hugo Cheverly say quietly:

"Forget it. This is one of the things best forgotten and never again thought about."

"I shall never forget your kindness," Camilla said.

"Kindness?" he queried, and added in a low voice: "I too shall have memories of tonight."

There was something in the tone of his voice which made her feel shy and unable to look at him. Once again she was conscious of her appearance, and how shocked her mother would have been at the thought of her talking intimately with a gentleman she scarcely knew, and wearing nothing but her nightgown and a satin wrap.

She turned away with her head bowed and Hugo Cheverly, lifting the candle from the table, followed her. They entered his bedchamber, and he put down the taper by the bed, lifted a wing-sided armchair from the hearth through the doorway into the passage and set it down quietly. It almost filled the passage so that it would have been impossible for anyone to pass that way without touching him. He then shut the window, closed the heavy wooden shutters and thrust the bolt into place.

"Now you are secure," he said. "I am prepared to swear that no one will disturb you, however bad their intentions."

"I too am convinced it would be impossible," Camilla smiled.

"Then sleep well," he said. "It has indeed been an upsetting day; for looking after the Baroness you have not travelled in the coach as comfortably as you should."

He paused a moment and then, in so low a voice that Camilla could hardly catch the words, he added:

"I would want Meldenstein to see how beautiful you are."

She looked at him in astonishment and then, before she could answer, he had gone from the room, closing the door quietly behind him. She heard him settle himself in the armchair and then, after a moment, she resolutely crossed the room, slipped between the sheets of the bed and lay down against the soft pillows.

For a long time she could not sleep. She found herself vividly conscious of the man outside the door. Once she heard him move his feet, but otherwise there was silence, and yet she was so aware of him it was almost as though he were sitting beside her.

She found herself repeating his last words over and again in her mind. So he did think she was beautiful! Despite the angry words he had addressed to her, despite the cynicism in his eyes and that ugly twist of his lips that had told her he was sneering at her, he thought her beautiful!

The thought was strangely comforting and finally at last she fell asleep, only, it seemed to her, to be woken almost immediately by a soft knock on the door.

Despite the shutters being closed she could see a chink of light above and below them, which told her the sun was rising. She slipped out of bed and pulling her wrap up closely around her opened the door. He was standing waiting for her.

"No more intruders," he said with a smile, and she forgot her shyness and was able to smile back. "There is no one in your room, I promise you, and already the ostlers are awake in the stables and the chambermaids are moving about downstairs. You will have no more unwelcome visitors."

"Thank you," she answered, "thank you for looking after me."

He did not reply, but there was something in the expression on his face which made her turn quickly away and hurry to her own bed-chamber. Only when she had shut the door did she feel a sudden flutter in her breast which was quite unaccountable and which made her feel a little breathless as she moved towards the bed.

She saw at once that while she slept he must have removed the pillow which had been pierced by the dagger; it was no longer there. It was considerate of him, she thought, to remove the evidence of the crime, which might have upset her. Then she realised that perhaps he had done it so that the housemaids would not immediately notice the pierced linen and any goose feathers which might have fallen loose.

She wondered where he had hidden the pillow, and then, still very drowsy, she slipped into bed without feeling any revulsion or recurring horror. He was still near her should she cry out to him, still ready to protect and sustain her, and the knowledge was infinitely comforting.

Owing to the fact that Camilla was unpunctual for breakfast they were late in setting off. The Baroness, looking heavy-eyed after taking laudanum, was for once noncommunicative, and when Camilla arrived downstairs it was to find Hugo Cheverly had already breakfasted and left the sitting-room.

She had schooled herself before leaving her room to meet him without embarrassment, but she had wondered all the time while she was dressing what he must have thought of her. How reprehensible to have rushed into his bedchamber in the middle of the night wearing nothing but a nightgown! To have clung to him in her terror in a most unmaidenly manner!

At the time it had seemed utterly natural, but now when she thought it over she decided he must have found her behaviour shockingly forward and unladylike. Yet what would anyone else have done in such circumstances? Even in the daylight she had only to remember the silent, murderous Chinaman to feel herself tremble and the panic of terror sweep over her again.

"You are looking pale, my dear," the Baroness said, after a second cup of coffee had seemed to revive her and erase some of the dark lines from under her eyes.

"I did not sleep as well as I might," Camilla said lightly but truthfully. "I trust you spent a good night?"

"I remembered nothing until my abigail woke me," the Baroness replied. "One blessing is that this hotel is very quiet. I am sincerely grateful that we did not have to

186

spend the night in the town for I am usually a very light sleeper."

Camilla was thankful that the Baroness had not woken during the night. Indeed she was still weak and heavy-headed from the laudanum; so when they started their journey again she showed no inclination to gossip.

Camilla noticed that today Hugo Cheverly did not go ahead. He rode with their small cavalcade, sometimes taking to the fields beside the road but keeping always within ear-shot. Knowing why he did so she felt grateful. It was a tremendous comfort to know he was there and that should anything happen he would instantly be at her side.

As the day progressed she came to the conclusion that he was right: it must have been just pure chance that the killer had chosen her room. Yet even when she told herself this she could not help remembering Hugo Cheverly's sudden tenseness and the look in his eyes when she had told him that the man was a Chinaman.

Puzzle though she would, she could find no clue to help her solve the problem, and there was no chance of her discussing it when they reached their rendezvous for luncheon. She found that they were to partake of this meal in a castle belonging to a cousin of Prince Hedwig's, who was unfortunately away from home.

They were entertained in his absence by his mother, who was old and rather deaf, but they had the comfort of enjoying a well-cooked and well-served meal in a room where the walls were beautifully painted with ancient murals.

"They at least could not be taken away by the soldiers," their hostess told Camilla when she had admired them. "All our pictures were stolen or destroyed, and the few pieces of furniture which you see here have since been brought by my son from farms or houses in the vicinity, which the peasants had collected from the rubbish heaps left by Napoleon's soldiers after they had stripped bare every house in the neighbourhood. Luckily much of their spoil was left behind."

The old lady spoke bitterly. Then, before Camilla could commiserate with her, she continued:

"I am French. My father was guillotined during the Revolution, my son was conscripted when Napoleon overran our country. You in England have no idea what we have suffered during the years of war. The peasants were near starvation and Napoleon cared for nothing but men who could provide him with cannon-fodder. How my son survived I shall never know, for I never expected to see him alive again."

With tales of so much unhappiness to listen to, it was not surprising that the meal was not a very cheerful one. Camilla was glad when luncheon was over and they could return to the coach and with fresh horseflesh between the shafts set off once again on their journey.

"Do not forget that we stay the night with the Margrave of Westerbalden," Hugo Cheverly reminded her as they went down the steps of the castle to where the coach awaited them.

"I hope he is not as unhappy as this poor lady," Camilla said.

"I hope so indeed," Hugo Cheverly replied, "but it is true these small principalities have suffered a great deal, as I have seen all too clearly while I have been in northern Europe since Waterloo."

"Do you speak their language?" Camilla asked.

"Enough to make myself understood in most places," he replied. "I like the peasants; they have endured more and complained less than the so-called aristocrats. There are not many of the latter left in France — the Revolution saw to that — but the Margrave was half French on his mother's side and managed to ingratiate himself, I believe, with the Napoleonic regime. He has certainly not suffered in the pocket as much as most of his contemporaries have done."

"You know him then," Camilla remarked.

"I have met him," Hugo Cheverly replied, "and he is one of those socialites who always manages to be in the right place at the right moment. By entertaining you tonight he ensures a front seat at your wedding. Do not forget that when he overwhelms you with his hospitality!"

She laughed at his words and said reprovingly:

"I am sure it is extremely kind of the Margrave to accommodate us."

When they reached the Palace of Westerbalden she found that her defence of her host was quite unnecessary. The Palace was enormous, standing in extensive parklands. There were ornamental lakes and waterfalls, with a fountain in the courtyard and white doves fluttering around flower-filled ornamented urns.

The Salons were worthy of the Palace. There were tapestries, brocade hangings, gilt-framed pictures, and inlaid marble-topped furniture which Camilla found particularly beautiful.

The Margrave was fat, red-faced and jovial. He did not appear at all like a conventional aristocrat, and she could well understand how he had managed to ingratiate himself with Napoleon and the new regime in France.

"Welcome! Welcome!" he exclaimed in tolerably good English. "It is a great honour and a privilege, Miss Lambourn, for me to receive you on this very auspicious occasion. I have only to look at you to realise how very fortunate my friend Prince Hedwig has been in securing such a beautiful and charming bride who will capture the hearts of all his countrymen."

His effusiveness made Camilla feel rather shy, but she was extremely interested in the Palace and had a quick look through many of its more formal rooms before she went upstairs to change for dinner.

" 'Tis very grand, isn't it, miss?" Rose asked in awe-struck tones. "Do you think the Palace of Meldenstein will be bigger than this?"

"I have really no idea," Camilla replied, "but this seems very palatial to me."

"I've never seen so many servants," Rose went on, "and all chattering away tho' I can't understand a word of their lingo."

"I am sure Mister Harpen will explain to you anything you want to know," Camilla said with a smile.

She had heard so much about Mister Harpen from Rose that she had begun to feel he was one of those men who would never be at a loss.

"Mister Harpen gets everything he wants," Rose said with satisfaction, "but he does not care much for foreigners — frogs and bullfrogs he calls them — the bullfrogs being the people in this country."

"Oh hush, Rose," Camilla said hastily, "someone might be listening to you. You must not say anything which might offend those who are offering us hospitality."

"Well, we beat them all, didn't we, miss?" Rose asked. "Mister Harpen says the people here hadn't the guts to square up to Boney, however bad he treated them. But we beat him and all those ahanging on to his coat-tails single-handed."

"Yes indeed we beat Napoleon," Camilla said, "and now that we are victorious we must be magnanimous. We must not remind Europe that we are their con-querors, that would be sadly impolite."

"I can't say that this place looks as though anyone has conquered it," Rose said, "and do you know what they offered me when I arrived, miss? Wine!"

"It is usual in France," Camilla said, "so I suppose it is the same here. But I should not drink too much, Rose, it will not suit you."

"I didn't drink the stuff," Rose said hastily, "I asked them for ale. They brought it eventually and they seemed to think they were adoing me a favour."

Camilla could not help laughing, but she felt that Rose, with the help of Mister Harpen, would be able to hold her own in the household, whatever language might be spoken.

After bathing in rose-scented water poured into a silver bath, and drying herself in towels scented with lilac, she concentrated on making herself as pretty as possible for the dinner party which lay ahead.

She was glad she had a gown which matched in grandeur and elegance the palace itself. It was in silver gauze embroidered all over with little turquoise beads, and there were turquoise ribbons to tie round her tiny waist and also to twist in her hair. These Rose secured with the diamond brooch which Lady Lambourn had given Camilla as a wedding present.

It was not a very large or expensive jewel, but Camilla had thought it the most magnificent thing she had ever seen until she had looked on the jewellery sent her by the Prince. She half thought she should wear his necklace tonight, and imagined that was one reason why he had sent them to her. But perhaps he would rather she wore them first on her arrival at Meldenstein.

When she opened the case she could only remember them lying on the floor at Hugo Cheverly's feet, and the way he had ranted furiously at her and the bitterness in his voice. She shut the velvet case with a little snap.

"I think this dress requires no jewellery, Rose," she said.

"Not even the diamond necklace, miss?" Rose asked.

Camilla shook her head and stared at her reflection in the mirror.

"Not tonight," she said. "I dare say I shall have to wear it often enough in Meldenstein for me to get heartily tired of diamonds."

The thought struck her that this was the last night of their journey. Tomorrow they would arrive, and then Hugo Cheverly would no longer be her escort. He would go back to England and she would be left in Meldenstein.

She shook the thought away from her as though it were a burden on her shoulders, and after thanking Rose for her trouble she did not wait for the Baroness but proceeded slowly down the staircase to the Grand Salon, where she had been told they were to meet before dinner.

She came down step by step, conscious that in her new gown and skilfully arranged hair she was looking her very best. She wondered a little breathlessly if Hugo Cheverly would think her beautiful.

With a sudden leap of her heart she saw he was waiting for her, standing in the hall at the bottom of the stairs, exceedingly elegant in a grey satin evening coat which fitted without a wrinkle, white breeches and a cravat that could only have been tied by a master-hand.

"No other man," she thought, "could look such a dandy and at the same time so strong and manly."

As if her thoughts were communicated to Hugo Cheverly, he turned and looked up at her approach. There was a smile on his lips and she thought the laziness, the cynicism and the indifference had gone. She felt herself smile back, and resisting an inclination to hurry she forced herself to proceed smoothly down towards him.

Suddenly there was the sound of wheels outside, a commotion at the door, and into the hall came a Vision in a driving-coat of strawberry-pink velvet edged with sable. A bonnet tied with ribbons the same colour framed an exquisitely beautiful face with dark slanting eyes and a crimson pouting mouth.

"Are you surprised to see me, Hu-go?" the Vision asked, both hands outstretched, her face alight with mischief.

"Anastasia, what brings you?" Hugo Cheverly ejaculated, clearly astounded at her unexpected appearance. "What does this mean?"

Anastasia gave a cry of sheer amusement.

"I knew I should surprise you!" she exclaimed. "And I should have been here earlier had not my cock-brained coachman lost his way."

"But how can you have managed it," Hugo Cheverly exclaimed in bewilderment.

"I recalled that the Prince of Meldenstein is a cousin of mine," Anastasia replied. "A distant cousin, it is true, but nevertheless it is blood that counts. So I decided it would be very inconsiderate of me not to wish my relative happiness on his wedding day. I despatched a courier to Meldenstein to tell His Supreme Highness to expect me, and I also sent a message here to my dear friend, the Margrave, that I would make all speed to be with him tonight — the same time as you would be present."

"But how did you know I was coming here?" Hugo asked. "I swear I never told you."

Anastasia gave a little gurgle of laughter. As she did so she put out her hand to draw him a little closer to her. Then she spoke very quietly, intending what she said only for Hugo Cheverly's ear; but Camilla — who had drawn nearer to them with every step — overheard quite distinctly.

"My sweet, unsophisticated Hu-go," Anastasia whispered, her face raised to his, "have you not yet learnt that women always read letters that men leave lying about? You carried your instructions from the Princess, my dear innocent, in your coat-pocket!"

8

"I must offer you my felicitations, Miss Lambourn, on your approaching marriage," the Countess of Wiltshire said formally as the ladies met in the Grand Salon after dinner.

Camilla inclined her head and murmured her thanks. She felt overwhelmed by the exotic beauty of the woman speaking to her.

Anastasia was wearing a gown of blood-red satin, so vivid in colour and shaped so seductively to her figure that she made every other woman in the room look drab and un-interesting. There were rubies sparkling in her hair and round her long ivory-white neck, and Camilla could understand why the gentlemen clustered round her and seemed to have eyes for no one else.

It was a large dinner-party, nearly all of the guests being *en route* for Meldenstein and the wedding which was to take place two days later. The Margrave made a great fuss of Camilla. Remembering Hugo Cheverly's words she realised that he was indeed one of those people to be found in every country in the world who must always be involved in the latest excitement, primed with the newest gossip, and an intimate friend of everyone distinguished or notorious.

Owing to her future exalted rank, Camilla found herself seated on the Margrave's right at dinner, and he regaled her with the names of many of the important people he knew both in England and in Meldenstein.

"His Serene Highness — your future husband — is a close friend of mine," he answered boastfully.

"Do tell me about Prince Hedwig," Camilla begged. "You realise I have not yet even met him."

"A patrician of the first blood, with whom I am convinced you will enjoy a most happy marriage," the Margrave answered. "His country is only a trifle larger than mine, but I flatter myself that together we can wield great power in the negotiations which are taking place with regard to Europe."

"The Prince is interested in international politics?" Camilla questioned.

"Naturally," the Margrave replied.

"When did you last meet His Serene Highness?" Camilla asked.

She did not know why, but she had the suspicion that the Margrave was not such an intimate friend of the Prince as he was insinuating. Her question certainly made him shift a little uncomfortably.

"As you well know," he replied, "his Supreme Highness had the misfortune — or perhaps it was good fortune — to go abroad during the armistice of 1802. He could not return when Bonaparte was rampaging over Europe once again. It was indeed fortunate that in his absence his mother was a most commendable ruler, otherwise I cannot imagine what might have happened to the delightful country over which you will soon reign."

"Have you seen the Prince since his return?" Camilla asked.

"Actually we have not met," the Margrave admitted. "We have, of course, communicated with each other. I wrote to His Serene Highness only a few weeks ago on a matter of boundaries, something which I consider it imperative that we should decide for ourselves before any Council of Europe starts telling us what we should or should not do."

"It seems strange," Camilla said reflectively, "that so few people have seen the Prince since his return. My father, of course, knew him before the war, and Captain Hugo Cheverly was continually at

Meldenstein when he was a boy. I just wondered if His Supreme Highness's sojourn in the East has changed him at all."

"Changed him? Why should it?" the Margrave asked. "I can assure you, my dear Miss Lambourn, that His Supreme Highness is a fine and upstanding young man. We used to have many good times together in the old days, and I have no doubt we shall enjoy a great many more in the future. And now we shall have the delight of your presence at our parties, and it will not be long, I hope, before you both come to Westerbalden as my guests."

"That is very kind of you," Camilla said, thinking it must be a misnomer to describe Prince Hedwig as young.

She realised now that the Margrave was not really as intimate with the Prince as he pretended. At the same time she wondered why the Prince was so elusive, why no one seemed to have anything to tell her about him, save from their knowledge of him before he went to the East.

"Fifteen years is a long time," she thought, "in it a man could alter completely and become, to all intents and purposes, a different person."

She hardly dared voice the suspicion to herself, but she had the feeling that there was some mystery about the Prince, something about him which was being kept from her. Yet whom could she accuse of deliberate deception?

She glanced down the table at Hugo Cheverly. He was seated beside the Countess of Wiltshire, and she saw they were talking together in a manner which made it all too obvious they were old friends. She felt a sudden constriction in her throat and was no longer hungry.

"Was the Countess with her seductive beauty the reason why Hugo Cheverly had seemed so cynical and aloof when he arrived at her home?" she wondered. "Was she the cause of his obvious boredom at the prospect of escorting the Prince of Meldenstein's future bride across the Channel? Could she also be responsible for the manner in which he had sneered at women who desired wealth?"

She found herself watching for Hugo Cheverly to come into the Salon, and when he did so she noticed he would have crossed the room to her side had he not been circumvented by Lady Wiltshire.

"Hu-go," she called in that soft, fascinating voice with its Russian accent which Camilla felt no man could resist, "I want you. Come here! I was just relating to these gentlemen the latest *on dit* about Lady Hertford. Come and tell them what Mrs. Fitzherbert said about her."

It would have been impossible for Hugo Cheverly to refuse. Even had he wished to escape, Lady Wiltshire's arm was through his and she was laughing up at him as she drew him into the circle which was ready to applaud anything she might say or suggest.

An elderly woman, who Camilla had learnt was a French Duchesse of the old Regime, sat down beside her.

"Who is that over-jewelled, under-dressed female?" she enquired, raising her lorgnettes to her tired eyes.

Camilla made no pretence of not understanding to whom she was referring.

"That is the Countess of Wiltshire, ma'am," she said respectfully.

"Not English, is she?"

"No indeed, Ma'am, she is Russian."

"Oh, Russian!" the Duchesse snapped in tones of contempt. "I might have known it. Those half-caste Mongolians never know how to behave with propriety — she is no exception."

Camilla could not help giggling, there was an autocratic tone in the old lady's voice which made her words as sharp as vinegar and her wit as stinging as a whiplash.

"So you are travelling to Meldenstein, I understand," the Duchesse went on.

"I am to marry the Prince, ma'am," Camilla answered.

"He has good taste," the Duchesse approved. "It is a tradition in Meldenstein that the reigning Princess should always be English. Are you looking forward to sitting on a throne?"

"No, indeed," Camilla answered in a low voice, "I am frightened at the whole idea. Besides, to be honest, ma'am, I have never been abroad before and I fear I shall make many mistakes."

"You are pretty enough to get away with them," the Duchesse said drily, "but it would be an ordeal for any foreign wench, however attractive. Why have your father end mother not accompanied you?"

"My mother is sadly indisposed," Camilla explained, "and is too ill to travel. My father is taking her to Bath, otherwise they would have been with me. I wish with all my heart that they were!"

"Poor child, I am sorry for you," the Duchesse said sympathetically. "Let me give you a piece of advice."

"Please do," Camilla answered.

"Do not let anyone trample on you," the Duchesse said. "I married into a noble family of great pretensions. I was young and inexperienced — good blood, mark you — but not up to their standards. They made my life a hell until I decided I would have no more of it. I stood up to them, I fought them and eventually I beat them."

There was so much satisfaction in the old lady's voice at what had evidently been a great victory that Camilla could not help smiling.

"Yes, I too can smile at it now," the Duchesse went on, "but I suffered agonies when I was young. I was shy and utterly lost amongst a crowd of social-climbers, philanderers and hangers-on. You will find them always around the wealthy. I felt they were suffocating me, I had almost ceased to exist, and then like a phoenix my spirit came to the rescue."

"What made you so brave, ma'am?" Camilla asked. She was listening attentively to the Dowager, for she felt that the advice she was giving her would be very applicable to her future life.

"Perhaps I should not tell you the truth about that," the Duchesse replied unexpectedly.

"Oh, please, ma'am, you are helping me more than you know," Camilla pleaded. "Nothing is more degrading or humiliating than to be afraid! But I shall try to do as you say and not be crushed, whatever lies ahead of me."

"Good girl!" the Duchesse approved. "I like your spirit. I lived in England for some years after the Revolution. There is an inner strength in the English which they can always draw on in times of trouble. Remember that, it is there inside you if you wish to use it."

"You have not told me what changed you, ma'am," Camilla prompted.

The Duchesse's old eyes twinkled.

"Well, if you insist," she said, "I will relate the truth — I fell in love! It was not with my husband, of course. I respected him. I was grateful to him for the position he had offered me, for all he was able to do for my family. But I never loved him — he was not a very lovable man. The one I did love was different."

"What was he like?" Camilla asked softly.

The Duchesse did not answer for a moment. She seemed lost in her memories. Then with a start she said:

"It is not at all *comme il faut* that I should be speaking to *une jeune fille* in such a strain. Try to love your husband, my child, that is always the wisest and very much the safest manner in which to conduct a marriage."

"But if I cannot?" Camilla asked in a whisper.

The Duchesse chuckled.

"With your looks there will always be compensations. But whatever happens do not be afraid. Hold that little English chin of yours high! The old always try to assert a despotic authority over the young, and when one is young one is vulnerable and ultra-sensitive. I know! But you will find the meek do not inherit the earth or anything else — I never could abide that verse in the Bible!"

Camilla laughed out loud, she could not help it. As if the sound of her mirth reached him, Hugo Cheverly turned and looked across the room towards her. She looked back at him and almost as if she compelled him he left Lady Wiltshire's side and came towards her.

"I can see you are in good hands, Miss Lambourn," he said, bowing to the Duchesse.

"Who is this young man?" the Dowager asked, raising her lorgnettes.

"May I present Captain Hugo Cheverly, ma'am?" Camilla asked. "He has been most obliging to escort me to Meldenstein."

"I should imagine it has not been a very hard task," the Duchesse said drily as Hugo

Cheverly raised her hand to his lips. "Cheverly? I seem to have heard your name when I was in England."

"My cousin is the Duke of Alveston, ma'am," Hugo Cheverly replied.

"Ah, now I recollect," the Duchesse exclaimed, "but I had no liking for the Duke, a tiresome, sanctimonious man! I remember now who you are, I knew your father. A handsome man, you do him credit."

"Thank you, ma'am," Hugo Cheverly said. "I am sure my Papa danced attendance on you. He always had an eye for a lovely woman!"

The Duchesse chuckled, delighted with the compliment.

"You should be in the Diplomatic Service, young man," she said. "Look after this pretty girl, though I do not suppose I have to tell you to do that."

"No indeed, ma'am," Hugo Cheverly answered, "but my duties will be over on the morrow."

"Then I must commiserate with you," the Duchesse said.

She rose with difficulty to her feet and tapped Camilla on the shoulder with her fan.

"Do not forget what I have told you," she said, "and when you are bored with

Meldenstein you may bring your husband to stay with me."

Camilla curtsied.

"Thank you, ma'am, you are very gracious."

The Duchesse looked at her smiling face.

"You remind me very much of what I was at your age," she said with a little sigh. "Try to fall in love with your husband, my child. It will save so many problems in the future."

She moved away, leaning heavily on an ivory-handled stick, and Hugo Cheverly looked at Camilla with a question in his eyes.

"What did she mean by that?" he asked.

"She has been giving me the good advice of one woman to another," she answered. "It was a secret — I cannot repeat it."

"That she was telling you that you must fall in love with your husband," Hugo Cheverly insisted.

"She said it would be the wisest thing to do," Camilla replied. "You do not agree?"

There was a moment's pause, and then he said with a strange expression in his eyes:

"I think that . . ."

"Hu-go."

Anastasia was at his elbow, the strange exotic perfume which she used seeming to envelop both him and Camilla.

"You have deserted me," she pouted. "Come, we are to play faro in the gaming-room."

"I think I should look after Miss Lambourn," Hugo Cheverly replied, his eyes on Camilla.

Camilla looked away from him as she replied:

"It is indeed gracious of you, Captain Cheverly, but I am fatigued. It would be best, I think, if I retired. We have, I understand, a long day ahead of us tomorrow."

"That is true," Hugo Cheverly agreed, "but it is still early. Would you . . . ?"

"No, no, Hu-go," Anastasia interposed, "you must not persuade Miss Lambourn to miss her beauty sleep. As she says so rightly, it will be a long day tomorrow. No doubt she is fervently anxious to meet the man to whom she is to be wed."

"Of course you are right, ma'am," Camilla said, dropping a small curtsy. "I shall retire immediately."

She moved away, and as she did so she heard Anastasia say:

"Do not be so stupid, Hu-go. I want you with me."

The words seemed to repeat and re-repeat themselves as she went up the grand staircase towards her bedroom.

"Why should the Countess of Wiltshire appear so possessive with Captain Cheverly?" she asked herself, and hated the answer that her heart gave her.

"He must be in love with her," she decided, and wondered why she suddenly felt that her head was aching and that a cloud of misery encompassed her.

Rose was waiting in the bedchamber.

"Have you had a pleasant evening, miss?" she asked.

"Rose, who is the Countess of Wiltshire?" Camilla enquired, the words seeming to burst from her lips before she could repress them.

"She arrived tonight, miss, soon after we got here," Rose replied.

"Yes, I know that," Camilla said.

"She has an English maid, a real chatterbox. She is much easier to get on with than that Fräulein Johann."

"Did she tell you anything about the Countess?" Camilla enquired as Rose unbuttoned her dress at the back.

She knew she should not be asking questions like this. She knew her mother would find it sadly reprehensible, and yet she could not prevent herself. She had to talk to someone about it, and who else was there but Rose?

"Well, I did not have much time to talk to Miss Andrews," Rose replied, "but she did tell me that they had a terrible rush to get here. Her mistress made up her mind at a moment's notice. 'Pack, Andrews,' she commanded, 'pack quickly. We are going to Meldenstein.' Miss Andrews said you could have knocked her down with a feather she was that surprised! Her Ladyship made plans to stay in London all through summer."

"I think she knows Captain Cheverly well," Camilla said in a low voice.

"I think perhaps she does, miss," Rose replied, "as Miss Andrews says to me, 'Is Captain Cheverly not escorting your mistress?' When I said he was, she said, 'Oh, that is what it is all about! I had a feeling he was behind it!' "

"Did she say if they were very great friends?" Camilla enquired.

"No, miss," Rose replied, "but I did hear her say to Mister Harpen that his master had left his fob behind at Lady Wiltshire's mansion. When Mister Harpen thanked her, she said, 'I have put it away in a safe place so no one should see it.' "

"What did she mean by that?" Camilla asked innocently, and then seeing the expression on Rose's face felt the blood rising to her cheeks.

She remembered the stories she had heard when she was in London of the different liaisons current in the Beau Monde: the scandal over the Prince of Wales and Maria Fitzherbert; the talk of Lady Jersey's long procession of lovers; the whispering about the Princess of Wales and Sir Sidney Smith, and her supposed relationship with her adopted son — Willikin. These tales and dozens more caused laughter and sneers, chatter and comment from morning till night.

She remembered how she had hated the feeling that there were always intrigues going on, which somehow made real love seem besmirched and dirty. She dreamt about the love she herself would one day find, the happiness she would know in the arms of a man who would love her as she loved him, and the world would be well forgotten.

She resented the encroachment of these sordid affairs on her dreams, and now she thought of the Countess of Wiltshire with her slanting eyes and red lips, and hated her. How had she been able to take a letter from Hugo Cheverly's coatpocket without his being aware that she was doing so?

"The Countess is very wealthy," she heard Rose say. "Her carriage is smarter than anything I have ever seen, and Miss Andrews says they have stables of fine horseflesh in England."

Camilla felt as though the information made it hard for her to breathe! So it was Lady Wiltshire's money that had made Hugo Cheverly speak so vehemently. That was why he resented the mere mention of riches, why he had sneered at the diamonds which had been sent to her, and why he had ranted at her for refusing to turn the yacht back when he had suggested it.

"He must love her very much," Camilla told herself miserably as she crept into bed between the cool sheets and felt the tears coming to her eyes.

She felt lost and alone; she felt as though she was no longer taking part in an adventure but a nightmare; she felt as though there was something cold and hard hurting her within her breast. Then as Rose blew out all the candles but one and went quietly from the room she knew that she could no longer hide from herself the truth — she loved him!

It was no use to pretend that it was just a passing fancy: she had loved him ever since she had seen him win that race on her thirteenth birthday, ever since she had prayed that he and Apollo would come thundering home the winners, leaving the rest of the field behind.

"I love him," Camilla said to herself, and despairingly buried her face in the pillow.

Downstairs Hugo Cheverly followed Lady Wiltshire obediently into the card-room. Already the older members of the party were seated with piles of golden coins stacked up in front of them.

"You see that?" Hugo Cheverly asked sourly. "That is quite beyond my touch, as you well know."

"I knew that," Anastasia said calmly, "I only wanted to pry you away from the pale-faced milk-sop. You must be tired by now of playing nursemaid."

"It is a mistake to speak like that among strangers," Hugo Cheverly retorted sharply, "and especially foreigners. You know what store they set by protocol."

"Poo-Poo!" Anastasia laughed. "Do not put on airs and graces with me, Hu-go! I am a foreigner, do not forget."

"I am not likely to," he replied.

"Let us go somewhere quiet," Anastasia said in a low voice, "I wish to talk with you."

"No, Anastasia, it would be most incorrect," he answered.

"Are you afraid of your reputation?" Anastasia taunted him. "Do you not think they are talking about us already? And if they are I do not care."

"But I do," he replied. "You are married to an Englishman, Anastasia, and I will not have a countryman of mine be made to look a fool."

"Do you mean that you are concerned with Wiltshire's reputation?" Anastasia enquired incredulously.

"No, indeed," Hugo Cheverly replied, "I am concerned with his wife's. I would not have these people say that you have come to Meldenstein, Anastasia, not because you wished to attend the wedding of your cousin, but because you followed your lover."

Anastasia's eyes flashed dangerously at his words.

"You insult me," she declared angrily. Then with one of her volatile changes of mood she added with a smile: "But it is true!"

"I am on duty," Hugo Cheverly said stiffly. "While we are in Meldenstein, Anastasia, we will behave with all possible propriety."

"Perhaps in public," Anastasia conceded, "but no one will know if you come to my room."

"Do you really credit that," he queried,

"in a Royal Palace where everything is known, where one cannot cough without some servant scurrying with information about it to his master?"

"Then why did I make the journey?" she asked sulkily.

"Because you read a letter which was not intended for you," Hugo Cheverly said sternly. "That was most reprehensible of you, Anastasia, as you well know."

"Bah!" she replied with a little grimace. "Women do not have to be gentlemen. It is something you would not do, I quite agree, but then I did not go to Eton. I am just an ignorant, savage Russian."

"Savage perhaps," Hugo said with a twist of his lips. "But, Anastasia, while you are in Meldenstein you will play no tricks."

She looked at him out of the corners of her eyes, her lips parted provocatively.

"I wonder if you will take a wager on that?" she said in a voice that had an irresistible enticement.

"We should not stand here talking," Hugo Cheverly said, "it is inviting comment. Come, Anastasia, let me settle you at the card-table, or if you would prefer, take you to join a party of ladies."

In reply Anastasia came a little closer to him.

"In half an hour I will retire," she said softly.

"No, Anastasia," Hugo said before she could go any further. Her eyes narrowed.

"You cannot mean that. We are on the same floor, my maid has already discovered which is your chamber. It will not be difficult for you to find me."

"No, Anastasia."

"What has come over you?" she asked angrily. "I have never before known you behave like this."

"I am thinking of your good name," he said.

"It is something that has never worried you in the past," Anastasia replied. "Why is it only about me that you have such scruples? What about all those women you loved before we met? What about the times you have defied convention, when you slipped down dark, unlighted passages and up long flights of stairs to find me when everyone else was asleep?"

"That is in the past, Anastasia," Hugo Cheverly said firmly. "I have already told you we cannot put back the clock."

"Why can we not be alone tonight?" she insisted. "All this talk of my reputation and being in a foreign country is just fustian, and you know it. I shall be waiting for you, Hugo, do not make me wait too long, my hand-

218

some, strong, wonderful lover."

"I shall not come," Hugo said, a steely note in his voice.

She looked up at him incredulously. Then he felt her fingers dig sharply into his arms.

"What has happened to you?" she asked. "You have changed. I did not realise it at first, but now I see that something has occurred. You are quite different from when we were together in London. You were sometimes angry with me, but you could not resist me. Now something strange has come about. Can it be, is it possible, that you have fallen in love with that chit, that insipid wench who is pledged to my cousin? I cannot credit it! It seems impossible! And yet in such a short time you have become a different man. Are you in love, is that the truth, Hu-go?"

He attempted to laugh.

"No, of course not!" But even to himself his protestation sounded false.

9

There was a tap at the door and Camilla raised her head from the pillow. She realised that by now it must be half after one in the morning and she wondered who could possibly be calling on her at such an hour.

The knock came again — not loud, almost as though the caller did not wish to be heard. She slipped out of bed and went to the door.

"Who is it?" she asked in a whisper.

" 'Tis I — Hugo Cheverly," was the reply.

She opened the door a crack.

"I have retired," she murmured.

"I must speak with you," he said urgently. "Dress as quickly as you can."

She did not argue with him. Instead she shut the door and by the light of the candle which, left burning by Rose, was now guttering low, she hurriedly put on the gown that she had worn for dinner that evening. It was lying over a chair where Rose had left it so that it could be packed first thing in the morning.

She went to the mirror. Her ringlets curled softly on either side of her face and she pinned the rest of her hair on the top of her head. Then, feeling it was not very elegantly arranged, she pulled a long, white chiffon scarf from one of the drawers and draped it over her head and shoulders before she opened the door.

She half-expected the corridor to be in darkness, but the candles in their silver sconces still lighted it brilliantly. She glanced about her, afraid for a moment that she had been so long in robing herself that he was no longer waiting. Then, from the shadows of a room on the other side of the corridor, he came towards her.

The expression in his eyes made her heart turn over in her breast, and all the miseries of the last hours, when she had wept so bitterly in her pillow, were forgotten.

He took her hand in his.

"Come," he said in a low voice, "we must not be seen."

He drew her down the corridor, walking so swiftly that she found it hard to keep up with him. They passed the top of the grand staircase, and then came to a small, less significant staircase down which Hugo Cheverly led her.

They were now at the back of the Palace,

and at the foot of the stairs was a glass door leading, Camilla guessed, into the garden. It was locked, but Hugo Cheverly turned the key, then put it in his pocket. He opened the door and the warm, still air of the night touched Camilla's cheeks. She looked up at him enquiringly.

"Where are you taking me?" she asked.

"Somewhere where we can talk," he answered. "I must speak with you."

She was content to let him lead her by the arm down a grass glade, turning away from the formal gardens which she had seen from her bedroom window, and winding through flowering shrubs till they came to a place where Camilla realised they were out of sight of the palace.

There was a small fountain surrounded by a yew hedge, in which was set an arbour covered with roses and honeysuckle. Hugo Cheverly drew her past the fountain to where under the fragrant shelter there was a wooden seat. They were not in darkness because the moon rays shone directly on them, and Camilla could see the expression on Hugo Cheverly's face quite clearly as she looked up at him, her eyes wide in surprise.

"What has occurred?" she enquired anxiously.

"Nothing dangerous," he said quickly,

"there is no need for you to be afraid."

"I am not," she answered untruthfully, "I only supposed that something must have happened, something you felt you must relate me."

"No anarchists, no Chinese, no daggers," he smiled, "only the desire to see you alone — to say good-bye."

"Good-bye?" she queried. "But you will be here tomorrow."

"I shall be here," he answered, "but I doubt if you will have time to speak to anyone so insignificant as myself. The Margrave informed me tonight that a troop of his cavalry will escort you from his Palace to the border of Meldenstein, where you will be met by the Prime Minister and most of the civic dignitaries. You will process through the crowds to the capital."

There was a sharpness in his voice, almost of anger. Camilla felt that he looked again at her with that contempt in his expression which she had grown to dread.

"Must it be like that?" she said childishly.

"Of course," he answered. "What else did you expect?"

Despite herself his tone brought the tears back to her eyes. She looked away, but not before he had seen them, and putting up his hand he took her little chin in his fingers and raised her face up to his.

"You have been crying," he said accusingly. "Why?"

She would have turned her face away from him, but he held her captive.

"Why?" he repeated.

"I . . . I was . . . homesick," she stammered.

"Anything else?" he asked.

Her lip trembled but she did not answer. After a second he released her, turning away to stare at the fountain, his face in profile.

"This is madness," he said abruptly. "I should not have brought you here, but I could not bear that we should part without a word of understanding."

Camilla did not speak and after a moment he went on:

"I saw your face when you said good-night, and I knew I could not bring myself to leave you unhappy."

"And if I am . . . unhappy . . . tomorrow," Camilla said in a very small voice, "I shall not . . . be able to . . . tell you about it . . . then."

"That has been your choice," he said, and his face was raw. "Oh, my dearest love, why did this have to happen?"

At his words it seemed almost as though an explosion of light flooded the garden, and Camilla caught her breath. Then she said as she trembled:

"What . . . what did you call . . . me?"

"Hell and damnation!" Hugo Cheverly exclaimed violently. "I love you, you know I love you, and there is nothing I can do about it except get out of your life as quickly as it is possible to do so. I shall leave immediately after the wedding. I would leave before if it would not cause comment. You will never see me again."

"No, why must you say that?" Camilla cried, a sound which seemed to come from her very heart.

He turned then to face her, looking at her hungrily with an expression she had never seen in a man's face before. The moonlight was on her face, making her seem curiously pale, glittering on the tears which still hung on her lower lashes, on the beauty of her parted lips and sudden brilliance of her shining eyes.

"God, you are lovely!" he exclaimed, almost beneath his breath as though he spoke to himself, "lovelier than I believed it possible for any woman to be! And I have brought you here to marry a man you have never seen, a man from all accounts who . . ."

He stopped suddenly, and she saw that he

clenched his hands until the knuckles showed white.

"How can you do this?" he asked. "You of all people."

She looked away from him, knowing that despite every instinct of caution she must tell him the truth.

"I am doing . . . this," she said in a small voice, "because the . . . offer from His Serene Highness saved us all . . . my father, my mother and myself . . . from a . . . debtors' prison."

He stiffened, then he seized her by the shoulder to turn her round to face him.

"It is not true," he said. "You are trying to humbug me. How could such a thing be true? I saw your home myself. I stayed there."

"You saw our house redecorated with . . . Meldenstein money!" she answered. "You saw flunkeys dressed to the part, locals from the village, garden boys decked out in old liveries! You ate food cooked by a chef from London — also paid for by Meldenstein. The performance was put on to trick you, so that they should not know that the bride you have brought so carefully to a new country is really a beggarmaid whom those who worship money would . . . despise if they knew the truth about . . . her."

Camilla paused. Then with a voice that broke on a sob she added:

"Even as . . . you despise . . . me."

"Oh my God, was there ever such a toil!"

He released her and dropped his head in his hands.

"Forgive me," he said.

"There is nothing to forgive," Camilla said quietly. "You could not have known . . . the truth . . . you were not meant . . . to know. Perhaps it is unwise of me to have told you now."

His head came up at that and he said:

"Do you believe — could you credit for a moment that I would harm a hair of your head?"

His eyes rested despairingly on her face as he said:

"Answer me something? If you had not been impoverished; if you had indeed come to Meldenstein without coercion, of your own free will, would you — when I asked it of you in mid-Channel — have let me turn the yacht back? Answer me, answer me true!"

There was no need for her to reply. He saw the answer in her eyes before Camilla said softly:

"You know . . . that I would have . . . begged you . . . to do so."

He looked away from her as if the light in her face hurt him.

"I think I loved you," he said after a minute, "that first moment when I walked into the Salon and saw you standing by the window. The setting sun was on your hair and you looked so small, so exquisite, a creature from another world. It seemed impossible that you would sell yourself for money, as all the women I have ever known have done in one way or another. I tried to hate you, I tried to vent all my loathing and contempt of your sex on you. But I failed, Camilla! You captured my heart so that it was no longer mine, and I could no longer resist you."

"I have . . . loved you longer than . . . that," Camilla said very softly.

"You love me!"

The words were almost like a pistol shot.

"Ever since . . . I saw you . . . on Apollo," she answered, "I have . . . dreamt about you, thought about . . . you, believed that . . . one day I should find . . . you."

"Oh my darling — my dearest love!"

He spoke the words beneath his breath, and then he said:

"I worship you but I dare not touch you. You must understand, Camilla, that if I touched you now I would never let you go.

Whatever the consequences I would carry you away with me. You would belong to me and you would never escape me again."

She felt herself thrill at his words. His eyes were on her lips and she felt as though indeed he were kissing her. She must have swayed a little towards him with the intensity of her feeling, for suddenly he turned away.

"I cannot look at you and not take you in my arms," he said roughly. "Do not tempt me too far, Camilla, for I am only a man and I love you more than life itself. I could kiss you and die. I would be happy to do so!"

"No, you must not . . . say things like . . . that," Camilla said in a frightened voice. "Perhaps one day we shall . . . find each other again. Who knows what . . . the future may hold?"

"Are you content with that?" he asked. "I want you now. I want you as my wife. The thought of another man touching you drives me mad, even though you have not seen him or he you."

"Do not . . . speak of it," Camilla begged. "I was frightened and apprehensive before this journey began, before I met you, before I knew . . ."

She paused.

"Say it," Hugo Cheverly prompted, "say

it for me, Camilla. Remember it is all that I shall have in the years to come — the memory of your words and the expression in your eyes."

"Before . . . I loved . . . you," she whispered.

"And now?" he asked.

"I love . . . you with all . . . my heart," she answered softly. "I did not know that . . . love could be like this! And I do not know . . . how I can face the future when . . . you will not be . . . there."

"When you turned to me last night," he said, "when you were afraid, I felt you trembling against me. You trusted me because you felt I would protect you. I vowed to myself that that was what I would do — protect you from the world. That is why, my little love, we must do nothing that would impair your reputation. That is why, and God knows how difficult it is, I have to protect you from myself."

She drew in her breath and once again he gently lifted her face up to his.

"I want to remember what you look like at this moment," he said, "I want to keep it with me in my heart when I am far away from you. I love you, Camilla, and because I love you I will let you go untouched and unspoilt to another man."

She wanted to cry out that she wanted above all things to be in his arms, to feel his heart beating beneath her cheek, to know that he had the power to waken within her a sudden ecstasy that was beyond description. Then as he released her she could only remain staring up at him dumbly, conscious that there were no words in which to express either her love for him or her fear of what life would be without him.

"Now I will take you back," he said. "If anyone sees us they will think you have come from the gaming-room where they are still gambling."

"Must we . . . go?" Camilla pleaded. "Please let us stay . . . a little while . . . longer."

"My darling," he answered, "I promised to protect you. It was wrong of me to bring you here in the first place, but I knew that I could not face leaving you with the unhappiness I saw in your eyes when we parted this evening."

"I was . . . jealous," Camilla said simply.

"Of Anastasia?" he asked. "Oh, my darling, there is no need. I will not pretend to you, I was wildly enamoured with her before I went with my regiment to the Peninsula. I even asked her to marry me. But she wanted money. Wealth was what counted with Anastasia, and I thought all women were like her."

"Including . . . me," Camilla said in a low voice.

"Including you," he agreed. "That is what hurt me, that is what made me attempt to loathe and despise you as I have learnt to loathe and despise all your sex until now."

"But I think . . . Lady Wiltshire still . . . loves you," Camilla said unhappily.

His lips twisted in a cynical smile.

"My darling, my innocent little love," he said softly, "that is not love. That is something wholly physical that men and women feel for each other, and which often makes life amusing. But it is not love such as I have for you and which I am persuaded you have for me. Let me ask you something. If it were possible, if you would not hurt your father and mother by doing so, would you come away with me now? Would you brave the scandal it would entail, would you face being socially ostracised perhaps for the rest of your life, or would that be too much to demand?"

Camilla did not hesitate.

"I would come now, tonight, if you asked me," she replied. "Do you think the social world means anything to me, or could mean anything besides our love? And as for money, I would be content with you in a cottage. I would be happy to work for you, serve you. Would we want the world outside if we had each other?"

Hugo Cheverly shut his eyes for a moment as though he must shut out the beauty of her face as she spoke, and then he said and his voice was raw:

"That is love, Camilla, but it is not for us."

"I am used to poverty," Camilla said simply, "but I dare say you would be uncomfortable."

"You adorable little goose," he replied, "do you think I have been nurtured on comfort? I can assure you there is not much comfort in Portugal! There is not much comfort either in knowing one has but a pittance to exist on when one moves amongst people with heavy pockets. If only I could swear to you that I could care for your father and mother, perhaps even now it would not be too late. But, Camilla, I have little but a drawer full of debts to offer any woman. I had thought to buy myself out of the Army, but now I shall remain with the regiment and pray that they send us to some outlandish spot where there is fighting. I have a great desire to fight somebody or something at this moment."

"You must not take any risks," Camilla said hastily.

"Would you care if I were killed?" he asked.

"I think I too . . . would want to . . . die," Camilla answered. "Can you not understand that though we shall not see each other, we shall know that the other is there . . . somewhere in the world. There is always the hope that . . . one day some miracle will occur and we . . . can be together."

"Oh my love, when you speak like that it makes me frantic to think that I cannot prevent you going on with this wicked, senseless sacrifice," Hugo Cheverly said. "But what can I do? Once, when the duns were after me, I went to see my cousin the Duke. My father was ill and I could not help him myself, and I believed that my cousin would at least advance me a loan so that I could make my father's last years a little more comfortable."

"And he refused?" Camilla asked.

"He told me that he had no use for impecunious relations, any more than he had any use for decrepit old pensioners."

"What a cruel thing to say," Camilla exclaimed.

"I learnt that he was, in fact, refusing to help the pensioners that my grandfather had always cared for on the Alveston estate," Hugo Cheverly said. "I told my cousin what I thought of his mean, cheese-paring economies. I spoke forcibly and he has never since acknowledged our relationship."

"He sounds despicable!" Camilla said.

"Old friends of my father's contributed to his comfort in the years before he died," Hugo Cheverly went on. "Their kindness was to me a debt of honour, something I have pledged myself to pay back, and which actually I am doing little by little every year. I am only telling you this, my dearest, so that you will understand that I have nothing I can offer you."

"I would not mind for myself," Camilla declared. "But just as you wanted comfort for your father, so I must do everything in my power to provide it for my father and mother. My mother is ill, and what I shall send back from Meldenstein will alleviate her suffering and perhaps enable her to live a few years longer."

"I understand, you know I understand," Hugo Cheverly said, "but that still leaves us — you and me — caught up in the treadmill of this accursed money! While I want to cry out be damned to it, you know there is nothing we can do."

"Except say . . . good-bye," Camilla said

with a little catch in her breath.

She put out her hand and laid it on his. She felt him stiffen at her touch, and then he kissed the palm — a long lingering kiss which made her quiver.

"Somewhere . . . some day . . . perhaps we shall both . . . meet on my . . . enchanted sea," she said, but the tears were running down her cheeks as she spoke and her voice broke on the words.

"That is the only thing which will keep me sane," Hugo Cheverly said, "the thought that perhaps one day we may meet again in different circumstances."

He rose to his feet without looking at her and she knew it was because he did not trust himself any further. Without speaking they walked together back through the garden to the door in the Palace. Hugo Cheverly opened it.

"You had best go up alone," he said, as they stepped inside.

For a moment she did not move. She could only stand looking up at him, her face very white and strained, her eyes dark with pain. They were both very still. It seemed as though something magic flowed between them, something which without words, without their even touching each other, made them invisibly one.

"Good-bye, my sweet, my little love, the only woman I have really found who was perfect and unspoilt," he said.

"I love . . . you," Camilla answered through her tears, "I shall . . . love you . . . always."

She turned without another word and went up the stairs. She knew he was looking after her and thought that if she looked back she would be unable to prevent herself running down again and throwing herself into his arms.

She was aware that not to touch her had subjected him to an almost superhuman strain; so it would be wrong for her to add to the burden he had imposed upon himself. And yet she wanted him so much that her ache for him was already a physical pain, and she wondered dumbly how much the agony would increase in the years that lay ahead.

She reached the top of the staircase and moved silent-footed along the corridor which led to her bedchamber. She let herself in, closed the door and threw herself face downwards on the bed — not to cry as she cried before, but to remember, to feel and to quiver with a strange, bitter-sweet happiness because he loved her, which in itself was a glory beyond words, even though she must lose him.

Downstairs Hugo Cheverly stood for a long time after Camilla was out of sight, still staring up the now empty staircase. He felt suddenly exhausted by the sheer force of his feelings, by the effort of control to which he had subjected himself.

Feeling thirsty he thought he would return to the gaming-room for a glass of wine. Then he knew he could not face the laughing, chattering throng which would still be wagering thousands of gold coins on the turn of a card.

Money! Money! He hated the very sound of it. It was money which was taking away from him the one person who mattered to him in his whole life. It was money that had made him suffer so acutely when he had been infatuated with Anastasia. He thought now how stupidly adolescent he had been to think for a moment that for her his love could ever have been any compensation — even a small one — for the great wealth she enjoyed with her present husband.

"How vulnerable we are when we are young," Hugo Cheverly said beneath his breath, and dismissing Anastasia from his mind, his thoughts were only of Camilla as he climbed the staircase and moved down the now deserted corridor towards his own bedchamber.

Deep in his own thoughts he opened the door of his room, to be assailed by the fragrance of an exotic perfume which he recognised. The door was half open as he paused, realising there was a candle alight by the bed, guttering low but still illuminating the sombre hangings of the big carved four-poster.

He remembered that he had told Harpen not to wait up for him. Harpen would not have left the light burning as he always considered it dangerous. Moreover the scent was unmistakable. Very quietly Hugo Cheverly moved a little further into the room. As he suspected, Anastasia's jet-black hair was spread fan-wise over the pillows. She had obviously waited for him but had finally fallen asleep.

Moving almost silently Hugo Cheverly went from the bedchamber and closed the door behind him. Then he retraced his steps down the corridor. There was, he remembered, an empty bedroom in which he had waited while Camilla dressed. In the morning, if there were any question, he would say that he was so foxed when he came upstairs that he had forgotten where he should be sleeping.

"It is perhaps," he thought to himself, "a retreat in the face of the enemy, but sometimes an open combat is unwise and to be avoided at all costs."

In the empty bedchamber he flung back the curtains and opened the casement. The pale moonlight that he had seen glinting on Camilla's hair gave him enough light to find the bed. He took off his coat and his shoes and flung himself down on it. He doubted if he would sleep: he wanted to think of Camilla's eyes and the wonder in them as she had said softly "I love you".

Camilla also was not asleep. After a while she rose and took off her evening gown and set it back on the chair where Rose had laid it.

She did not think of the morrow or what lay ahead. She slipped between the sheets to think only of Hugo and the words he had said to her, words that she felt were engraved on her heart for all time. At last the dreams she had dreamt for so long now had become reality.

"I love you, I love you," she whispered to herself, and felt as though he could hear her say them.

She must have fallen asleep, because when Rose came to call her she had difficulty in remembering where she was.

"We have to leave early, miss," Rose said. "It is quite some miles to the border and you are to be accompanied by soldiers. Fancy

240

that, miss, just like the King!"

Camilla got out of bed and went towards the washing-stand.

"I expect they will make a terrible dust," she said disparagingly, "and I shall arrive in Meldenstein with a brown face which will not be at all becoming."

"I'm sure they will take care not to do that," Rose said reassuringly. "And now, miss, you are to wear one of your best gowns, the Baroness says, and the diamond necklace that the Prince sent you."

"No!" Camilla said sharply without thinking. "No, I will not wear that."

She saw the surprise in Rose's face and added quickly:

"What does it signify? Yes, of course I will wear it."

"His Serene Highness'll want you to be wearing his present," Rose said reprovingly, "he'll be disappointed if he thought you didn't like it."

"I must remember to express my gratitude for such a magnificent gift," Camilla sighed.

She went to the window and looked out on to the sunlit garden. Was it really only a few hours ago that she had sat in the moonlight and heard Hugo Cheverly tell her that he loved her? Had that been true or had she indeed dreamt it?

She felt herself quiver a little as she remembered the expression in his eyes when they rested on her lips, when he kissed the palm of her hand and when, with that raw note in his voice, he had said that he dare not touch her.

Rose broke in on her reverie.

"Oh, miss, there's no time for dawdling," she said, "we'll all get into trouble if you keep their horses waiting. And what'll they think in Meldenstein?"

"I will hurry," Camilla said obediently.

"What does it matter," she thought to herself, "what happens to me now?"

She had lost the man she loved and she knew he had been right in saying that never again would they be alone together, never again would they be able to talk as they had talked together on the yacht, at the inn where they had lunched without the Baroness, and last night.

"Nothing matters now," Camilla told herself, and permitted Rose to dress her without even glancing in the mirror on the dressing-table.

Only when finally there was a knock on the door did she realise she was wearing a gown of white, elaborately decorated with lace, and décolleté enough to display the magnificent diamond necklace to advantage. On her head Rose had arranged an extremely modish bonnet of white crêpe decorated with tiny white feathers just tinged with pink. It was the only touch of colour with the exception of the very pale pink ribbon which clasped round her waist.

"Come in," she called, rather expecting it to be the Baroness.

To her surprise the door opened to reveal the wife of Herr von Kotze, the Master of Ceremonies to the Margrave.

"Good morning, Miss Lambourn," Frau von Kotze said, dropping a curtsy. "My husband asked me to ascertain if you were ready to depart."

"Yes, indeed I am ready," Camilla replied.

"You look lovely," Frau von Kotze remarked warmly, but the expression on her face was wistful. "There are no gowns to be bought in Westerbalden to equal yours."

"I thought perhaps I was overdressed," Camilla said a little anxiously.

"No indeed!" Frau von Kotze replied. "You will be the cynosure of all eyes, and it would be a pity if they were disappointed by someone drab or dowdy. Queens and princesses should always play the lead at any appearance they may make in public."

Camilla gave a little laugh.

"Except, of course, when a King or a prince is there," she said. "They always outshine us poor females."

"That is true," Frau von Kotze agreed, "and I am quite certain that you will be impressed by His Serene Highness. His decorations are dazzling!"

"I am sure they are," Camilla smiled.

She had a feeling that the Prince, if nothing else, would be pompous and very full of dignity. Her father had said that the protocol at the Palace of Meldenstein was not overpowering, as at some other Courts in Europe, but Camilla was certain that this was the moment when the door of the golden cage in which she had reluctantly agreed to incarcerate herself would close behind her, and the future held no escape.

She thought of the times she had ridden wildly alone over the fields and grasslands at home; when she and Gervase had swum in the lake without permission; when she had climbed trees or played truant from her governess by escaping into the woods and felt an inexpressible happiness because she was alone. All that was finished — in the future she would be confined, chaperoned and, to all intents and purposes, imprisoned.

"You look a real princess, miss," she

heard Rose say. "All you want now is a crown."

Camilla laughed.

"Another shackle, Rose," she said without thinking, "I am quite sure I shall get one."

It was only when she saw the startled, shocked expression on Frau von Kotze's face that she realised how indiscreet her remark had been.

"I am sorry," she said hastily, "I was, of course, only speaking jokingly."

"I will tell my husband you are ready," Frau von Kotze said stiffly.

She curtsied and went from the room. Camilla stood for a moment as if steeling herself for a tremendous effort. Then she moved slowly towards the door. She felt as if she were going to the guillotine.

10

Camilla had only taken a few steps down the corridor when she saw the Baroness hurrying towards her. She had been surprised that the Baroness had not called on her earlier to see if she needed anything or had anything to discuss before they set forth on the journey to Meldenstein.

She thought that perhaps the older woman was still fatigued, but now she saw by the Baroness's manner and by the expression on her face that she was in a state of extreme agitation.

"I must speak to you, Miss Lambourn, in private," the Baroness said breathlessly as she reached Camilla's side.

"Of course," Camilla agreed. "Will you come into my bedchamber. I will send Rose away."

"There is no need," the Baroness replied. "You have a boudoir, we will go in there."

She opened the door adjacent to the bedroom, and Camilla saw a delightful small sitting-room that she had not previously discovered. There were flowers arranged on the tables and she thought it was remiss of her not to have realised that the boudoir had been assigned for her use.

The Baroness shut the door, and Camilla noticed that she was most elegantly garbed in a gown of pale lilac silk trimmed with lace. There were nodding plumes in her bonnet and her long kid gloves matched the whole ensemble.

"I am deeply distressed, Miss Lambourn," the Baroness began, and Camilla, from her appearance, had already seen that this was the truth.

"What has occurred?" she enquired.

"The Margrave sent for me a short while ago," the Baroness answered. "He informed me it was with a perturbation and astonishment that he had learnt that last night, after I had retired to bed, you walked to the garden alone with Captain Cheverly."

The Baroness's words were unexpected, but Camilla managed to receive them without betraying the consternation that they caused her.

"Indeed," she said cooly, "and is there anything particularly wicked in that?"

"Wicked?" the Baroness queried. "I do not suggest it was exactly wicked, Miss Lambourn, but certainly it was exceedingly indiscreet for someone in your position and on the very eve of your arrival in Meldenstein. Of course, I should have been in attendance, and there is no one else to blame, but when I saw you ascend the stairs I was convinced that you were retiring."

"But of course that was the natural thing for you to suppose," Camilla assured her, "and indeed I should have said good night to you. That was most remiss of me. But I had a slight headache and went in search of some lavender water to ease it."

"I blame myself," the Baroness said, "I should have come to your room and asked if you had indeed finished with my services. But, to be honest, Miss Lambourn, I was still feeling indisposed and glad of the opportunity to escape the heat and noise of the Salons."

"And who shall blame you?" Camilla asked lightly. "When my headache had eased a trifle I felt that the one thing I needed was fresh air. If you recall it was very warm last night, and Captain Cheverly was obliging enough to show me the way to the garden. I cannot see there is anything reprehensible in that."

"The Margrave has always been a trouble-maker," the Baroness remarked. "He is certain to carry the story to the ears of the Princess as soon as he reaches Meldenstein. She will be incensed with me for neglecting my duty and I may be dismissed from Court and no longer able to retain my position as her lady-in-waiting. If that happened, my life would come to an end! I swear it, Miss Lambourn, I would no longer wish to live."

Tears gathered in the Baroness's eyes and she dabbed at them pathetically with her handkerchief.

"Pray do not fret yourself," Camilla said gently, "I promise you I will relate to the Princess how grateful I am to you for your kindness and consideration on this journey. There will be no need to make any mention of your indisposition, and I am convinced that the Princess will listen to me rather than to the Margrave."

"I am not sure if she will," the Baroness said miserably. "Oh, Miss Lambourn, how could you have done anything so distressingly unconventional — and in this Palace of all places?"

"I cannot see it is any concern of the Margrave's if I wish to converse with a fellow countryman under whose protection Her Highness has felt fit to place me," Camilla said.

The Baroness shook her head.

"Ah, my dear, you are so young, so trusting and innocent!" she said. "You have no idea how spiteful people can be at Court. They see evil in every action, they hear it in every word that is spoken. How I reproach myself for allowing you to take what you consider an entirely natural and commonplace action but which can be sadly misconstrued by those who wish to cause trouble."

"But why should the Margrave wish to cause me trouble?" Camilla asked.

The Baroness made a gesture with her gloved hand.

"He has always been jealous of Meldenstein," she said. "At this moment, after Napoleon's defeat, it will in most countries on the Continent be considered extremely advantageous if their Prince should wed an Englishwoman."

Camilla smiled.

"You give me a new sense of importance."

The Baroness did not smile back.

"There will be jealousy and envy amongst all the princelings who attend your marriage tomorrow," she said. "You are not only English, my dear, you are also very beautiful."

Camilla had an idea.

"Listen!" she cried. "If I am so important, or will be as soon as the wedding ring is on my finger, I will untangle this skein. Ask Captain Cheverly to attend me immediately."

The Baroness looked aghast.

"I dare not!" she exclaimed. "How can you think of such a thing? It would be most uncomfortable for you to speak to him alone."

Camilla's little chin went up.

"Either I am of some consequence or I am not," she said. "I wish to speak to Captain Cheverly, and the Margrave can think what he pleases. He is obviously a malevolent old chatterbox and I am out of all patience that you should be upset in this manner."

"Oh, my dear, pray consider before you do anything more to flout the conventions," the Baroness begged.

"I am English," Camilla said, "and I am not yet concerned with the conventions of Meldenstein, or, indeed, of Westerbalden. Ask Captain Cheverly to speak to me here or I will send Rose."

Her words threw the Baroness into a tumultuous flutter.

"That would not do, it would not do at all!" she cried. "I will go, I will try my best. But indeed, Miss Lambourn, I shiver with trepidation as to what will be said. They will talk! I know they will talk!"

"Let them talk," Camilla declared firmly.

But already the Baroness had gone agitatedly from the boudoir, and Camilla turned to the window to await Hugo Cheverly. It seemed that fate was not allowing them to part so dramatically or so unhappily. It would be wonderful to be near him again, if only for a few moments, and she felt her heart leap at the thought.

Woman-like, she ran to the mantelshelf to stand on tiptoe and peer at herself in the mirror that surmounted it. Her bonnet, with its pink feathers and silk ribbons, was extraordinarily becoming, and yet as she stared at her reflection she saw her mouth pathetically drooped a little and there were lines under her eyes from her tears the night before.

It was then that some words of her mother's came back to her. Lady Lambourn had been dressing for a dinner party, when she had obviously been in pain from the rheumatism in her leg, and Camilla, seeing her wince as her maid helped her into her gown, had exclaimed:

"You are suffering, Mama! Must you go to this party? You will not enjoy it if you are not in good health."

"Your father would be very distressed if I did not accompany him," Lady Lambourn replied. "Men are always bored with women who are either ill or sad."

"I am sure Papa could never be bored with you," Camilla protested.

Lady Lambourn had smiled.

"Sir Horace was a very handsome man when I married him," she said, "and he still is. He is also, Camilla, a very charming flirt. So many great ladies have cast sheep's eyes in his direction, but he has always disregarded them. If I am not beside him he might find it more difficult to resist their blandishments."

"Oh, Mama!" Camilla had exclaimed, laughing, "what a reputation you are giving poor Papa."

"Poor Papa is no different from any other man," Lady Lambourn had replied. "They are very easily led astray."

"But Papa adores you," Camilla had objected.

"I know he does," Lady Lambourn said, and her eyes were soft, "and I love him very deeply. That is why, Camilla, it is worth while suffering a trifle, and your Papa must never know about it."

"You mean you will not tell him that you are in pain?" Camilla asked.

"Not if I can help it," Lady Lambourn had replied. "As I have already told you,

Camilla, it is something you should re- member all your life: gentlemen like to be entertained, they also like to be the centre of attraction. A woman who is continually harping on her disabilities and striving to evoke their sympathy is a dead bore."

"And you say that a man will also think of a woman as a bore if she is unhappy," Camilla persisted, trying to understand.

"Look round any assembly," Lady Lambourn said, "and see who are the women around whom the men flutter like foolish moths — the gay, the amusing, the witty ones. They may not be beautiful, they may not even be elegant, but if they amuse that is all their attentive males ask of them."

Camilla had remembered her mother's words when she was in London. It was not always the pretty girls who were the most sought after or had the most eligible offers; it was the ones with a gaiety and a *joie de vivre* which imparted itself to those around them.

Camilla had felt herself woefully inade- quate. She found it hard to be amusing when everything was so new and strange, and she did not know of what the Beau Ton were gossiping or with whom she con- versed.

It was only when she returned home from

these parties that she realised how far she had fallen short of her mother's advice. It was one thing to chatter away with Gervase, with her papa, or even the young squires of the neighbourhood; it was quite different to find anything to say when confronted with the bland, bored face of a Tulip of Fashion, and the indifference with which the Dandies condescended to the young girls.

"I was a complete mutton-head!" she told her Mother cheerily. "Not that it signifies! I had no desire to linger in London, finding the dressed-up gentlemen at the assemblies as much a yawn as they found me."

"I cannot believe that either my daughter or your Papa's would ever make anyone yawn," Lady Lambourn had replied, "and I promise you, Camilla, that you will enjoy it more next time."

But there had never been a next time. Lady Lambourn had grown increasingly helpless, and not only were Sir Horace's pockets to let, but the duns were threatening him. Then came the closure of the country banks, and there was not enough money for food, let alone social roistering.

Looking at herself in the mirror now Camilla saw it all pass before her — the unhappiness, the penury and the fear of the future.

"I have got to make the best of things," she told herself.

She spoke aloud. Then, watching herself in the mirror, she put up her chin and forced a smile to her lips, knowing that she did it for the man for whom she was waiting.

At that moment the door opened. Camilla turned quickly. The Baroness entered the room followed by Captain Hugo Cheverly. She saw by the look in his eyes that he was concerned lest something should have gone amiss, and with her new-found courage Camilla said to the Baroness:

"I would speak with Captain Cheverly alone. Would you be obliging enough to wait outside to prevent anyone interrupting us?"

"I should not leave you alone," the Baroness replied, thrown into an immediate agitation by Camilla's request.

"I know that," Camilla said quietly, "and that is why I have asked you to wait in the corridor. Should anyone approach, please join me immediately. I should not wish there to be any further criticism of your chaperonage."

"No, of course," the Baroness agreed, bemused by Camilla's words into thinking that perhaps it was the right rather than the wrong thing for her to wait outside.

"I will do as you ask. I will wait outside," she agreed in a slightly hysterical voice, and going from the boudoir she closed the door.

For a moment neither Camilla nor Hugo Cheverly spoke. Then, with two quick steps, he was beside her, and taking her hands raised them to his lips.

"Is there an upset?" he enquired. "I should not be here; you are well aware of that."

"I expect the Baroness made that clear," Camilla smiled, "but I no longer mind what is said or what is thought. I am determined I will not be crushed by these people."

She saw the question in his eyes and continued:

"We were seen last night. The Margrave has given the Baroness a great scold for having left my side. She imagined, poor woman, that I had gone to bed, which indeed is what I had done before you knocked on my door."

"So the Margrave is interfering?" Hugo Cheverly muttered. "Will he make trouble?"

"That is what the Baroness has informed me he will do," Camilla replied, "and that is why I wish you to speak to him. Not on my behalf! I am not in the least concerned what he thinks about me, but if the Baroness is reported as being lax in her duties she might lose her position at Court. That would be something which we cannot permit."

"We?" Captain Cheverly asked with raised eyebrows.

Camilla dimpled at him.

"After all, it is you and I who have got her into this toil," she said.

"You shall not blame yourself," he said quickly. "It is I who was at fault, as you well know."

"And I was a willing accomplice," she said softly.

He looked down into her eyes and for a moment everything was forgotten. Then, with an effort, he looked away from her and said almost harshly:

"What would you wish me to do?"

"I want you to tell the Margrave that you are extremely surprised that he had not appointed one of the ladies of his Court to be in attendance on me last night. He knew that the Baroness is not young and had been travelling at breakneck speed for two days. It would have been a considerate and natural action for the Margrave to arrange that her duties should be taken over by someone of his own choosing."

She saw the sudden smile dawn on Hugo Cheverly's face.

"Tell him that you realised I was in that nervous, almost hysterical state," Camilla went on, "which is to be expected of any prospective bride. I wanted soothing and needed to be given confidence about the ceremonies which lay ahead, quite apart from the ordeal of meeting a bridegroom with whom I had not yet any acquaintance. Tell him that if it were not for your intervention I could easily have been so afraid and nervous of the future that I might have demanded to be returned to England."

"When did you hatch this little plot?" Hugo Cheverly asked, his eyes twinkling.

"Just at this moment," Camilla replied demurely. "Ingenious, is it not? And do not forget to add that you do not intend to say anything in Meldenstein of his neglect of their future Princess. That will ensure he will not be in a hurry to criticise the Baroness."

Hugo Cheverly threw back his head and laughed.

"I called you incorrigible," he said, "but the word should have been incomparable. There was never anyone like you."

"Do you mean that?" Camilla asked softly.

"You know I mean that," he said, a grim seriousness replacing his laughter. "Oh, my darling, how shall I deal with life without you, for I swear you have made every other woman seem pale and insignificant."

"And how shall I fare when there is no one to laugh with me?" she asked.

For a moment there was a mist before her eyes. Then resolutely she added:

"I have been thinking that perhaps we were both rather faint-hearted last night. We were too ready to accept that everything we cared for was finished and that we had reached the end. I have a feeling — it is a little crazed, illogical and quite without foundation, but nevertheless undeniable — that we should have faith."

"Faith?" Hugo Cheverly asked.

"Yes, faith in ourselves, in our destiny," Camilla replied. "It cannot be for nothing that we have found each other — it must be fate."

"Oh my dearest, if I could only believe that!" he said. "I have been casting round in my mind ever since I left you for some way of escape, some loophole; but I feel as though we were walking into a darkness in which there is no light and only an eternity of emptiness."

"No, No!" Camilla protested. "We must not think of it like that. I know it is wrong of me, but I cannot give up hope — some hope

— that we shall meet again. If I did not believe that . . ."

She paused and knew that with his eyes on her face he was waiting for the end of her sentence.

"If that were so . . . I should want to die at this moment," she finished in a low voice.

"If you speak like that," he said, "I shall take you in my arms and then I swear before God, Camilla, I will never let you go."

There was a sudden wildness in his voice and a look in his eyes that told her she had tried him too hard. Woman-like she knew that she must save him from himself, and with a deep sigh she crossed the room and opened the door.

"Will you come in, Baroness?" she asked.

"We must go downstairs, Miss Lambourn," the Baroness said hastily. "The Margrave will be waiting, and I am apprehensive that we are already late."

Hugo Cheverly had not moved. He was still staring at Camilla, a fire smouldering in his eyes as though he contemplated something desperate. Now the Baroness's words recalled him to his duty. He glanced at the clock on the mantelshelf.

"We are ten minutes late," he said, "which is most reprehensible of us, and doubtless the Margrave will be in a tremendous flip-flap about it. I will make him your apologies, Miss Lambourn, and speak with him on the matter you and I have discussed. I suggest that you wait, for another five minutes."

"We will do that," Camilla said, "and I think a glass of wine would do both the Baroness and me a power of good before we set out on our journey."

"Oh indeed no, Miss Lambourn! I could not think of taking such refreshment at this hour in the morning," the Baroness protested.

But when the bell was answered and the wine brought, she drank a glass without further ado.

"Captain Cheverly will see to everything," Camilla said. "He will speak with the Margrave and I promise you not a whisper of what occurred last night will reach the ears of the Princess. It is all arranged."

"But how have you done it?" the Baroness asked in bewilderment.

"Just a little subterfuge," Camilla replied. "I am beginning to believe, after what you have told me, that I will need all my wits about me if I am to preserve anything of my own identity at court."

"I did not wish to distress you," the Bar-

262

oness said hastily, "or to make you apprehensive. There is no need, I assure you, so long as you conform to the rules."

"That is something I have never been good at doing," Camilla confessed, and she smiled at the elderly woman who looked, in her feathers and frills, rather like a ruffled hen.

"I have a feeling," she said, "that I am not going to be as frightened as I anticipated I might be."

She knew it was love that had given her courage, it was love that made her suddenly less nervous of what this petty little Court might think.

"What right have they," she asked herself, "to criticise or condemn an Englishwoman?"

She had believed herself trapped for all time, and yet already she was thinking that perhaps there might be a possibility of escape. She did not know how or why, it was only that there was an irrepressible hope in her heart as she went downstairs to where her first Royal procession was waiting.

The Margrave's cavalry was a flutter of feathered helmets, flagged lances and jangling harness. The troopers were a brave sight as they rode ahead of the coach, and Camilla could see them trotting round the bend of the drive, the sun glinting and flashing on the colour and high polish of their accoutrements.

The coach in which she had travelled from Amsterdam had, during the night, been decorated with flowers. It was now drawn by six horses instead of four, and the coachmen wore new livery which was dazzlingly colourful.

Camilla found that she was to ride with the Margrave beside her, the Baroness and his aide-de-camp seated opposite them, while Hugo Cheverly was once again on horseback, immediately behind her coach with another squadron of cavalry, followed by several other coaches, one of them containing Lady Wiltshire.

Anastasia had been waiting in the Hall when Camilla came downstairs. While looking extremely elegant in coral silk with a magnificent parure of diamonds and a hat which made every other woman in the procession green with envy, she was obviously in a bad mood. As everyone curtsied to Camilla she made not the slightest effort to do so, and merely remarked:

"If you had been much later, Miss Lambourn, we should have been constrained to think that you were a reluctant bride."

There was no doubt of the acid in her tone as she looked at Camilla, her eyes smouldering, and Camilla could not help wondering whether the Margrave had most indiscreetly voiced his disapproval of what had occurred the previous night before Hugo Cheverly had had a chance to caution him.

"I must express my regret, madam, if my tardiness has in any way inconvenienced you," Camilla said.

Now that Camilla had appeared the Court officials were busy shepherding the party into the coaches awaiting them. Her name had already been called, but Anastasia lingered. She came a little closer to Camilla.

"Leave him alone," she said almost below her breath, but distinctly enough for Camilla to hear the words.

For a moment Camilla was disconcerted. Then with a little smile she turned to the Margrave, who was a few steps away.

"Your Highness, Lady Wiltshire is complaining she must travel alone. I hope that she has been misinformed and that someone will accompany her in her coach."

"But of course," the Margrave replied. "There are four people in every coach, I have seen to that."

"Then Your Ladyship need have no fears," Camilla said kindly, but with a condescension in her voice which she thought to herself was very effective.

Anastasia gave her a look of sheer venom, and walked out from the hall on to the steps. Hugo Cheverly was standing there watching the company enter the coaches, and Camilla saw Anastasia put her hand on his arm. She looked up at him, her lovely face seeming irresistible under the flurry of feathers which surmounted it.

What she said Camilla could not hear, but suddenly she felt as though a dagger had been driven into her heart. When Hugo Cheverly returned to England Lady Wiltshire would be there to see him, to talk with him and entice him as she was trying to do now. And she would be left behind in Meldenstein — a princess in a gilded cage.

For one moment she wanted to cry out at the injustice and the cruelty of it; she wanted to run to Hugo Cheverly to take his arm in hers and defy Anastasia; she wanted to tell her to whom he belonged, to dismiss her so that she no longer had the power to hurt with her barbed words and the hatred in her eyes. And then Camilla knew she could do none of these things: they were waiting for her in the leading coach and the

Margrave was offering her his arm.

With an effort she kept control over her feelings; she even answered with a smile something he said, although she had no idea what he replied. She stepped into the coach and there was a cheer from the courtiers and servants standing on the steps as they drove off. In the roll of the wheels, the clatter of the horses' hooves and the jingling of the harness, Camilla knew that her new life had begun — and there was no escape.

They travelled at a good pace considering the size of the procession. The Margrave talked incessantly throughout the journey, telling interminably dull stories of his respect and admiration for Great Britain, of his plans to reconstruct and improve his country in the future.

His voice droned on and on till Camilla saw that the Baroness sitting opposite her was growing sleepy and that the aide-de-camp, who doubtless had heard everything that was said a dozen times before, had long ceased to pay attention.

She too ceased to listen, reliving over and over again those enchanted moments in the garden, when Hugo Cheverly had told her of his love and she had known how deeply she loved him in return. She wished now that he had forgone his scruples and taken her in his arms. She longed above all things to feel the touch of his lips and she wondered whether, if he were never to kiss her, her regret at never having felt his mouth on hers would be with her all her life.

On and on they travelled. It was hot and dusty until the Margrave sharply commanded the aide-de-camp to shut the windows. Then it was hotter still, and Camilla felt it was almost impossible to breathe. At last, when she felt she might faint from the lack of air, the Margrave said:

"Now we are crossing the border," and she saw a wide river beneath a stone bridge over which they were passing.

"That is our boundary," the Margrave said, "and now, Miss Lambourn, you must be ready to receive the Prime Minister of your new country."

Camilla, as she stepped from the coach, felt that she knew Ludovick von Helm already, he was so exactly like her father's description of him. There was a huge crowd of courtiers and statesmen with him, and she listened attentively while the Prime Minister read her a long address of welcome. Fortunately he spoke in English, and then the company were presented to her.

"They seem rather ordinary," she thought, "just like the politicians of any country." And she felt, perhaps unjustly, that they were shorter of stature than they would have been had they been of British blood.

She was presented with a bouquet, and then, emerging from the seclusion of the place where she had been received, they proceeded through crowds of cheering people to a fine building where she was told that luncheon would be served.

She had a few moments in the retiring-room with the Baroness before the other ladies came upstairs.

"Oh, Miss Lambourn, Captain Cheverly tells me that the Margrave will make no mention of my indiscretion. How can I thank you for your kindness? If there is anything I can do for you, I swear you have but to command me."

"I am so glad that you need not be anxious any more," Camilla said. "It would be a sad beginning to my new life in Meldenstein if my first friend were to be in disgrace on my account."

"Your first friend," the Baroness repeated, obviously very touched. "Is that what I am to you, Miss Lambourn?"

"But of course," Camilla said. "Let me thank you again for your kindness, and please remember that I will rely on you to be my support and help in the future."

Camilla kissed the Baroness, who was overcome almost to tears, and then in the retiring-room they were joined by the other ladies of their company, all shaking out their silks and satins, complaining of the heat and making the air fragrant with the perfumes which they had produced in tiny bottles from their reticules and dabbed behind their ears and on their wrists.

They seemed like a clutter of songbirds. Camilla had eyes only for Anastasia and she found with relief that the Countess seemed too preoccupied with her own reflection in the mirror to have time for anything else.

"Let us go down," Camilla whispered to the Baroness. She was afraid that another encounter with the venomous Russian might find her at a disadvantage.

"Yes of course," the Baroness agreed and raising her voice said: "Pray do not be long, Ladies. Miss Lambourn is desirous of starting luncheon, and I have already been informed that the meal must be curtailed owing to our late arrival."

Camilla fancied she heard someone ask whose fault that was, but already she had turned away, eager to go downstairs, hoping for a sight of Hugo Cheverly.

He was, as she had expected, amongst the

gentlemen drinking in the ante-room, and she thought how handsome and distinguished he looked. He would have been outstanding, she knew, in any company. Here he seemed like a being from another world, and she knew that world was England.

When at last they were seated in the huge hall which had been turned into a banqueting-room, she sipped the wine which was placed before her in a crystal goblet.

She felt it was going to be a long day before finally they reached the palace. It was obvious from the notes that the Prime Minister was consulting that be intended to make another speech, and glancing down the table she guessed that he was not the only one.

She was not mistaken. The meal, which included dozens of dishes, many of them unknown to Camilla, proceeded slowly, and then one after another the statesmen rose to their feet. As the majority of them spoke in a foreign language which she could not understand, Camilla found the hours passed slowly. At last even the audience grew restless; only those who were speaking and who seemed utterly satisfied with themselves and their lengthy orations were entertained.

Finally, the banquet coming to an end,

the company were shepherded towards the doors, and Camilla found that the order of the procession was now changed. An open carriage, so bedecked with garlands of flowers that it was almost impossible to see the vehicle itself, carried her, the Prime Minister, the Baroness and Hugo Cheverly. Camilla was so overjoyed that he was to accompany them that her spirits rose and she managed to make sparkling, gay retorts to the Prime Minister's remarks. It was even enjoyable to wave to the cheering crowds when she knew that Hugo Cheverly was watching her with a look of admiration in his eyes.

There was no chance of their exchanging a word of intimacy, but it was enough to know that he was there. She realised that they must be extremely circumspect, but it was such a comfort to have him near her that she could view Meldenstein with a pleasure and interest of which she would not otherwise have been capable.

It was a pretty enough country through which they were passing — wooded, sparsely inhabited and with a natural beauty that had been sadly lacking in the flat country though which they had passed after setting out from Amsterdam.

The Baroness, following her good lunch,

was drowsy; the Prime Minister, having made two speeches, was not as talkative as he might otherwise have been; so Camilla, after the first mile or so, found it unnecessary to make any particular effort at conversation. She was content with stealing a glance every now and then at Hugo Cheverly, feeling as she did so that they were so close to each other in their thoughts that it was almost as though he held her in his arms.

The crowds of sightseers grew thicker and now there were houses on either side of the road. Finally they entered the capital.

There were arches of flowers and flags. "Welcome to the Bride" was inscribed on banners overhanging the roadway or on the houses, or even chalked on walls or bridges. Many of the women in the crowds were in national costume, and Camilla admired their heavy full skirts gathered round the waist, their black velvet bodices over blouses with huge puffed sleeves. They had starched lace and muslin caps with streamers and many of them wore pretty lace aprons and carried children dressed in the same manner like little dolls.

The cheering grew louder as the crowds increased, and Camilla's arm was getting quite tired from waving when finally the

Prime Minister said:

"There is the Palace ahead of us."

She saw huge ornate gilded gates through which the horses passed a few seconds later. Then they were drawn along a drive bordered by magnificent formal flower-beds with a dozen marble fountains throwing their water, iridescent in the sunshine, towards the sky.

Beyond was the Palace, an enormous building of white stone, the front ornamented with balconies, carved palisades and an immense flight of stone steps on which were grouped a large company of people in brilliant uniforms, elegant gowns and glittering jewels.

For a moment Camilla found it difficult to take it all in. There were statues on top of the Palace; hundreds of glass windows shining in the sun; garlands on posts and poles; and flags, which included the British, were fluttering everywhere.

For a moment she felt afraid: it was all so grand, so overwhelming. Then she looked at Hugo Cheverly and felt her fear evaporate. He had told her she had courage, that she would always do what was right under any circumstances. Well, she would not fail him now!

She gave him a little smile, and regardless

of what the Prime Minister might think she bent forward and offered him her hand.

"I would like to thank you, Captain Cheverly," she said formally, "for escorting me on my journey here. You gave me every consideration, as did the Baroness, and I am extremely grateful."

"It has been a privilege, ma'am," Captain Cheverly replied in even tones, but she felt the pressure of his fingers on hers.

She longed above everything to cling to him, to beg him not to leave her. But even as she looked at him with pleading in her eyes, the horses turned to bring the carriage alongside the steps where the company was waiting.

Camilla felt her lips go dry.

"Now I shall see him," she thought, "now I shall meet for the first time the man I am to marry, the man who will be my husband."

The carriage door was opened. Hugo Cheverly alighted to stand stiffly to attention as Camilla, the light rug taken from her knees, moved forward and was helped by a flunkey on to the red carpet which covered the steps.

She realised that hundreds of eyes were staring at her curiously, and because she was shy she lowered her own as she walked step by step up to where she knew someone was waiting for her.

It was only when she reached the last step that she looked up. An extremely handsome woman was standing with her hand out-stretched. She was not wearing a hat, Camilla noticed, but on her grey hair spar-kled a resplendent tiara. Row upon row of pearls encircled her neck, and many orders and decorations were pinned on her breast.

Camilla sank down in a deep curtsy. Then the Princess, drawing her to her feet, bent and kissed her on both cheeks.

"Welcome to Meldenstein, my very dear daughter-in-law-to-be!" she said. "This is a very special occasion for us all, and I wel-come the daughter of my old friend Sir Horace Lambourn, for whom I have always had a deep affection."

"Thank you, ma'am," Camilla managed to say in a very small, shy voice.

"And now," the Princess said, "you must meet Hedwig, my son, the ruler of Meldenstein and your future husband."

For the first time Camilla looked at the man standing beside the Princess. She saw a white uniform covered with a multitude of jewelled decorations, before apprehensively she raised her eyes to the Prince's face.

It was then she drew in her breath sharply, so sharply that she was half-afraid that it was audible to those standing around her. Prince Hedwig was not in the least what she had expected. He looked old — very old and ill.

11

The long procession of people filing past Camilla seemed endless. The stentorian voice of the announcer somehow deadened her mind so that she could think of nothing save the extended hand, the automatic smile, the murmured "Thank you" to the congratulations, all of which she had to repeat afresh as each of the notabilities was presented.

"Der Baron und Die Baronin von Luckdenner. Der Margrave und Die Margravine von Bassewitz. Der Comte und Die Comtesse de Maubeline . . ."

The names jangling in her mind created a pattern represented by the tall, the short, the fat, the thin, the old, the young, all having one characteristic in common as they went past — eyes goggling at her curiously as if she were some exhibit in a zoo.

After the first quarter of an hour Camilla got used to the conventional bow of the gentlemen and a perfunctory bob from the ladies. She realised she was not yet being accorded the Royal curtsy — that would doubtless come after tomorrow's ceremony — but they swept to the floor for the Princess and again to Prince Hedwig, and she could not help thinking that for some of the older women it was a remarkably ridiculous posture.

There was a little pause in the proceedings while a guest, unable to walk without two sticks, held up the ceremony. Camilla turned to her future bridegroom.

"My hand is already fatigued," she said brightly. "I wonder how many more guests are to be greeted."

He glanced down at her. Then in a chill, flat voice which was somehow repellent he replied:

"Shaking hands is a barbarous English custom. One should never be obliged to touch a stranger."

The answer was so rude that Camilla stared at him in astonishment, for a moment at a loss for words; but before she could think of anything to say the announcer's voice had started again.

"Der Baron und Die Baronin von Bigdenstein."

At last, when it seemed to Camilla that she would go on shaking hands in her sleep, the procession of guests ended, and now the Princess escorted her through the reception rooms, pausing every so often to speak to some chosen acquaintance and present them once again to Camilla.

The Prince walked behind them, making little effort, Camilla noticed, to speak to anyone or to make himself pleasant. She wondered if this was his usual behaviour or whether he had perhaps taken an instant distaste to her personally. She could not help feeling that he rather than his mother should have taken the initiative and presented his subjects to her, but it was obvious from the very first that the Princess, as she had anticipated, was the dominating character.

Camilla found it quite irritating that while she was still wearing the gown in which she had travelled, the Princess was arrayed in what appeared to be Court regalia, bejewelled, tiaraed and looking not only wonderfully impressive but extremely handsome. She must, Camilla thought, have been very lovely when she was young. Simultaneously she felt with a sudden droop of spirits that perhaps in thirty years' time people would be saying the same of her when she was performing the same type of duty for one of her children.

As they moved from room to room, Camilla realised that many of the guests present were not privileged enough to be greeted personally by their Royal family. This impression was confirmed when, as they reached the third Salon, the Princess said in a low voice:

"The townspeople. We need only speak to a few of them."

Camilla thought on the whole these looked more interesting and more alive than those of noble blood; but after a brief word with the Mayor and several Aldermen, who were obviously extremely gratified at being presented to her, the Princess led the way through two huge carved doors. Camilla found they were now in a long corridor with flunkeys stationed every six yards, but without any more guests in sight.

The Princess turned briskly to her son.

"Now that ceremony is over, Hedwig, we can go to the Drawing-Room, where I am sure Camilla would like a cup of English tea."

"I regret I cannot accompany you, Mother," the Prince replied with the same flat voice which made him sound as though he were only half-alive.

A little frown appeared between the Princess's eyes.

"I thought that was what we had arranged," she said, and there was no mistaking the note of irritability in her voice.

"I regret it is not possible," the Prince replied. "Nevertheless I will escort you to the Drawing-Room."

The Princess, pursing her lips, flounced ahead, obviously extremely put out. They entered a room which overlooked the garden. It seemed to Camilla enormous, but the Princess said:

"This is my own private little sitting-room. As you see, it contains many personal treasures and many photographs."

There was indeed a great number of them, Camilla noticed, ornamenting the piano, the side-tables and the mantelshelf. Many were framed in silver surmounted by a crown, and on most the donor's signature was written across the corner.

At a table in front of the hearth was a sparkling array of silver, which was typically English. With a hint of nostalgia Camilla observed the tea-pot, kettle, milk-jug, sugar basin and, of course, the locked tea-caddy, just like her mother used at home.

Looking round the room again she realised how very English everything was. The Princess might rule Meldenstein, but it was obvious she had not become anything other than British in her taste and her affections. Camilla lost a little of the awe and warmed towards her future mother-in-law.

"How delightful all this is!" she exclaimed, and was rewarded by a smile from the Princess.

"Come, Hedwig," she coaxed her son, "change your mind, sit down with us, if only for a brief while."

"I have already told you, Mother, I have made other arrangements."

"In that case it is unlikely that you will see Camilla again."

"We shall meet tomorrow," he said indifferently, speaking directly to his mother and not even glancing at Camilla.

She looked at him curiously. He certainly looked far older than the age he was reputed to be. He must at one time have been extremely good-looking in the Germanic way that she could see repeated in the portraits of what were obviously his ancestors round the walls. They all had square heads, fair hair, which in Prince Hedwig's case was now turning grey at the temples, and pale, somewhat cold blue eyes.

Strangely enough in Prince Hedwig, his eyes — or was it only his pupils? — seemed extraordinarily dark. It was hard to tell; for his eyelashes were very fair and his eyes, as he talked to his mother, seemed to be half-closed as though he were sensitive to the sunlight coming in through the windows.

It was the colour of his skin that was so strange, Camilla decided. It was sallow to the point of yellowness, and she wondered if he had contracted a fever while he was out in the East which had not only changed the shade of his complexion but given it the dried-up parchment appearance which was so definitely ageing.

She had drawn off her gloves as she listened to the Princess talking to her son. Now, with a click of his heels, Prince Hedwig bowed, lifted his mother's hand towards his lips and turned to Camilla.

"We shall meet tomorrow," he said formally, taking her hand and raising it as he bowed. His fingers were almost ice-cold.

"It was like touching a corpse," Camilla thought, and with difficulty prevented herself from shuddering.

Then without another word the Prince turned on his heel and walked from the room. Camilla looked after him in astonishment. She was just about to speak when the Princess's voice, soft and soothing, said:

"Come and sit down, my dear child. I must apologise for Hedwig, but he is very overwrought. He has had a great deal to worry him these past weeks, there have been so many preparations to make for your marriage."

Camilla took a deep breath and said bravely:

"You must forgive me, Your Highness, but are you convinced that His Serene Highness is really desirous of making me his wife?"

The Princess put out her hand and drew Camilla down beside her on the sofa.

"My dear," she said, "I know only too well what you must be feeling. I am really out of all patience with Hedwig, but he is very shy. He finds it hard to express himself in public. When you are alone you will find he is a very different person."

"Surely we shall meet again before to-morrow?" Camilla said. "How can we be married knowing we have hardly exchanged a word with each other?"

"I assure you it is best that way," the Princess said complacently. "When I came here from England I never even saw my husband until we met at the altar steps, and yet I lived extremely happily with him until he died."

"What I asked, Your Highness, was whether the Prince is really anxious for this marriage to take place?" Camilla insisted.

The Princess busied herself with opening the silver tea-caddy and spooning the sweet-scented tea into the silver pot.

"My son," she said after a moment, "has expressed to me in most ardent terms his desire not only to be married but to marry you in particular."

She closed the lid of the tea-pot with a little snap and continued:

"He had, of course, a very wide choice of brides, but you were the girl he wanted from the very moment he heard of your charm and your attractions."

"But who can have told the Prince about me?" Camilla enquired.

The Princess gave a little laugh.

"What a sensible girl you are," she said. "I can see you are not only intelligent but that you have a delightfully frank and open manner which will endear you from the very start to your subjects."

The Princess poured the tea into a cup.

"Now, what will you have with it," she asked, "milk or lemon?"

"Lemon please," Camilla said quickly, trying to concentrate on the conversation which she felt somehow was important.

"You have not told me the name of your informant, Your Highness," she prompted.

The Princess laughed again.

"Your persistence shall be rewarded," she said. "Not only have I many friends and relatives in England, but when the Army of Occupation came to our little country a short while ago, there were many English officers to relate that you were the prettiest girl in England! Now having seen you I know that they spoke the truth."

Camilla looked down at the cup of tea in her hand. The Princess was lying: there was no one in the Army of Occupation who would have spoken of her. But what could she do about it?

As if she realised what Camilla was thinking, the Princess chatted away light-heartedly about the Palace, the people Camilla had already met at the reception and the splendour and the magnificence of the hospitality which was arranged for the morrow.

"We will sit down two hundred person-ages for luncheon," she said. "Mainly rela-tives, of course, with the exception of the rulers of our neighbouring states, and after-wards you and Hedwig will process through the streets. I will not spoil the surprise of what has been prepared for you by telling you about it now. But I assure you, my dear Camilla, you will be entranced by the fore-thought and the warmth of our people. Their delight that the Prince is to be mar-ried is touching. I know that you will soon grow to love them as he does."

Camilla very much doubted if Prince Hedwig loved anybody, but of course it was impossible for her to say so.

The Princess brought out photographs showing her son as a baby, as a small boy and then as the young man whom Sir Horace had liked and who in those days undoubtedly had not only good looks but charm. There were pictures of him laughing with his friends on the steps of the palace, there were pictures of him shooting, riding a spirited horse or driving a four-in-hand. It was hard to recognise in the carefree, light-hearted young Prince the pale-faced, ageing man who had greeted her so coldly on her arrival.

Camilla was debating with herself whether she dare ask for a postponement of the marriage until she had had further conversation with her future husband, when the Princess rose to her feet.

"I expect, child, you are tired after your journey," she said. "It is important that you should rest because you will find tomorrow strenuous in the extreme. I suggest that you now retire to your bedchamber and lie down. Dinner will be at 7.30 p.m., a small meal with only myself and our closest relatives. My son will, of course, have his bachelor party as is traditional."

She touched a little silver bell lying on a side-table. Instantly the doors opened and two elderly women, obviously ladies-in-waiting, came bustling into the room.

"Will you accompany Miss Lambourn to the bridal suite, Countess?" the Princess asked one of them.

"It will be a pleasure, Your Highness."

The lady-in-waiting swept to the floor and Camilla, realising what was expected of her, curtsied very low to her future mother-in-law. As she rose, the Princess bent to kiss her cheek.

"You and my dear son will be very happy together," the Princess said. "I have no doubts on that score, and indeed I shall pray for you both."

Camilla was escorted upstairs to an enormous room. She had a quick, rather terrifying impression of a colossal gold-canopied bed draped in blue brocade and covered with priceless lace. It was raised on a dais and seemed to occupy almost the whole of one wall of the room. There were cupids carved on the canopy, cupids on the gold gilt tables on either side of it. In fact all the furniture in the room was gilt. There were huge mirrors festooned with flying cupids and cupids intertwined with hearts formed the pattern of the needlework carpet which covered the floor.

"A very beautiful room — is it not?" the Countess asked in broken English.

"It is delightful," Camilla replied, trying to force some enthusiasm into her voice.

At any other time she knew she would have been full of admiration for such a decorative bedchamber, but now she could only think of the man with whom she was to occupy it.

"Your boudoir is next door," the Countess said, "and there is also a small room containing a bath. Fancy a room for bathing! When I first came to this palace we had never heard of such a strange idea."

"It is truly magnificent," Camilla agreed.

She looked up in relief to find Rose entering the room carrying some of her clothes over her arm.

"I expect you desire to rest," the Countess said. "I will attend you, Miss Lambourn, five minutes before dinner so that you can be in the ante-room before Her Highness appears."

"That will be very kind of you," Camilla said.

The Countess curtsied and withdrew. Camilla waited until she had shut the door, then looked at Rose.

"What do you think of it all?" she asked, her voice uncertain and worried.

"Oh Miss, it's ever so strange and you'll never believe it," Rose replied, "but what do you think I sees just now in the corridor as I came from the servants' quarters?"

"I have no idea," Camilla answered. "What did you see?"

"A Chinaman," Rose told her.

"A . . . China . . . man!"

Camilla found it hard to pronounce the words.

Rose nodded.

"With a pigtail," she giggled, "a long pigtail, miss . . ."

Dinner was so interminably long that Camilla was half afraid she would fall asleep from sheer boredom. It was indeed, as the Princess had told her, an intimate party. It consisted of eight people, most of them so old that Camilla wondered how they could ever have reached Meldenstein, let alone expect to take part in the ceremonies the next day. They were all aunts or cousins of Prince Hedwig's and they ate very, very slowly, speaking when they were not eating in cackling, high-pitched voices which made their foreign language sound even more unintelligible than it would have been anyhow.

When they said anything of importance the Princess translated it to Camilla. Otherwise she appeared to find them as dull as Camilla did and contented herself with giving her future daughter-in-law a long and glorified account of the splendours of Meldenstein and the bravery of her late husband's ancestors.

There was one cousin who could speak English. She was a spinster of about seventy who spoke of the marriage in such a coy manner that it made Camilla squirm to listen to her.

"I expect, Miss Lambourn, you are wishing that your handsome bridegroom were here beside you," she said to Camilla with an archness which made every word seem an intrusion.

Camilla felt this called for no answer, and anyway before she could reply the Princess said sharply:

"Hedwig has his bachelor party tonight."

"You have been misinformed," the cousin replied, delighted to be first with the news. "I hear that your naughty Hedwig has refused to have one! Cousin Rudolph was extremely incensed not to have been invited, but when he enquired Hedwig said he had no interest in such out-of-date tom-foolery."

There were cries of protest from the other guests and the Princess looked angry.

"Hedwig is of course of an age when he can employ his time as he thinks best," she said acidly.

"But not to have a bachelor party with all his men friends is against all tradition," the cousin persisted. "Perhaps he would rather have been here with his pretty bride. Did you invite him?"

The Princess rose at the head of the table.

"If you have all finished," she said, "I suggest we should withdraw to the Salon. Camilla has had a long day, it is best that she should have an early night in preparation for tomorrow's festivities."

"She must certainly look her best for the wedding . . . and the honeymoon," the cousin giggled.

Camilla followed the Princess thankfully from the room. At the foot of the Grand Staircase she was allowed to say goodnight and accompanied by one of the ladies-in-waiting to proceed to her bedchamber.

It was not many minutes past nine o'clock, Camilla noticed, and as Rose came hurrying in response to an instruction that must have been sent her, she said:

"Come back in half an hour, Rose. I will write to Mama before I go to bed. There will certainly be no time on the morrow."

"No indeed, miss," Rose answered. "Would you wish to change your gown?"

"No, I will not trouble to do so," Camilla answered. "I will go to bed as soon as I have finished my letter. I saw a *secretaire* in the boudoir, I expect it will contain writing paper and quills."

"Yes indeed, miss," Rose answered. "After you had descended to dinner the housekeeper looked to see if there was everything you would require."

"I am glad the Palace is so well run," Camilla smiled. "I cannot imagine how I would begin to cope with such an enormous place."

She opened the door which led into the boudoir, then paused and looked back.

"You have not seen the Chinaman again, have you, Rose?" she asked in a low voice.

"No, miss, not a sign or sight of him," Rose answered quickly. "Perhaps I was mistaken, the corridors in the servants' quarters are none too light."

There was something in the way the maid spoke, and the manner in which she turned her head away so that Camilla should not see her face, which showed all too clearly that she was prevaricating.

Suddenly Camilla felt there was no point

in pursuing the subject. What did it matter if there were Chinamen or any other Orientals in this big Palace with its rude, unapproachable Prince and his dull, boring relations? Would she have to sit night after night at meals such as she had endured this evening — or worse still be alone with her husband?

She felt herself shiver at the thought, as she recalled his voice which had repelled her with the first words he spoke, the coldness of his hands, the strangeness of his eyes and the dark hollows under them.

"He must have been gravely ill," she told herself. "Why cannot his mother be honest and say so? She must think I am a nitwit to be taken in by all that chatter of how much he loves the people and how he is shy only where I am concerned."

She told herself she did not believe a word of what the Princess had said, then considered despairingly if there was any point in not believing her. There was no one she could turn to, no one with whom she could discuss it.

She knew that even to think of Hugo Cheverly was dangerous. All through the evening she had forced herself not to recall consciously the times they had been together, or the words he had said to her the night before. But she knew that she was only pretending to herself. He was a part of her, he was inescapable. With every breath she drew he was present in her mind.

She sat down at the *secretaire* and wondered if she dare write to him. She could see the words forming before her eyes on the white paper surmounted with the crown of Meldenstein.

"My darling . . . my love . . . how can I live without you?"

How could she write such things? It would be an offence against all propriety, and yet her heart cried out for him.

Then came a sudden knock at the door. Camilla stiffened and then, almost hoping against hope, she wondered if her need for Hugo Cheverly had brought him to her. Could it be that in some miraculous way he had managed to escape surveillance and come in search of her?

The knock came again, and now she forced herself to say in a normal tone as she rose:

"Please enter."

The door opened slightly. The tapers in the chandeliers were unlit and the boudoir was lighted only by the candles on the secretaire. For a moment Camilla thought she must be dreaming as into the room came a small, dark woman in the stiff, heavily embroidered robes of a Chinese. Then she saw that in the dark, high-coiffured hair there sparkled the ornamental combs which she knew indicated someone of high rank.

The thought flashed through her mind that this was perhaps one of the visitors attending the wedding. In a strange silence the Chinese woman looked Camilla up and down with a close scrutiny which was positively insulting. Her enamelled face was expressionless. It seemed to Camilla standing voiceless and embarrassed that she exuded an aura of evil.

"You wished to see me?" she faltered, despite herself considerably frightened at the woman's silent and insolent appraisal. The black slit-eyes looked at her enigmatically. She was answered in English, but the high sing-song voice was oriental.

"His Serene Highness asks for you. Come."

"Now?" Camilla questioned.

"At once."

Camilla put down the quill pen she still held in her hand.

"I thought His Serene Highness had a bachelor party?" she remarked, merely for something to say because she was wondering whether she should or should not obey this strange summons. The Chinese woman had come to her room certainly without the knowledge or the approval of the Princess.

"Come!"

The Chinese woman beckoned, and Camilla felt it was impossible to refuse such a command. She found herself wishing that one of the ladies-in-waiting were with her. Then she told herself that she was being ridiculous. Her future husband had obviously changed his mind and wished to converse with her before the ceremony tomorrow. There was indeed no reason why, as if they were children, they should ask his mother's permission to meet.

The Chinese woman led the way down the corridor. They walked for some distance and Camilla guessed that the Prince's apartments were in a special wing.

They came eventually to a huge door, outside which were two sentries. The Chinese woman walked past them without a glance. They stood to attention staring straight ahead of them. The woman knocked, when instantly the door swung inwards and Camilla saw that the servant who opened it was also Chinese.

She stepped inside and could hardly check

298

herself from exclaiming aloud. The place was decorated in Eastern fashion. The walls were black, there were strange coloured hangings, huge gilded Chinese dragons, and pervading it all the fragrance of incense. There was very little light, only an occasional torch set in a wrought-iron holder.

Another door now faced them. The Chinese woman stopped and stood once again staring closely at Camilla, at her hair, her face, her breast, her feet.

"Now you will see the man you would marry," she said at length. The tone of her voice was so horrible that Camilla knew she had been right: this woman was evil!

She wanted to turn and run away, but it was too late. The door in front opened silently and she saw that inside it was lighted only by two great candles at the far end of the room.

Seated between them on a dais was a man wearing mandarin robes, his hands hidden in the wide embroidered sleeve. Somewhere a gong boomed. Camilla stood there astonished. Then gradually she found it easier to see in the dimness and recognised who sat there. It was the Prince!

"You sent for me?" she asked, and even as she spoke her voice sounded very small and lost.

The incense seemed almost overpowering. In the dimness she saw a movement at the side of the dais and realised it was a Chinaman. There were several of them kneeling in the shadows, their slit eyes watching her.

"They are going to kill me," she thought in sudden terror and wanted to run to Hugo Cheverly.

The very thought of him brought back her courage. She would not show her fear, she would not be intimidated by the Prince or by the Chinese woman who had brought her here. She walked forward across a soft rug, which made her steps noiseless, until she reached the dais. It was then, as she almost reached him, that the Prince rose to his feet.

"How dare you approach me without permission?" he cried. His voice was no longer flat and lifeless as it had been when he spoke to her before; it was now deep and strong, rough and brutal.

Instinctively she stopped, staring up at him in perplexity. He seemed immensely tall; his eyes were no longer black but alight with a strange fire and his whole face seemed transfigured. She saw there was a mandarin's many-folded hat on his head, which gave the impression of a dark crown and made him seem almost satanic.

"I am your King, your Emperor," he shouted, his voice echoing round the room. "You may not move without my command, you kneel in my presence. Kneel!"

It was an order and he pointed to the ground at his feet. But Camilla stood looking up at him, making no effort to obey.

"I am Camilla, your future wife," she said. "Do you not recognise me?"

She felt he must be in some sort of trance to speak to her in such a manner.

"I recognise you," he replied. "You are a woman and you will obey. Down on your knees, you are in the presence of your master."

"This is ridiculous," Camilla answered, a sudden feeling of anger sweeping away her fear. "I have no intention of kneeling to you or to any man. If you wish to speak to me I will sit down and talk to you, otherwise I shall retire."

"You will obey me."

This time he did not shout, the words were almost spat at her. He snapped his fingers and to Camilla's horror suddenly two Chinamen sprang one from each side of the dais. They took her by the arms and forced her down on her knees. She had no time to struggle against them, she was too astonished. When she was kneeling they took their hands away from her arms, but they did not leave her side. Instead they stood sentinel on her right and on her left.

"How dare you let these men touch me! How dare you treat me like this!"

"Bow your head," the Prince commanded.

Now, looking up into his face, she realised he was mad. Only a madman could have spoken in such a manner, only a madman could have eyes shining like balls of fire, a face that was somehow contorted out of human recognition.

"I will not," Camilla replied, and she knew as she spoke that she was defying not only an order to bow her head but the man himself; a man, terrifying, awe-inspiring, whom she had come from England to marry; a man who was crazed and no fit husband for any woman.

She saw the fury in his face as she spoke. Afterwards she was not quite certain what happened. She thought it was the woman who put the whip into his hand, she knew the two Chinamen standing by her side had fallen flat on their faces and then she felt the long lash of a leather whip, such as the Egyptians might have used on their slaves, crack through the air and catch her across her bare shoulders.

The suddenness and the agony of it took away her breath. Then the lash came again and she screamed. With a terror that was beyond thought, she now saw him towering over her. He dragged her to her feet, and while one hand held her helpless, the other pulled at her gown as if he would tear it from her. She struggled and screamed, but she was powerless. She was in the grip of a maniac. As she thought fearfully he would strip her naked she heard a quiet voice say:

"That is enough — for tonight."

It was the Chinese woman who spoke. The Prince at once released her, letting her slip from his clutches as if she were a puppet. She fell to the ground and her terror and horror must have made her momentarily lose consciousness. When she opened her eyes again neither the Prince nor the Chinese woman were in the room.

With her breath coming sobbingly between her lips she scrambled to her feet, feeling dizzy and light-headed. She knew the Chinamen were watching her, but she could see no one and no one moved as she staggered across the room, holding her torn dress across her breast. The first door opened without her touching it. She went down the passageway and the man who had let her in opened the outer door.

When she found herself once again in the lighted corridor she started to run. Sobbing with fear and pain she sped towards her own bedchamber, meeting no one on the way. Only when she opened the door to find Rose standing by the dressing-table did she collapse on the floor, conscious that she could go no further.

"Oh, miss, what has happened? What have they done to you?" Rose cried.

It took a moment or two for Camilla to force her voice from between her lips.

"Go and fetch . . . him," she sobbed, "bring him here . . . to me . . . whatever they may say . . . whoever may try to . . . stop you."

"Do you mean Captain Cheverly, miss? But I cannot leave you like this."

"Go now . . . quickly . . . Rose. Tell him that he . . . must come to me . . . at once."

"Please let me help you first," Rose pleaded.

"No! Go . . . go!" Camilla cried in panic.

The maid ran from the room, and after some minutes Camilla dragged herself from the floor to sit on a chair. She felt so faint she knew she dare move no further. She sat with her head down, feeling waves first of faintness and then of nausea sweep over her as she waited — and waited.

The agitation in her breathing was easing a little when she heard a sound, not at the door but at the window. Instantly she stiffened. Could this be some other danger to threaten her? Then the curtains parted end Hugo Cheverly came into the room.

"This is madness," he said, "but I understood from the message I received that it was desperate . . ."

He stopped suddenly. Camilla rose shakily to her feet and he saw her white face and torn dress. Then, before he could speak again she was in his arms.

"Take me . . . away," she sobbed, clinging to him in desperation and with a terror in her voice such as he had never heard before. "Take me away . . . take me home . . . He is crazed . . . and I . . . cannot marry . . . him . . . take me . . . home before it is too . . . late."

Hugo Cheverly's arms tightened round her.

"It is all right, darling," he said quietly. "Tell me what has upset you. How can anyone have reduced you to this state?"

She dropped her head against his breast and when she did so he could see the terrible weals across her naked back caused by the leather whip.

"The Devil take it!" he exclaimed furiously. "Who has done this to you? I will kill them for it!"

"No . . . no," Camilla wept, "take me . . . away. I cannot stay . . . here. He is not . . . human."

Hugo Cheverly picked Camilla up in his arms, carried her across the room and set her down against the soft pillows of the great bed.

"Listen, my darling," he said, "you must try to tell me what has happened."

In a broken voice, stammering over her words and still trembling from the shock, Camilla told him what had occurred, but all the time she clung to him, her fingers holding desperately to the lapels of his evening-coat.

"The Prince is . . . mad," she finished.

"No, drugged," Hugo Cheverly corrected her. "Oh my God, that you should have gone through this! I should have taken you away the moment I learnt of it."

"You knew?" Camilla ejaculated.

"Not that he was in the state you have just described," Hugo Cheverly answered, "but at Meldenstein last night they laughed about his — Chinese harem."

"The Chinaman . . . at the inn!" Camilla whispered.

"The woman is his mistress and I can understand that she wishes to be rid of you," Hugo Cheverly said. "It must have been of her planning that this occurred tonight."

"And they told you . . . that . . . he takes . . . drugs?" Camilla questioned.

"It was hinted at," Hugo Cheverly replied, "enough to make me worried and apprehensive. But how could I act on such scanty information and what could I do?"

"You will . . . take me . . . away?" Camilla said with a catch of her breath.

"Yes, I know I must do that," he agreed. "But you understand that we run a great risk? For my part it does not matter, I would die willingly for you, Camilla — but if they catch us they will not kill you."

"Then I shall kill . . . myself," Camilla whispered, "for I could not . . . live under such . . . circumstances."

"No, no, I see that," Hugo Cheverly said, "but now we have to be clever. Whatever happens we must not be seen."

"You will take me . . . away . . . at once?" she pleaded.

He bent down and kissed her on the mouth. For a moment she was too astonished to respond. Then she felt a sudden flame wake within her body and she clung to him, knowing that all that mattered in the world was that he loved her.

"Are you strong enough, my darling, to face what lies ahead?" he asked as he released her. "God, if anything should happen to you!"

"Nothing will," she whispered, "as long as I am with you."

He turned his eyes away from her as if with an effort.

"There is much to be done," he said sharply.

He opened the door of the bedroom and beckoned to Rose, who Camilla saw was standing outside.

"How did you reach me?" she asked.

"From the balcony," he said, "I could not be seen entering your bedroom. As we learnt at Westerbalden, everything that happens in a Palace is seen."

"But the balconies are not connected," Camilla objected.

Hugo Cheverly smiled.

"I jumped," he said. "It is something at which I used to excel at Eton."

"You might have killed yourself," Camilla gasped.

"But I did not," he answered. "Now, listen to me, Rose. Go and find Harpen. Tell him I must have two fast horses saddled immediately. He must somehow contrive that they are ready when we reach the stables. As you go, look to see who is about and if your mistress is likely to be seen as she goes down a back stairway."

"There are very few people about, sir," Rose answered. "There is a party tonight for all the Palace servants and, I believe, for most of the stable-hands."

"Then luck is our way," Hugo Cheverly said. "Go, Rose, and when you return take your mistress to the bottom of the third small staircase leading off this corridor. By chance I came up that way tonight and I know it leads to an outer door through which we should be able to reach the stables."

"You will meet us there, sir?" Rose enquired.

"I will be there," Hugo Cheverly answered, "and now hurry, girl, there is no time to be lost."

Rose disappeared.

"Put on a riding-habit," Hugo Cheverly said to Camilla. "Can you dress yourself?"

"I have always managed to do so," Camilla replied with a little laugh.

She felt suddenly alive and happy beyond expression. She was going away with the man she loved, and she knew with the surety of the faith which she had spoken of the night before that somehow they would escape the terror and the evil she had found in the Palace.

"I will be waiting for you," he said, "but make all haste!"

She had risen from the bed and now he swept her into his arms and held her tight. He did not kiss her, only looked down into her face, his eyes searching hers.

"I adore you," he said very softly. "Tell me that you are mot afraid to go away with me."

"I am only afraid to stay behind," Camilla answered. He pressed his lips to her forehead, then walked towards the window.

"Take care," Camilla begged him, "oh, my love, take care."

He turned and smiled at her, then he was gone. For a moment she could not move, waiting with a kind of sick horror for fear that she should hear a sudden cry as a body slipped and fell from the balcony. But there was only silence, and she ran to the wardrobe and started frantically to seek the riding-habit which had been one of the items in her trousseau.

She was dressed by the time Rose returned. Instead of wearing the smart velvet hat with its coloured plume which went with the habit, she had tied a dark chiffon scarf over her fair hair, pulling it forward over her forehead so as to hide her face as much as possible.

"Have you found Harpen?" she asked Rose as the maid entered the room.

"He was not surprised, miss," Rose answered. "He had warned me that he had heard no good of the Prince."

Camilla did not answer. What was the point of speaking about it now?

"Harpen will bring you home, Rose," she said. "You will find gold in my reticule."

"Yes, miss, do not worry about me. Mister Harpen will look after me."

"And leave the diamonds behind," Camilla said as Rose opened the door.

"Move quickly, miss," Rose said urgently. "There is no one about. They are all adrinking themselves under the table downstairs and singing songs as gay as crickets."

"Let us pray that no one sees us," Camilla murmured.

She did indeed pray as they moved swiftly down the corridor, passing first the grand staircase and then two others, until they came to a narrow flight of stairs dimly lit by only an occasional taper.

There seemed only silence and darkness when they reached the bottom, and Camilla felt a sudden constriction in her heart in case something had gone wrong. Then a figure moved in the shadows. She put out her hands to him with a little cry of gladness.

"The horses are there," Hugo Cheverly said in a low voice. "Harpen has told the stable-boys that they are needed by the Margrave, who desires that one of his aides-de-camp should escort a sick lady-in-waiting back to Westerbalden in case she infects the guests during the wedding."

"A clever story," Camilla said.

"Let us hope they will believe it long enough for us to get away," Hugo Cheverly said.

Camilla took his arm.

"Good-bye, Rose," she said softly, "and thank you."

"God speed, miss," Rose replied.

It was quite a long walk round the wing of the Palace and then over the cobbled stones which led to the stableyard. Hundreds of horses were stabled there and innumerable carriages belonging to the visitors were drawn up down the centre, there not being enough shelter for them all.

At the far end of the yard Camilla saw two saddled horses waiting. She would have quickened her pace had not Hugo Cheverly said quietly:

"Not so fast, remember you are ill."

"Yes, of course."

There was only an elderly groom and two stable-boys in attendance on the horses, and Harpen hovering anxiously in the background, saying nothing because he knew he must not be heard speaking English.

It was in their own language that Hugo Cheverly thanked the stable boys and gave the groom a piece of money. Then he lifted Camilla up on to the saddle and mounted his own horse.

She noticed he had changed his clothes and wondered how, in his superfine grey whipcord coat and polished boots anyone could mistake him for anything but an English gentleman. But she guessed that the stablehands were not too bright and they certainly did not seem particularly curious or interested in the two foreign guests who had dragged them away from the festivities, to which they would now doubtless return.

Hugo Cheverly led the way slowly out of the stable-yard and then down a back drive from the Palace.

"We must not travel too fast," Hugo Cheverly said warningly. "We do not want to draw attention to ourselves. There is nothing more arresting than a man and a woman galloping together as though all the fiends in hell were after them."

"I feel as though they were," Camilla murmured.

It was fortunate that Hugo Cheverly had been in Meldenstein before. He seemed to know how to avoid the main streets, which were crowded with people staring at the decorations or already taking their places on the roadside so as to have a good view of the morrow's procession. Instead they twisted and turned down narrow alleys until finally they were out of the city.

"Now for the fields," Hugo Cheverly said, "And then we can give the horses their heads."

Camilla felt the wind on her face and pushed back the scarf she had worn over her hair. The heat of the day had passed; there was now a delightful freshness and fragrance in the air, and the light of the moon, not yet at its full height, made it easy for them to see where they were going.

"We have escaped!" she cried. "We have escaped!"

"Not yet," he answered soberly. "We have a long way to go, but I swear to you that if it is humanly possible I will get you to England."

His words were almost lost in the thunder of the horses' hooves as they tore over the soft grassland. Then, as they rode neck and neck, he looked at her and cried:

"I love you, Camilla! Damn it, you were right! This must have been fate!"

12

They reached the river which was the boundary with Westerbalden in about two hours. As they reined in their sweating horses Camilla said:

"The bridge is on our left. I can see the flares."

"I think we would be unwise to use the bridge," Hugo Cheverly answered. "We must try and ford the river lower down."

"Surely they will not yet have discovered we are missing," Camilla exclaimed.

"We cannot be sure of that," Hugo Cheverly replied. "When a flunkey approached me to say that Harpen wished to speak to me urgently I was in conversation with the Margrave. I saw a look of curiosity on his face, and when I do not return he will be certain to enquire what was the reason for such urgency. After what happened at his Palace he will suspect I am with you."

"Do you think they will come at once in search for us?" Camilla asked in a frightened voice.

"Yes! Unfortunately that is one thing we can wager will happen," Hugo Cheverly replied grimly. "Come, we must not waste time."

He turned his horse downstream and Camilla followed. Soon they came to a place where the banks were not so steep, and he reined in his mount.

"To cross here will undoubtedly mean that the animals will have to swim. But we must get clear of Meldenstein. Cling to your pommel, you must not fall — the current is strong."

Camilla had never ridden across a river before, but she was horsewoman enough to be able to coax her animal into the water and then cling tightly, as Hugo Cheverly had suggested, to prevent herself from being swept away.

Fortunately the horses could not have been entirely inexperienced at this sort of exercise, for they reached the other side without much difficulty. Camilla and Hugo Cheverly dismounted to squeeze the water from their clothes, and the animals shook themselves dry.

"We must not linger," Hugo Cheverly said almost sharply. "I calculate we should ride on for about two hours. Can you manage it?"

"Of course I can," Camilla said proudly, determined he should not think her weak or failing under the strain.

The cold water had refreshed the horses, and they set off at tremendous speed. The going would have been dangerous had it not been for the light of the moon, and it was only after nearly two hours hard riding that the sweating beasts began to slow their pace. Hugo Cheverly drew up in a small wood.

Camilla was glad when he lifted her down from the saddle and she was suddenly experiencing an overwhelming weakness. For a moment he held her close, then he busied himself in undoing the girths and taking the saddles from the horses' backs.

"Are we going to stay here long?" she asked as she pulled off her boots.

"I have an idea of how we can obtain fresh mounts," he replied. "I noticed when we came this way from the Palace that there was a large posting inn. Many of the guests travelling to Meldenstein will have changed their horseflesh there."

"Surely it will be dangerous for you to go to the posting inn?" she asked.

"The horses will be out to grass," Hugo Cheverly replied with a smile. "I was always told a fair exchange was no robbery."

"You mean you will leave these horses in exchange for two other fresh ones!" Camilla exclaimed. "But suppose someone sees you?"

"That is a risk I must take," he replied.

He sat down beside her under a pine tree and pulled off his riding-boots in turn to empty the water from them.

"I think it will be safe," he said, "to make you a small fire, and then when I have gone you can dry out your riding-skirt. It would not help to have you down with a fever."

"I have been wet before," Camilla answered with a smile.

"You are wonderful!" he said softly. "At the same time you have to be strong enough to endure this ride. It will tax the strength of a man, let alone a frail woman."

"You will not find me failing," Camilla said gently.

He took her hand and raised it to his lips. She felt herself quiver at his touch. Then, remembering what lay behind them, she said: "We are in dire danger, are we not?"

She knew he would answer truthfully, and he replied:

"If they catch us they will take you back, and that is something which cannot be contemplated."

"What will happen to you?" Camilla enquired.

"As I am a British subject," Hugo Cheverly answered, "I will undoubtedly suffer a regrettable accident."

Camilla shuddered and clung to his hand.

"We must not be captured," she whispered. "Where shall we be safe?"

"In the British Embassy in Amsterdam," he answered. "It is a long way, my little love."

"It will not seem so long if we are together," Camilla answered.

He kissed her hand again, this time his lips lingering passionately first on the palm, then on her wrist, where her pulse beat beneath the little veins which showed blue against the whiteness of her skin.

"Can we be married in Amsterdam?" Camilla asked softly.

"You know that is what I want above all things," Hugo Cheverly replied. "Have you thought what it will mean, my darling? I have nothing to offer you, there is also your father and mother to be considered."

"They will understand," Camilla said passionately, "I know they will understand. They love me, they would not wish me to be subjected to the insane fiend who struck at me tonight. Why, oh why is he like that?"

"I have been wondering myself," Hugo Cheverly answered. "Perhaps the explanation lies in the fact that the Prince must always have resented the fact that his mother is the dominating character in his life. Even when his father was still alive she was virtually the ruler of Meldenstein. His resentment of her must have festered, and then when be went to the East he found how completely a man can assert his mastery over an Eastern female. You saw his mistress. I dare say she loves him in her own way, for it must have been she who sent one of her race to the inn to murder you so that you would never arrive in Meldenstein."

"Did you not suspect that the Chinaman might have something to do with the Prince?" Camilla asked.

"I had heard vague stories of his deterioration after his sojourn abroad," Hugo Cheverly replied, "which was one of the reasons why I tried to hate you, my darling, when I believed you were selling yourself to him."

There was a little pause and then he added:

"That was something I found impossible to do, as now you well know."

"When did you suspect the truth?" Camilla persisted.

"I learnt at Westerbalden from the Margrave that the Prince had an oriental mistress," Hugo Cheverly continued, "but I still do not credit that he personally was involved in the plan to murder you."

"Perhaps he was not," Camilla said, "yet I believe he would do anything when he is in the condition he was in tonight."

"It must have been the Chinese woman who taught him to take drugs," Hugo Cheverly said. "To suit her own ends she would have pandered to the worst instincts within him — a Germanic desire for dominance over those who surrounded him. She would have also fostered his unborn contempt for women and his desire to humiliate them."

Camilla felt herself tremble.

"Thank God . . . you could rescue . . . me!" she stammered. "What otherwise would . . . my life have . . . been?"

"Do not let us think about it," Hugo Cheverly said, rising to his feet, "it is something we must leave behind us. Let me make you a fire."

He kindled one in an open space round which the pine trees stood sentinel. Then, taking the bridles of the two horses in his hand, he turned to smile at her as she sat watching him.

"I will not be long," he promised.

"Take care, I beg of you to take the

greatest care," Camilla implored him. "If you do not return in a short while I shall be distraught."

"I will return," he said confidently as he led the horses away.

Camilla took off her riding-skirt and set it near the fire to dry. She had already emptied the water from her boots and now she placed her wet stockings near the flames. The petticoat she wore under her skirt was only damp at the hem and she dried that by holding it near to the fire and then put it on again.

Still waiting for her skirt to dry, she lay down on the soft moss-covered ground, and almost before she had settled herself her eyes closed and she fell asleep. The events of the past forty-eight hours, the emotional strain and now the exertion of four hours' hard riding had taken their toll.

She was still fast asleep when Hugo Cheverly returned. In the light of the fire she looked very young and very innocent, almost a child, with her fair hair in disarray and her hands crossed over her breasts.

There was a reverence in his eyes as he looked at her which no woman had ever seen. Then gently he knelt down beside her and kissed her lips. She responded almost without waking and then, as she opened her eyes, found that he was holding her close.

"My darling, we must go," he said, and his voice was deep with emotion.

"You are back!" she exclaimed, and he saw the sudden joy in her eyes.

"I am back and we must set out while there is still moonlight," he urged, resisting an impulse to hold her close and to tell of his love.

Almost roughly he helped her to her feet. She looked around her drowsily.

"I must have . . . fallen asleep."

"It will have done you good," he smiled. "Dress yourself quickly."

"Oh my skirt!" she exclaimed in confusion, and blushed to think he should have seen her in her petticoat.

"I will not look," he promised with a smile on his lips. "I have plenty to occupy my attention."

He started to saddle the horses. When finally they were ready he heard Camilla say:

"I have not kept you waiting?"

"No," he replied, "you are the most punctual woman alive. You will make a very exceptional wife on that count if on none other."

She laughed as he swung her up on to the saddle, and at once they were off again. The horses were fresh and had obviously not been used the day before. Camilla thought that her mount had a touch of Arab in it. It had certainly been expertly schooled, and she liked the way it responded to the slightest touch of her hand or the spur of her boot.

The moon was fading and dawn was just creeping up over the horizon. It was a warm, fresh day and Camilla could not help wondering what the crowds lining the streets in Meldenstein would feel when they learnt that the wedding would not take place. Would there be consternation in the palace? She wished she had instructed Rose exactly what to say. Then as she worried about it she felt sure that her remissness must have been remedied by Hugo Cheverly, who would have told his valet to speak for both of them.

They had been riding nearly three hours before Hugo Cheverly drew in his horse and pointed to a small farm nestling among trees in an apparently isolated spot.

"Dare we ask them for breakfast?" he suggested.

"I was just wondering if I would sound a frail woman if I informed you I was hungry," Camilla replied.

"I am ravenous," he admitted. "Come on, we must risk it. I cannot believe that,

325

even if the Meldenstein cavalry have caught up with us, they are likely to find us here."

It was about a mile to the farm, and when they arrived Hugo Cheverly made the woman understand what he required. They were taken into a large kitchen, where there was a well scrubbed table and the flags on the floor were spotless. There were big pans on the walls and long strings of onions hanging from the ceiling. Soon there was the delicious aroma of eggs and bacon frying in a pan held over the open fire.

"I do not think food has ever tasted so good," Camilla said, watching the man she loved stowing away half a dozen eggs accompanied by innumerable slices of lean ham.

There followed the dark brown bread which the peasants baked for themselves and golden butter with which to finish off their meal. Although their hostess was obviously delighted with the coins that Hugo Cheverly gave her, Camilla felt no recompense was enough for the enjoyment they had both had from the simple but excellent fare.

On again, and now Hugo Cheverly would allow no rest until, when the sun was high in the sky, they stopped at a farmhouse for another meal.

This time they were not so lucky. The food was indifferent, the farmer surly and inclined to ask questions. Camilla gathered that he disliked foreigners. He had fought for Bonaparte, and what he had suffered in the Army was, he believed, directly the fault of those who had prolonged the war by preventing the French armies from being victorious.

"An unpleasant fellow," Hugo Cheverly said as they left the farm and cantered on.

He had explained to Camilla, who had not understood what was being said, how the man had ranted against the privations his country had suffered, but was not incensed against the man who had caused the suffering.

"I thought they all hated Napoleon," Camilla said.

"Not all," Hugo Cheverly replied. "Many admired him tremendously for his courage, and for the fact that for a very long time he was the victor. Everyone likes to be on the winning side, they all hate being the loser."

"I loathe war and everything connected with it," Camilla said. "You will not stay on in the Army, will you?"

"There is a very easy answer to that," he replied, "I could not afford it even if I wished it. Not with an extravagant wife to support."

"I am not extravagant," Camilla began hotly and then realised he was teasing her. "You will not mind leaving?"

He shook his head.

"I ask for nothing but to be with you," he replied. "I will strive to find some employment for which I will be recompensed, but, God knows, when we reach safety we shall have to do some hard thinking."

"I have been thinking too," Camilla said. "Papa and Mama will have enough money to last them to the end of the year. Papa told me that before I left. I do not think that even he will expect us to give back to Meldenstein the ten thousand pounds they advanced for my trousseau."

"No indeed," Hugo Cheverly replied, "but Sir Horace may take a little persuading. Even on my short acquaintance with him I could see he was a man of tremendous integrity and honour."

"I will not let him return it," Camilla said determinedly, "And anyway, Mama will persuade him to do what is sensible — she always does."

"And do you think you will have the same influence over me?" Hugo Cheverly enquired.

She flashed him a smile which seemed to unite them for a brief moment, but there was no time for further conversation. They were off again, too tired to speak to each other, and their horses were flagging visibly.

It was then they came in sight of another Posting Inn. This was after they had passed the Dutch border, where Camilla felt, with an inexpressible relief, that tomorrow they should reach Amsterdam. They had dragged on because Hugo Cheverly was determined to find another inn. Having located this one he left Camilla, as he had done before, hidden in a small spinney. This time, however, tired though she was, she did not fall asleep.

She sensed instinctively that the man she loved was in danger, and she sat almost holding her breath until he returned. When he did so she started up with a glad cry and ran towards him.

"I was frightened — I was frightened you would not come back!" she cried, and then gave an exclamation of horror.

There was blood on Hugo Cheverly's face, and the knuckles of his right hand were bleeding.

"I was seen," he said simply, "and I had to give a man a leveller. You may be sure he will be warning the countryside. Come, we must push on."

He saddled the fresh horses which he had purloined and they were off again, Camilla listening as they rode for the sound of pursuing hooves, shouts or even a bullet whistling past them.

They must have ridden for an hour before Hugo Cheverly brought his horse to a standstill and turned his head in the direction from whence they had come. There was only the quiet of the night, and after a moment he said:

"I think perhaps we may have given them the slip. You must rest a little; this strain is too much to expect of any woman."

"I can go further," Camilla assured him.

He did not reply but found a haystack in an empty field and insisted that she lie down.

Her whole body was aching with fatigue and the weals from the whip the Prince had used on her felt like red-hot bands round her shoulders. Even so she fell asleep instantly. It seemed to her as though she had only just closed her eyes when she felt his hand on her shoulder and realised it was dawn.

"We must be away," Hugo Cheverly said.

Still dazed with sleep, Camilla found herself in the saddle. The horses he had procured the night before were not as good as those on the previous exchange; nevertheless they were of robust stock and covered the miles well. On . . . on . . . on . . . until finally, to Camilla's relief, they stopped and watered the horses in a winding stream.

"We dare not risk going to a farmhouse for breakfast," Hugo Cheverly said. "Our pursuers may not be far behind. Are you very hungry, my love?"

"I will not think about it," Camilla smiled, and then she pointed to the ground. "Look, there is our breakfast!"

Peeping from between their green leaves were a profusion of wild strawberries. Dismounting at once they ate avidly, finding the fruit ripe and sweet, and unexpectedly satisfying.

"If I do not find you something substantial to eat," Hugo Cheverly said as he lifted Camilla on to the saddle, "you will grow so light that you will float away from me. Can you really endure to go on for a few hours until I feel we are out of danger?"

"Yes, of course," Camilla promised bravely.

At the same time she was thankful when Hugo Cheverly decided they could stop at a small inn situated in a tiny hamlet some miles from the main highway.

"I cannot believe last night's enemies or the Meldenstein cavalry will find us here," he said.

The proprietor was impressed by the obvious quality of his guests, even though they looked exceedingly dishevelled.

When Camilla went to the bedroom to tidy herself she exclaimed with horror at her appearance. Her face was dusty, her hair in disarray and her habit caked with mud and dust. She washed herself as quickly as she could, combed her hair and curled her ringlets, while the landlady, wondering at the rich velvet of her habit, brushed it until it was restored to some semblance of its former glory.

She cast Camilla many curious glances, and it was a good thing the woman could not ask questions. Anyway Camilla was too hungry for conversation and in a desperate hurry to repair downstairs to the private sitting-room where what appeared a sumptuous repast had been prepared on Hugo Cheverly's instructions.

They both ate until laughingly Camilla confessed she could not manage another morsel. They had been too famished even to talk while they were eating, and now Hugo Cheverly lay back his chair, a glass of wine in his hand.

"You look as though you have stepped into an assembly," he said. "How can you perform such a physical feat as you have just endured and yet look as though to pick a few flowers would tax your strength to the utmost?"

"Do I really look like that?" Camilla answered. "I assure you in reality I am very tough. I could always outride my brother, and when we used to walk miles over the countryside, which Mama considered very unladylike, I swear that he was more fatigued than I at the end of the day."

"It is that training which is standing you in good stead now," Hugo Cheverly said. "Oh my darling, had it been too much for you I would never have forgiven myself!"

"We are not in Amsterdam yet," Camilla said warningly.

"We have only another twenty-five miles to do," he replied. "The innkeeper has promised us a change of horses. Lord knows what sort of beasts they will be, but he swears they will be fresh. Would you prefer that I hire a cart and take you along the roadway?"

"You must be crazed," Camilla said. "You have said yourself the cavalry may be searching for us. Come, how can we linger here?"

"I am only ashamed of asking you to do too much," he said. "If you should collapse, I should be most blameworthy."

"Let us press on," Camilla urged. "I will not feel safe until I hear English voices and know that in the Embassy I am on English soil."

"Come then," he said, rising from the table and holding out his hand to her.

She took it and got to her feet. Then as if driven by some compulsion which moved them simultaneously she was in his arms. She put her head against his shoulder and he bent to find her lips. For a moment everything was forgotten, except the wonder of his touch and the feeling that she belonged utterly and completely to him.

"I adore you," he said, his voice deep and moved.

Their lips met and clung, then Camilla tore herself from his arms and they went out of the farm to the horses.

The pace was now unavoidably slower. The horses moved in the steady manner to which they were accustomed, however much they were coaxed or even given a touch of the whip.

It was as the afternoon wore on that Camilla began to feel a terrible exhaustion creeping over her. She had not dared confess to Hugo Cheverly how greatly her legs and back ached, since it was long since she had been in the saddle.

When her parents had become so poverty-stricken the horses had been sold, and in the stables there had been only an aged nag which carried messages to the village. It was far too old and too slow to be ridden, and Camilla had realised when she first mounted the horse at Meldenstein how terribly out of condition she was when it came to riding.

Now she knew it was only determination which could keep her from falling from the saddle. As on and on they rode, it seemed to her that the flat green fields interspersed with silver canals were endless. Suddenly, fearing that she could keep her seat no longer, she let the reins go loose on the horse's neck and clung to the pommel as she had done when they had forded the river.

Hugo Cheverly, realising what was happening, rode closer to take her horse's reins and lead the animal beside his own. Camilla did not protest; she only sat wondering how long she could endure fighting with every nerve in her body not to fail the man beside her at the last moment.

It was then, raising her eyes with an effort, that she saw a flash of blue and felt that it revived her like a sip of champagne.

"The sea!" she tried to say, and she knew that her throat choked with dust could not say the words.

"We are there!" she heard Hugo Cheverly cry.

Now she managed to take the reins in her hands as they clattered over the cobbled stones of Amsterdam.

Though it was only a short way to the British Embassy, it seemed to Camilla like a hundred miles, until suddenly they were outside the great porticoed front door and Hugo Cheverly had swung himself to the ground. She felt unable to move, as though she had been turned into stone, and as he lifted her down into his arms, her legs were numb and her hands dropped limply at her sides. He carried her up the steps past the surprised flunkeys into the hall.

"I wish to see the Ambassador at once," he said to the Major-domo. Then looking down at Camilla's white face and closed eyes added: "No — show me first the way to a bedchamber."

Camilla was only half-conscious, but she was aware that he was carrying her upstairs. She knew that she was now safe and that the strength of his arms was a protection that took away all fear. She felt him lay her down on the softness of the bed. Then, as his arms left her, she would have cried out to him to stay, but still she could not speak.

It was some time later that she found a glass of cognac being held to her lips, and the sound of water told her that a warm bath was being prepared. She opened her eyes to find herself attended by an elderly maid and two younger ones.

"Drink this, ma'am," the elderly woman said in English.

Camilla swallowed obediently and felt the fiery liquid rush down her throat to revive her and to bring her back to an awareness of her surroundings.

"I . . . am . . . sorry," she managed to say.

"Now, ma'am, there be nothing to be sorry about," the maid replied. "His Lordship has asked me to look after you. I understand you've had a long ride. You'll be stiff, ma'am, and a hot bath is what you need."

"I . . . am sure . . . it is," Camilla agreed. "It was stupid of me . . . to collapse at the . . . last moment, but I just felt as if my legs did not belong to . . . me any more."

"Another sip of brandy, ma'am," said the English maid in the tones of a nanny who expects to be obeyed without question and who knows exactly what is good for her charge.

337

Camilla drank what was given her, sipped the hot broth which was produced a few minutes later, then sank into the bath, which the English maid told her contained a special medicinal salt from one of the French spas.

"Her Ladyship always uses it after a long day," she said.

"I must thank Her Ladyship," Camilla said. "I can feel the stiffness going as I sit here."

"Her Ladyship is in England," the maid explained, "only His Lordship is in residence. He will be waiting downstairs to see you, ma'am, as soon as you feel better."

Camilla remembered who would be with the Ambassador and felt new life and energy coming back to her. She insisted on getting out of the bath as soon as she had washed, and permitted one of the younger maids to dry her with a soft, warm towel because she felt it would be quicker.

"Where are my clothes?" she asked.

"I have taken the liberty, ma'am," the elderly maid replied, "of providing you with one of the gowns belonging to Her Ladyship's daughter. She is about your size, and there is a deal to be done to your riding-habit before it will be possible for you to wear it again."

"That is most considerate," Camilla said, then gave an exclamation when the maid went on:

"His Lordship explained you were to be married, ma'am. This is most suitable for a bride."

"It is lovely!" Camilla cried, knowing that the dress of pure white silk, its puff-sleeves trimmed with Valenciennes lace to match the three frills round the skirt, became her greatly.

There was a knock at the door and one of the younger maids brought Camilla a bouquet of camellias. The older woman translated what the bearer had said.

"With His Lordship's compliments, ma'am!" she smiled. "They are his special favourites. Her Lady can seldom coax one out of him!"

"How kind, how very kind!" Camilla murmured.

The maid took three of the camellias from the bouquet and arranged them high on her head like a tiara. They gave her an ethereal nymph-like look, and she was as young and fresh as Persephone bringing in the spring.

"You make a beautiful bride, ma'am!" the maid exclaimed when she had completed her task, and her words were echoed in the admiration shining in the eyes of the two younger maids.

"Thank you," Camilla said, "but now I must make all possible haste."

"One moment, ma'am," the maid interjected. "There is a necklace of rare pearls which Her Ladyship's daughter always wore with this gown. I know she would wish you to wear it today."

"Oh no, I could not presume to borrow any more," Camilla protested.

"You'd not want the gentlemen to see you looking anything but your best, and I would be sadly lacking in my duty, ma'am, if I did not contrive to make such a lovely young lady as yourself truly presentable before you go downstairs."

Camilla smiled and made no further protestations. The necklace did show off the rounded perfection of her neck and the whiteness of her skin. She certainly longed for Hugo Cheverly to see her looking radiant. They had been through so much together yet now she felt suddenly a little shy of him.

It had been easy to speak intimately, even passionately, when they were in danger of their lives; but now they had returned to the English way of living and she remembered with some embarrassment how forward she had been in so blatantly declaring her love, and yet — she loved him with her whole heart!

There was a flush on her cheeks denoting the quickened beating of her heart as she went downstairs carrying her bouquet. A flunkey who was obviously expecting her opened the door and she found herself in an elegantly decorated Salon where Hugo Cheverly, washed, shaved and like herself attired in new and elegant borrowed clothing, sat talking with an elderly man.

They rose at her entrance and while Camilla dropped her eyes a little uncertainly before the look on Hugo Cheverly's face, she found herself smiling at the Ambassador, who took both her hands in his.

"My dear Miss Lambourn," he said, "I am indeed glad to find you are not further incapacitated by this terrible journey about which Captain Cheverly has been telling me. I have an acquaintance with your father and I am only so exceeding glad that you have reached here in safety."

"I must thank you for your hospitality, Your Excellency," Camilla replied, "and for the beautiful flowers you sent me."

"Now I must talk to you, my dear," the Ambassador said, drawing her near to the fireside and sitting down beside her on a sofa. "Captain Cheverly has asked that you should be married immediately. My private chaplain is here and the ceremony can take place as soon as you wish. But first it is beholden upon me to explain something to you."

"What is that?" Camilla enquired apprehensively.

"It is my duty," the Ambassador replied, "to point out the consequences which will inevitably occur if you marry, as I understand you wish to do, Captain Hugo Cheverly."

"What consequences?" Camilla asked in a frightened voice.

"You see, my dear," the Ambassador said, obviously a trifle embarrassed by what he must say, "the world is a very censorious place. It loves scandal, it is always prepared to distort or misrepresent the truth."

"What are you trying to say to me?" Camilla asked.

"You came to Europe," the Ambassador continued as if she had not interrupted him, "to marry His Supreme Highness the Prince of Meldenstein. From what Captain Cheverly has told me you are entirely within your rights in refusing to go through with a marriage which could only have been disastrous to your health and to your self-respect. If you return to London and tell your father what has occurred, he will be able to drop a few discreet hints in the right places about the situation in Meldenstein. On that score I feel sure that there could be no scandal, no censure of your withdrawal at the last moment from this marriage which is now so clearly unsuitable. In fact you will command the sympathy of all who learn what has occurred."

"I am sure Papa will understand," Camilla murmured.

"I too am convinced of that," the Ambassador agreed. "But on the other hand, Miss Lambourn, if you marry Captain Hugo Cheverly now, then a very different construction may be put — in fact will be put — on your action in leaving Meldenstein."

"You mean," Camilla said in a low voice, "they will think we . . . ran away because we . . . loved each other?"

"That, of course, is what I am trying to say," the Ambassador said. "The world is a hard place to live in when you are socially ostracised, Miss Lambourn. I would not be fulfilling my responsibilities to any British subject, especially to your father's daughter, if I did not explain to you what this action will entail."

"What he means, my darling," Hugo Cheverly said, speaking for the first time since Camilla entered the room, "is that if I were a person of consequence then all would be forgiven. But you will be marrying, Camilla, a penniless, unimportant young man who has quarrelled with his more respectable relatives and has nothing to offer you but his heart."

Camilla looked at him and the light in her eyes made both men draw in their breath.

"That is all I want," she answered. "Do you think anything else counts with me? I wish for one thing only — to be your wife."

The Ambassador smiled and put his hand on her shoulder.

"There is no need for me to say any more," he said. "I will send for my chaplain. There is only one thing I would add. Since you arrived a detachment of the Meldenstein cavalry has encamped outside the Embassy."

"They cannot touch us?" Camilla asked apprehensively, putting her hand out instinctively towards Hugo Cheverly.

He took her fingers, which were trembling, in his warm grasp.

"No, not while we remain in the Embassy," he said.

"Have they asked for me?" Camilla enquired, looking at the Ambassador.

"They informed me that they were here to escort Miss Lambourn back to Meldenstein," he said. "I have a feeling that they may depart when they know that there is no question of Miss Lambourn marrying their Prince since she has become Mistress Hugo Cheverly."

"Then let us be married quickly," Camilla begged.

"There is one other matter of which they informed me," the Ambassador said.

"What is that?" Camilla enquired.

"They are at this moment laying at the Town Hall a charge against one — Captain Hugo Cheverly."

"Of abduction," Hugo Cheverly suggested, finishing the Ambassador's sentence.

"On the contrary," he replied, shaking his head, "the charge is one of horse-stealing."

"Horse-stealing!" Camilla ejaculated.

"A charge that is exceedingly serious," the Ambassador said, "for it carries the penalty of death."

"Oh no," Camilla cried, "it was not stealing, it was an exchange!"

"That would be for the Judge to decide," the Ambassador answered. "But do not distress yourself, Miss Lambourn. I have a better idea. I cannot allow the soldiers of any State to threaten a British Embassy as they are doing at the moment. I have, in consequence, sent a messenger to the Colonel commanding a battalion of the Army of Occupation which is encamped on the outskirts of Amsterdam. They are, in fact, the 5th Dragoons."

"My own regiment!" Hugo Cheverly exclaimed. "This is my most fortunate day!"

"Your own men and doubtless a brother officer will escort you aboard the first English ship which enters the harbour," the Ambassador said with a smile. "Now, if you will pardon me, I will make arrangements for your marriage. My chaplain is waiting in another room."

"Oh thank you, Your Excellency, thank you with all my heart!" Camilla cried, sinking down in a deep curtsy.

"I am glad to be of service to you," he replied, "and also to Sir Horace's daughter. Your father is a man I have always admired greatly, and he once did me a favour many years ago when I was young and new to the Diplomatic Service."

He went from the room. Hugo Cheverly waited until the door shut behind him, then very gently he lifted both her hands to his lips.

"You are quite sure," he said in a low voice, "that you want to marry me?"

"Are you sure that you wish me to be your wife," Camilla replied, "a young woman who has behaved abominably to a reigning Prince and whose subsequent behaviour will be sniggered about and misinterpreted by everyone in London?"

"I do not think 'everyone in London' counts with either of us," Hugo Cheverly answered. "Oh my darling, if you only knew what this means to me, to know that you will be mine and that no one, no prince, no man in all the world, can ever take you from me again."

With that she lifted her face to his and he swept her into his arms, kissing her wildly, passionately with a fire and a passion she had never known in him before. She was not afraid, she only felt herself respond with a joy of ecstasy that was beyond words. With his mouth on hers she felt as though he lifted her up into a golden world of beauty and wonder, and she was conscious of nothing save they were one, joined indivisibly for all time.

Then, as the door opened, they moved apart, not hastily but slowly, as though they could hardly bear to be sundered from one another. They turned, expecting to see the

Ambassador, but a young gentleman stood there, an Exquisite garbed in the latest fashion, the points of his collar reaching over his jawbone, his cravat tied in meticulously intricate folds, his polished boots reflecting his surroundings, his pantaloons so tight and his coat so perfectly cut that they could only have belonged to a very Tulip of Fashion.

For a moment he stared at them and they at him. Then Hugo Cheverly exclaimed aloud.

"Charles!" he said. "You are the last person I expected to see here! How have you come?"

"By one of His Majesty's ships o' the line, as it happens," he replied, and advanced further into the room to clasp his friend's hand.

"But all that is wonderful," Hugo Cheverly declared, "you are sent from heaven itself! That is just what we need at the moment, a ship to carry us back to England. Camilla, let me present Sir Charles Fotheringdale, an old friend of mine. We served in the Peninsula together. And let me tell you, Charles, there is no one I would rather at this moment ask to oblige me by acting as my best man."

"Your best man!" Sir Charles ejaculated,

having bowed to Camilla. "You are about to be wed? My dear fellow, if so, why in this hole-in-a-corner manner?"

"It is a long story," Hugo Cheverly answered, "and shall all be related to you in time. At the moment just assure me that you were not funning when you said you had a ship o' the line in harbour."

"It is the truth," Sir Charles declared, "and I have been sent, I may tell you, Hugo, in search of you."

"In search of me!" Hugo Cheverly repeated. "On whose orders?"

"On the orders of He-who-must-be-obeyed — Prinny — the Regent himself!" Sir Charles replied.

"Good God!" Hugo Cheverly exclaimed. "What bats have got into his attic? Why should His Royal Highness wish to see me?"

"I had fancied that I would have to go as far as Meldenstein to tell you the news, dear fellow," Sir Charles said, "and it is extremely gratifying, I may say, to find that I have reached my goal and can carry you back with me to London. But if you take my advice you will delay your marriage until Prinny can be present. He will be extremely peeved to find you have performed such an important ceremony without his approval."

"Prinny to be at my wedding?" Hugo

Cheverly demanded. "Have you become turnip-brained all of a sudden? Why should Prinny wish to be present at my marriage?"

Sir Charles gave Camilla a sideways glance and then blandly, with his face deliberately expressionless, he said:

"It is usual, my dear fellow where Dukes are concerned."

"Dukes!" Hugo Cheverly ejaculated, his face suddenly paling beneath its tan.

"Yes, Dukes!" Sir Charles replied. "And let me felicitate you, old man. You are now — though the Devil alone knows you do not deserve it — His Grace the Duke of Alveston."

"My cousin is dead?" Hugo Cheverly asked in a low voice.

Sir Charles nodded.

"But his sons?"

"They were burnt with him," Sir Charles explained. "The west wing at Alveston caught fire. Apparently the Duke made an attempt to rescue both his boys who were on the second floor. The roof caved in, there was no hope for any of them."

"How terrible!" Camilla whispered.

"A tragedy indeed," Sir Charles said. "It appears the estate fire-engine had not been repaired for some years."

"You mean that my cousin had let it rust,

because as usual he was cheese-paring," Hugo Cheverly said. "My God, what a thing to happen! I had always believed that Alveston was well protected against the dangers of fire."

"There was, I understand, nothing anyone could do about the west wing," Sir Charles said, "although the rest of the house is intact. The Regent has decided you must return at once to deal with your affairs. He has also, overnight as it were, developed a new fondness for you, which is why I know he would wish to dance at your wedding."

"My wedding is not going to be delayed for Prinny nor for anyone else to dance," Hugo Cheverly said firmly.

He turned towards Camilla and put out his hand.

"That is to say, if you will still marry me, my darling."

She looked up at him, her face a little troubled.

"Perhaps you . . . no longer have . . . any wish . . . to marry . . . me?" she stammered.

He laughed down at her, his eyes twinkling.

"Do you really believe that, you adorable, most beloved little goose?" he asked.

She looked up at him and for a moment they forgot that they were not alone, that Sir

351

Charles was watching them.

"No," she said very softly, almost beneath her breath. "I do not think . . . any of it . . . matters."

"Then let us be married," Hugo Cheverly said, "then I can show you, my dearest dear, that indeed nothing matters except one thing — our love."

About the Author

Barbara Cartland, who sadly died in May 2000 at the age of nearly ninety-nine, was the world's most famous romantic novelist. She wrote 723 books in her lifetime, with worldwide sales of over one billion copies and her books were translated into thirty-six different languages.

As well as romantic novels, she wrote historical biographies, six autobiographies, theatrical plays, books of advice on life, love, vitamins and cookery. She also found time to be a political speaker and television and radio personality.

She wrote her first book at the age of twenty-one and this was called *Jigsaw*. It became an immediate bestseller and sold 100,000 copies in hardback and was translated into six different languages. She wrote continuously throughout her life, writing bestsellers for an astonishing seventy-six years. Her books have always been immensely popular in the United States, where in 1976 her current books were at numbers one and two in the B. Dalton bestsellers list, a feat never achieved before or since by any author.

Barbara Cartland became a legend in her own lifetime and will be remembered for her wonderful romantic novels, so loved by her millions of readers throughout the world.

Her books will always be treasured for their moral message, her pure and innocent heroines, her good-looking and dashing heroes and above all her belief that the power of love is more important than anything else in everyone's life.